# choo
## *woo*

Lloyd Jones is a full-time writer and journalist. His most recent book was the highly acclaimed *This House Has Three Walls*, and he is the author of *Biografi*, which was published in America, England and Europe. It received international acclaim and featured on the 1994 Best Books Lists of the *New York Times*, *Atlanta Journal Constitution* and US *Publishers' Weekly*. In New Zealand, it was shortlisted for the New Zealand Book Award in 1994. Lloyd Jones is also author of *Swimming to Australia and other stories* and *Last Saturday* (with photographer Bruce Foster), and editor of *Into the Field of Play*. He was born in 1955 in Wellington, where he lives with his wife and three children.

# choo
## *woo*

## LLOYD JONES

PENGUIN BOOKS

*The author wishes to thank Creative NZ for a writer's grant in 1996-97*

Penguin Books Australia Ltd
487 Maroondah Highway, PO Box 257
Ringwood, Victoria 3134, Australia
Penguin Books Ltd
Harmondsworth, Middlesex, England
Penguin Putnam Inc.
375 Hudson Street, New York, New York 10014, USA
Penguin Books Canada Limited
10 Alcorn Avenue, Toronto, Ontario, Canada M4V 3B2
Penguin Books (NZ) Ltd
Cnr Rosedale and Airborne Roads, Albany, Auckland, New Zealand
Penguin Books (South Africa) (Pty) Ltd
4 Pallinghurst Road, Parktown 2193, South Africa

First published by Victoria University Press, New Zealand, 1998
This edition published by Penguin Books Australia Ltd, 1999

1 3 5 7 9 10 8 6 4 2

Cover design by Nikki Townsend, Penguin Design Studio
Cover photograph courtesy of The Image Bank
Typeset in 12pt Garamond by Midland Typesetters, Maryborough, Victoria
Printed in Australia by Australian Print Group, Maryborough, Victoria

National Library of Australia
Cataloguing-in-Publication data:

Jones, Lloyd, 1955- .
Choo woo.

ISBN 0 14 028077 4.

I. Title.

NZ823.2

# choo
## woo

# ONE

Once I was so in love with a woman that I couldn't imagine a future without her. To begin with we worshipped this thing between us. I sat at her feet and she leant forward to cup my cheeks. We couldn't believe our good luck. Then something happened. One day it did – something like a flicker of irritation. She averted her eyes and when she looked back I was still there so she turned me into a chicken. It was all downhill after that. I was no use to her. She wanted a conversation and all I could do was squawk.

I told that to my daughter, Natalie, when she was ten

years old. I had just left her mother and I needed a fable. So I smiled like an anaesthetist. Better to speak of a chicken than spill the awkward truth that I couldn't stand to live with her mother a day longer. Vivienne could say the same thing about me – I'm sure she has. She was as unhappy as I was, of course she was, and I remember the day when I first became aware of it. Suddenly it felt like everything we'd done together we'd done too young. We'd met when we were too young, and because we were looking for the next thing we married when possibly we shouldn't have. The good times had passed too quickly, and before we knew it we were on to the nit-picking stage. I was thirty-one years old when I moved out, and yet it felt like we'd been living together for sixty years. Pick. Pick. Pick. And not just her either. I want to make that clear.

We were no longer even the same people who had defiantly exchanged vows to death us do part. More than one relative told Vivienne she didn't know what she was getting herself into, and they were right, but not for the reasons they gave. They couldn't see past the boy with the bad haircut and the amateurish gap tooth of his grin. True enough, you won't find me in a photograph with three generations of lawyers, the fingertips of my leading hand spread against the desk blotter. The self-taught start with a blank sheet and it showed in my appearance. That's why to this day I love Vivienne for seeing that in me and not shying away, for holding my hand all the tighter in front of the dinosaurs lined up behind the clicking cameras.

Back to the squawking chicken. Natalie laughed and laughed. Thank God for that sweet music. She loved the idea of her mother turning me into a squawking chicken. That's when I learnt about the value of story. We were sitting in the car outside KFC. She laid her head on my shoulder and squawked; we squawked together and laughed until tears rolled down our cheeks. 'Probably you shouldn't mention that to your mother,' I said. Events were still fresh. It was only a week earlier that I'd moved out.

I didn't spring it on Vivy. I told her I was going; just as soon as I found the right place. So she knew my intention but she hadn't properly prepared herself for it happening. The day duly rolled around. It must have been the sight of me standing in the hall with my bag because suddenly she just lost it. She threw herself at me, clawed at my trousers, held on for dear life. She begged me to reconsider. 'Don't go, Charlie. Please don't . . . I'll kill myself . . . I will . . . I will . . .' And no matter what she said or how much she begged and cried I felt the ugliness of the human spirit upon me. I should have stood her up. I should have slapped her dignity back on. After all, she was still my wife, and despite everything else, the constant pick pick picking and the dreadful rows that began in silence and ended in silence, I loved her. Instead, I stood there like a bloodless statue and when she tore open my fly all I did was reach behind to push the front door to a close in case the neighbours were looking in. I might have been standing over a shoe-shine boy. And it's true what is said about a man's penis. The world stands still for it and its possessor knows no shame. I'm trusting Vivienne will forgive me when she reads this. But if she swallows her embarrassment, if she is able to put aside what her shitty relatives might think, she will nod to herself at the truth of what I'm about to say.

I'm preambling here like crazy. Partly it's a result of the excited state I'm in. I expect some wise man has some clever words to say on the subject of revenge. I won't bother with looking them up. The same with grief. It's the same fruitless exercise. The dictionary provides a few pretty words. *Sadness, triste.* The words fall lightly but are as dead as bricks and say nothing of the cancer that grief really is.

Twenty minutes ago I learnt Ben Strang was back in town. I wasn't expecting that news. I never expected to set eyes on him again or hear his name spoken except as a thought in the eyes of others. I was watching television and someone rang with his whereabouts. The caller wouldn't give his name. I started to feel doubtful about what I was hearing. It didn't make sense for Ben to come back here. I couldn't imagine him believing he'd be welcomed back in an air of forgiveness. Once again I asked who was calling. There was a pause. Then he answered briskly, 'Cooper Street . . . over in Lansdowne . . .' He mentioned the house number then the line went dead. I put the phone down. The TV was still babbling in the next room. I'd been watching something with some interest but now I switched off the set, killed the programme that had so engrossed me just a few minutes earlier. I started to think about the caller, his motive. I didn't feel it was someone trying to disguise his voice. I didn't feel like it might be one of Vivy's smiling relatives or some sicko getting his kicks. I picked up my car keys, juggled them in my hand. I thought about calling Viv. If it were true, she needed to know. Definitely she would need to. On the other hand, if it turned out to be a hoax she'd be upset for nothing.

We were already living apart when Ben came into our lives. By this time things were on a more even keel. Vivienne had adjusted to the real likelihood that I wasn't coming back. Where I'd moved to wasn't far away. Michael Street is only three kilometres from South Road; just around the corner from KFC. My new abode was a small cottage with a sloping iron roof. It wasn't the greatest of neighbourhoods. More than half the houses in the street are unloved, and at night raised voices are heard. Dogs bark constantly, and during daylight hours an end-of-the-world bleariness clings to the street that not even the best planted garden can overcome. My cottage needed work, and when I wasn't painting I ploughed hour upon hour into re-lining the rooms, fixing the roof, and making the porch out front safe. I had plenty to occupy me. Other things I couldn't hurry. The butchered tree out front, for instance. Its sheared limbs needed careful nurturing; I needed its shade over the iron roof. But there was nothing to do but wait and let nature take its course. Best of all was the silence collected inside these four walls. Silence that was sweet and untroubled and knew only my rhythm. You don't think that anything so simple and free could ever be so important.

Once a week I stopped by the house on South Road. I re-entered my old life and Vivienne made dinner and we played happy families for Natalie's sake. A couple of times – this was at the start of our separation – I made the mistake of staying over and that just returned us to the tearful scenes of months earlier. I also saw Viv more times than she knew. Ours is a small town and it was easy to see her without Viv knowing I had seen her. I'd catch sight of her in my rear-view mirror – walking up the street. No, dragging herself up the street is more accurate. The dark rings around her eyes, the droop of her face. I'd feel awful. I felt responsible. But Viv wasn't helping matters. She wouldn't let go. She was still ringing me in the middle of the night. She'd call up about Natalie. Could I pick her up from school? Sure, no worries. Or she would want to talk about something that had happened at school. We spent more time talking about Natalie on the phone than we ever did when we were living under the same roof. There was always something. Some emotional problem she thought a girl Natalie's age might be having. Dizziness in class. Inattentiveness. It didn't matter what the subject was. The point was, Viv just wanting to talk. And she could talk. Upwards of an hour. Sometimes longer. I knew she was lying in bed, propped up by pillows. I could picture her twisting her hair around her finger as she spoke. Across town, I stood shivering in the hall with my hand in my pocket. 'Well, goodnight,' she'd say finally as if this was the most unnatural thing in the world. 'I still love you, Charlie. No matter what.' She'd slip that in at the end. Maybe she thought she had caught me in a dithering mood. The pause was for me to say something which would make everything right again. But I could never do that, and so these phone calls that had started out as a conversation about Natalie often ended on a miserable note.

Still, the idea of a second home began to appeal to Natalie. She helped me furnish it with stuff picked up from Mick D's Saturday morning auctions. I'd let her bid. She bought an iron for a dollar. A heater for five dollars. She stuck up her finger for a table going under the hammer at fifteen dollars. She loved the idea of her dad's house taking shape at the bidding of her finger. It was an inexpensive way of indulging her. The mat with the bathing tigers we bought and tossed out. Same with the antelope rug. Mick D's was an outing – a huge warehouse across the road from McDonald's where we'd drop by for breakfast first. Inside the warehouse swallows flew up against white painted brick walls; and Maori women in tracksuit pants sat around in armchairs still to be auctioned hooting and shrieking back at Bob the auctioneer who gave them cheek. Natalie loved it. She loved the world she entered at Mick D's. Life at South Road was boring, she said. And although I pulled her up for saying so I was secretly pleased to have her approval.

Things got better for Viv with time – just as everyone said they would. She stopped calling as much. Natalie called instead. On one of our goodnight chats she told me about Ben. It was such a surprise that I didn't know what to say. I could hear my daughter's excitement and I felt a twinge of sadness at that – of wonder, too. Of course she was happy for her mother and I couldn't begrudge her for feeling that, could I.

Vivienne had met him at the hotel where she worked at the front desk. Ben was attending a sales conference at the Solway. Doubtless there were plenty of opportunities for their paths to cross. Vivienne trotted out his credentials. Ben was a sales manager. Head office was in Auckland. He drove a company car. I nodded and offered noises of approval. Typically, Viv made it sound more glamorous than it really was. Ben sold and inserted towel dispensers for hotel and garage dunnies. When I heard that I found myself smiling into the receiver.

Ben was so different from me that I wondered what Viv had ever seen in me. Or maybe, as I was starting to think around that time, people change according to whoever they are with. Viv was one person when we were together; with Ben she became someone else. We didn't like each other, and that's all right. There's no rule compelling us to take to one another. It's just not humanly possible. But with Ben it was more than indifference. I actively disliked him. It was his arrogance. That smile of his – I couldn't stand his smile. I'd think of someone smiling down from a bus window at the others queuing outside in the rain. I thought that the first time I ever laid eyes on him. Vivienne said I would feel differently once I got to know him, that I'd see him for what he was. I wonder if she remembers that now.

Her new man was into theatre. And so too, now, much to my surprise, was Viv. On the nights they drove over the hill to a theatre in the city Natalie would sleep over at my place. In the morning I'd make her a special breakfast and get her off to school before going to paint houses. I enjoyed those sleepovers. There was endless opportunity to ask her about events in the house. What was happening? What was Ben like? Was he a storyteller at dinnertime? 'Ben's in a play,' she announced one evening. This was when we were still being polite to one another, and sure enough, a week later Viv sold me a ticket to a local production, *Heaven Can Wait*. Ben, who normally I wouldn't have said was a boxer's arse, plays a boxer killed in a car crash. The stage gave full reign to that condescending smile of his. He seemed to want the audience to know that while he was taking part in this show he could just as easily be smirking from a corner of the audience. Anyway – to the story. When Ben arrives in Heaven the guardians ask him what he's doing there. He wasn't down on their books to die just yet. So the messenger, played by Murray Parkes (the heat rose in my scalp when I ran across his name in the programme: I still owed Murray for the carpet he had laid in the cottage) goes down to Earth to find Ben a new body to inhabit, as the old car-wrecked one has already been cremated. At that point Ben's smile swept over us and I felt a quick passing chill, and again later when his smiling glance fell upon the section in which Natalie and I were sitting; and for some time after it was like he had slipped into my old life, sleeping where I used

14

to, on my side of the bed, apparently; eating at my old table, sitting in my old chair with his arm around the woman who used to be my wife. I felt like I had been burgled.

These days Ben stationed himself at the door when I came round to pick up Natalie. There was no invitation to come in and as I read it he seemed to be saying, 'This is my life now. You wait outside.' So I'd be left standing out on the porch. Even when Viv came into the hall I could have been the paperboy. She called out to Natalie, and I was left to hover under Ben's armpit, his arm extended against the doorway barring my entry. I felt like I had died and Viv had picked up the pieces and moved on.

At least she had changed from the sad, dispirited figure trooping through town, and I felt relieved of that burden. Natalie seemed to perk up as well. She was more energetic, for a while she was, and if there were genuine problems at school then I didn't hear about them any more. Viv had got their lives back on track – that's what this cool distancing seemed to be about.

After that I didn't pay nearly enough attention, and for the most selfish of reasons: I didn't want to see the fun my estranged wife and daughter were having with the new man in their lives. By the time they stopped showing signs of having such wonderful fun, well, by then I didn't want to know what was upsetting them either. With Natalie it was a little different. All of a sudden she seemed such a grim little thing. I prodded away. I asked if everything was okay. She just nodded (officially). She didn't gallop on to the next thought like she might have, as she used to, racing to cut through my questions to talk about the small, injured bird she had found and which she and her mate across the road, Pete Sutton, were looking after. She didn't give much away.

I wondered if this closing up had something to do with the onset of puberty, the way kids that age develop a secretiveness. Even when I scored the odd point at her mother's expense she didn't laugh or tick me off like she had on plenty of previous occasions. One time I dropped her back at South Road I drew her attention to the figure sitting alone in his car at the end of the drive. I said, 'Look, there's Ben waiting for Murray Parkes to turn up with another life.' She missed the point of the joke. At least that's what I thought at the time. Now I see a different possibility. When she looked across at me she had something on her mind that she was weighing up whether or not to mention. Her lips parted and closed, and I said, 'Murray Parkes, get it!' She replied with a sullen little nod and said goodnight.

I didn't give Vivienne an opening to unload either. She usually stopped in for a drink when she came to pick up Natalie. I thought she was preoccupied, that there were things she could have told me. But, knowing me, knowing what I would do, she must have held back, hoping that 'things' would blow over. She stared into her coffee and I fell about inwardly gloating. I watched her stir her coffee and thought Ben must have found someone else. Or else I'd catch her looking at me. Viv looking for the person she'd once known and slept with? Too late for that, baby. I gave her no opportunity to speak her mind. None whatsoever. I found myself acting up jaunty. I talked about me. My painting business was doing well. She listened and nodded at the right moments. She reminded me of someone sitting out in the rain. She said little, and stared wordlessly down at her knees. I couldn't wait for her to leave. After I closed the door I'd find Natalie lying on her bed in the dark, still in her clothes. 'Come on out here, you roly poly,' I'd say. I'd noticed her roundness. Viv said it was a passing thing. But her face too – she's always had a pretty face – was filling out. More than once I had a shouting match with her mother over what she ate or didn't eat.

One Tuesday night when I called round for Natalie the lights were out in the front of the house. Tuesday night was the night I had Natalie. Usually we'd go off to Burridges. It was set in stone. I hammered at the front door. Then I went around the back. The kitchen light was on and I could see Viv sitting by herself at the table. I stood outside in the dark watching her lean on her elbows and knead her forehead, then I let myself in. 'Remember me?' I said. 'It's Tuesday night.' I was filled with self-righteousness. 'You must have heard me knock. Surely to God . . .'

She raised her face and I saw the red rings about her eyes. She had been crying. One eye was wetter than the other. It was a scene I'd run away from in the past.

'What's happened?' I said. 'What's the matter, Viv?'

She started to tell but couldn't. She shook her head. Then she started to cry.

'Vivienne. Come on, mate.' I placed my hand on her shoulder and instantly regretted it. It didn't feel like my hand or like her shoulder. It was a gesture without any feeling in it. I took my hand away. I couldn't think of anything to say either. 'C'mon, Viv. Speak to me. What's the matter?'

She shook her head again. Then she started to cry again.

'Doesn't sound like nothing,' I said. 'Doesn't look like nothing.' I looked around the kitchen. I had just noticed the lovely cooking smell. On the stove was a lightly tanned apple crumble she'd just baked. A crisp chicken cooled in the baking tray and that, in some obscure way, set off the alarm bells.

'Where's Natalie?'

'He took her somewhere,' she said.

'He?'

'Ben.'

'Where did he? Come on, Viv. Jesus, will you stop crying!'

'I don't know,' she said. 'Out somewhere. He took her out to dinner.'

She looked up and I saw all that old grief, and all I could think of was, 'Please don't hang this on me, Viv. Please . . .' I couldn't give her a shoulder to cry on. I couldn't even pull up a chair and sit down and listen. I was too full of my own loss. Tuesday nights were supposed to be our time together. I couldn't understand Natalie just passing it up or forgetting, or worse, putting her mother's boyfriend ahead of me. I felt let down and disappointed.

There was no word from her, and the next Tuesday night I deliberately stayed away. I hadn't heard from her during the week and now I was out to punish her. It shames me to think about it now. The second Tuesday came and went. Still there was no word. Several more days passed and Ben turned into the traffic off the Mt Holdsworth road. It was just on dark but I could see Natalie in there with him. I could see the back of her head, the erect neck, shoulders. I thought she looked like someone's wife. I jumped the car in front and pushed up behind. I swear it was like looking at Vivienne, the way she had her arms folded; it was like she had grown into Vivienne. She sat where her mother ordinarily would. It filled me with wonder. Here was my daughter grown up. Here she was taking her place in the world. The wonder of it passed. I reminded myself that she was twelve. Twelve years old for God's sake. I considered flagging them over if only to disturb what I had seen – in the hope it would reassemble into some other, more acceptable arrangement. But I did nothing. I thought at the time it would be hard to do something, I mean to take some action, without making a fool of myself. I'd refrained from that so far. But I also had another reason in me. I had been punishing Natalie with my silence. Now I thought to punish her with my indifference. I overtook them and drove on without so much as a backward glance. Many months later I'd think back to that moment, and others like it, and feel ashamed to realise that I had seen the future and driven right by it. But that's hindsight making things more obvious than they appeared at the time.

Ben had been in town for more than eighteen months by this point. For twelve of those he had lived with Vivienne. That's not counting the two or three days a week he spent on the road driving up to Hawke's Bay and across to Taranaki. It was a large territory to cover. But he was around long enough for people to make up their minds about him. No one that I knew or spoke to thought he was a good guy. No one said he was an out-and-out bastard either. Of course, when people said anything they were aware they were speaking to Vivienne's ex. Still, I'd see it in their faces – a slight apologetic shift, and no matter what they said the truth of what they felt was there in their eyes. They didn't think much of Ben.

Ben had inherited my old life and that included my neighbours. On the south side, the Bennetts' place was still empty so he had only the Harrises to contend with. I knew Ron Harris didn't think much of Viv's boyfriend. I had seen them at a distance – Ron with his folded arms. I had the feeling that if Ron hadn't been able to fold his arms I don't know what he would have done; probably hit him. And Ben, of course, being Ben he didn't appear to notice anything. Unable to entertain any other possibility than that the world was in love with him. He leant back for more bearing, for more light and a slit-eyed smile. But Ron wasn't having any of it. Until his retirement Ron Harris had run a plant with twenty men. He knew what he liked and didn't like in people, and those people usually knew which way Ron felt about them.

Meanwhile, Viv's thing with Ben staggered on. I was beginning to think it wouldn't survive the summer. In the weeks leading up to Christmas I thought Viv looked more strained than at any time we were together. At the same time her misery didn't strike me as anything out of the ordinary. She'd been miserable with me. There was no reason why she shouldn't be miserable with Ben. It was just the same old wheel turning. Still I denied her an opening, and she didn't invite questions. We were still making a point to each other.

It all came to an end in February. Everything about that Sunday afternoon is crystal clear. She called me on Ben's cellphone. The cellphone must have been playing up because she faded in and out. Only the *Charlie* part came through loud and clear. *Charlie. Charlie . . .* One of the times the line went dead the cricket caught my attention. I poked my head round the door to the pictures from the Caribbean. Lara looked guilty of something. His grin was tacked to his chest. I watched him prod the ground with his bat. Fleming studied and picked at his fingertips. Then I realised I'd come in too late. The drama was over. Kennedy, the Dunedin storeman, stood at the bowler's end with his face turned up to the sky. Viv's shouting returned. And sounding like a man shuffling papers on his desk I asked her to wait. I held the phone until the replay came on, and there it was, as you might recall, Kennedy getting the edge of Lara's bat and a regulation catch flying at chest height to Fleming at slip and a rare chance going to ground. A cloud passed in the window, casting a shadow over the living-room carpet. Viv must have stepped outside for now she came through loud and clear. She was no longer shouting. She spoke with a kind of hushed urgency. 'Charlie, listen . . . Go to Bennetts'. Come now, okay. Charlie . . . ?'

I looked outside. The tar on the road was melting. I didn't want to go outside, let alone crawl into my van.

'Charlie. Please, just for once . . .' Then, with the same urgency as before she added, 'Don't go home, understand?'

*Home.* I thought about that on my way over. It sounded like a concession to something we hadn't ever discussed. Michael Street was my home. What did she mean by home? I drove along Pownall. Some kids were throwing stones at a battered duck in the swamp. It got to its feet then slumped again. I was at the York Street intersection before I gave any thought to what I had seen. Nine times out of ten I would have gone back. But Vivienne's strangely urgent message plus the arrival of a car behind me put that gesture out of range. I turned on the cricket and carried on. Kennedy was continuing to trouble Lara. At the top of South Road I slowed to get in another Kennedy over. He was everything but. I let my foot off the gas and looked over at Vivienne's. The front door was ajar. The front lawn was burnt and I noticed the weeds thriving in the bed along the drive. How Ben failed to notice them was beyond me. I cut the motor and listened: '. . . Kennedy turns at the top of his mark and runs in . . .' Viv's face appeared in the front door of Bennetts'.

She looked nervously back at her place – that is to say our old home. Then she cocked her head, wondering no doubt why I was stuck in the car. '. . . Lara more circumspect this time allows the ball to go through to the keeper.' I switched off the ignition and got out. Bennetts' place had well and truly fallen into ruin. The grass was long, the garden beds chocker with oxalis. Sarah Bennett would turn in her grave if she could see it.

'You didn't say you were shifting,' I said lightly. I might as well have saved myself the trouble.

'Go inside, Charlie,' she said.

The house stank of trapped air. I waved the air away from my face.

'The front room,' directed Vivienne. She took hold of my arm for a close word. 'Don't say anything to her, Charlie.'

'Say anything to who?'

'Just go in . . . Go in the door and don't say anything.' She pushed open the door to the front room.

The room was a mess. There was stuff on the floor, crap all over the place. Then I started to pick up the detail. The childish painting of a tree on one wall. A stuffed bird on a stand which gave me a start. Then I saw Natalie. 'Honey, baby . . . ?' I said. She was lying on her side. She must have heard me. She didn't look up though. 'Natalie . . . What's that you're holding, sweetheart?' She didn't stir. 'Natalie?'

Behind me Viv said, 'Don't yell at her.'

'I'm not yelling. I'm asking . . .' She was holding something like a tiny doll. 'Come on now. Let Dad see . . .' I stepped across the room and Natalie tried to shield the thing. 'Come on, Natalie, let me see . . .'

'Show Charlie,' her mother said then. 'It'll be all right. Let your father see.'

I pulled her arm away and saw what I thought had been a doll. I see it now in my dreams. Though not just in my dreams. It springs to mind in an endless number of situations. I might be in the shower, working, eating, or driving along, and the world will be filling in my head with itself – you know, the detail, the traffic, the lawns, the pavement, the trees, houses, maybe I'm thinking about a painting estimate, maybe I'm thinking about a faceless woman, and then this other detail will hove in there, I'll see the baby that I saw in my daughter's hands. Its eyes squeezed shut. A tiny, shrunken figure still attached to the placenta. Viv says I made an inhuman noise. I'm sure I cried out.

I recall backing off towards the door and Vivienne nervously trying to persuade me, 'Just take a deep breath, Charlie. Go on. Deep . . . Deep . . .' I reeled out to the porch where I looked across to where I used to live. Ben happened to be walking up the drive to his car. He looked across to Bennetts', saw me, and froze. I screamed across at him; and Ben walked quickly to the car, got in, and reversed out to the street. There are people who saw this at different stages. Ron Harris was driving past and he happened to look over and see me on the porch of Bennetts'. I don't recall his car passing. But Ron says he saw a man who'd had his view snatched from his eyes.

The Suttons. Natalie's little friend, Pete – they were witness to a man beside himself. Vivienne claims she tried to haul me back but that I flung her aside. I don't recall that. I ran for the van and turned on the key and the cricket came drawling on. Much, much later I would find the volume button on the floor mat. I had busted it clean off.

Ben drove up in the direction of town. There was no traffic. Sunday afternoon. Half the town was out at the coast or they were sitting in the shade of their living rooms. I caught up with him at the roundabout at the top end of town near the Castle Point turn-off. I saw him look up and catch me in his rear-view mirror and his wagon leap forward like a dog spooked in its sleep.

After that he hauled out to open road which was only averagely smart of him. He should have taken the Pahiatua Track over to Palmerston North. That way he'd have seen me off. But God was smiling down on the situation in a variety of ways. I was in my clapped-out painting van. It could manage seventy, seventy-five ks, top. Ben must have known that when he sailed by the turn-off for the Pahiatua Track. The hills flashed by. It felt like there was only me and Ben in the world that day. I concentrated on what I'd seen, stewed on what that bastard had done virtually under my eyes. I never doubted that I would catch up with him.

I came into Dannevirke just as he was ready to leave a service station on the corner. I saw his Mazda up ahead held up by a passing sheep truck. He just looked like a lawful driver waiting for the traffic to pass and let him in. I don't think he even saw me coming, and in any case I gave him no time to react. I cut across the station concourse and hit his right rear fender. Bang! The force pushed his vehicle round on an angle like a pick-up stick. I was out of the van before he knew what had happened. He looked out his side window and saw me. He didn't know what to do. Beg for mercy? Lock his door? Ben being Ben reverted to form and tried to smile through his window at me as if to say, 'Let's be reasonable about this.' Ben was splitting his hopes in too many directions. I got his door open. 'Hey, now. Charlie, please,' he said. 'Now look . . . wait a second. Please . . .' He had his seatbelt on and I couldn't drag him out. 'Charlie,

Jesus. Wait!' he said. I brought my knee up into his face and he made an indignant noise like who was I to do that. 'You've broken my fucking nose!' I got a hold of his hair and tried to ram his head into the steering wheel but he was resisting. So, with him still in harness, I pulled him out the door and beat his head on the ground (a dull pumpkin sound in case you were wondering) until, from all directions, unseen hands were dragging me off him.

In court I learnt that I had smashed Ben's head into the ground approximately thirty times. His skull received multiple fractures. The broken nose I've mentioned. Somehow (though I can't think how) I managed to break his cheekbone as well. The contusions on his neck the prosecutor tried to say was evidence I'd attempted to throttle him. Ben lost several front teeth. It must have been when I brought my knee up.

I was taken from Dannevirke to the Masterton police cells. When Viv came by later that night we hugged for a long time. We hadn't done that for a long while but it felt good and right. She was crying but there was only the one subject that interested me.

'How's Natalie?'

'At the Harrises'. I didn't want to bring her here.'

'God, that poor little thing. That poor girl. I've been pulling my hair thinking about it, Viv. She's twelve years old.'

'Thirteen,' she said.

'Like that makes a world of difference. Christ.' I parted myself from the embrace and shook my head. I was feeling angry again. If they'd said Ben was in the next room I would have torn the wall down. 'What about your boyfriend?' I said.

'Hospital, apparently.'

'I'm not sorry, Viv. No matter what you think.'

'Charlie, listen a moment. This is important.' She looked down at the floor then she looked up. She chose her words very carefully. 'Firstly, what happened to Natalie . . . our daughter, Charlie . . . I'm not proud of that.'

I wasn't sure I had heard correctly.

'You knew, Viv?'

'No. I'm not saying that.'

'Vivienne . . .'

She closed her eyes and held up a hand. 'Maybe. I wasn't sure. I didn't want to think it.'

'Vivienne. Surely to God, no . . .'

Some voices arrived in the corridor outside. Vivienne looked behind, then she continued in a whisper.

'I'm not asking this for me. I don't care about me. I could die tomorrow for all I care. This isn't about me.'

I nodded, though I wasn't thinking about what she was saying.

'Look at me,' she said.

'Just say what you want to say, Vivienne.' I couldn't bear to look her in the eye.

'All right,' she said. 'Here it is.' I listened to her take a deep breath. 'I don't want our little girl put through anything more. I don't want her hurt any more.'

'Well, of course,' I said. ' That goes without saying . . .'

She looked at me like she thought I might be dumb or something. Then I had an inkling of what was coming.

'Go on,' I said.

'They interviewed me. You probably know that.'

'I didn't but go on.'

'I told them it was jealousy, Charlie.' She watched my

26

face to see how I would react. Jealousy. That's a laugh. 'I did it for Natalie,' she said then, and I took a few paces away to think about what she said and the real truth, and I decided she had done the right thing.

'I didn't know what else,' she said.

'I know. I know. Natalie's the one.'

'She's suffered enough, Charlie. She's suffered.'

'I wish I'd killed him,' I said.

The funny thing is (if you can call it at all funny), it was Ben's surviving the attack that saved me. All things considered, I was given a light sentence – three months' jail followed by twelve months' periodic detention. The court seemed satisfied it knew the story and had dispensed justice accordingly. I had nothing of my own to say. I went along with Vivienne's story. There was everything to say but I chose not to say it. I said nothing because Vivienne asked it of me, as she was right to.

I was in low-security Rimutaka Prison by the time Ben got out of hospital. The whole time he was in there Vivienne didn't visit. She never saw him again. When he came out of hospital he didn't bother to call round to the house for his clothes and things. I suppose none of us were terribly surprised. Viv shoved everything into green rubbish bags and drove out to the tip.

Over the years we got word of Ben. He had been seen somewhere up north going into a picture theatre. One of Viv's hotel friends swore black and blue she had seen him on a beach at Surfer's Paradise. Ben in Dirty Dog sunglasses, so she said, propped up on an elbow to watch the swimmers come out of the water. There were two or three other sightings. In every case Ben was by himself. The fact that he had spent so much time with Vivienne began to feel all the more unusual, like it was even out of character for Ben. I wondered how I had missed so many obvious things. I wondered what had turned my head at crucial moments when a more deliberate glance would have told me everything. I wondered where the hell my head was during that year for a thing like that to have happened right under my nose.

# TWO

I meant to wait until dark, but then I thought I'd take a run by in the van first to make sure it was where I thought it was. I saw the Lansdowne Beauty Studio and realised I'd been in the area before. Years ago, Viv won a kindergarten raffle for a free consultation and later turned up home with her eyebrows tinted and shaped Egyptian style.

Cooper Street is pensioner land: semi-detached brick units screened by oak trees that begin at Te Ore Ore Road, and cross First Street to end in a cul-de-sac. I turned into Cooper Street. It was close to dark, and on lawns up and down the street elderly figures stooped to pick up the fallen oak leaves. I slowed down and counted the letterboxes. Ben's house had been set down on a subdivided section.

Cooper Street follows a dog's hind leg; the address given by the anonymous caller was the house at the bend. Brick pensioner units pushed up on both sides. A small strip of a drive went up the side of the house. But there was no car. Nothing in the windows suggested occupation. It was a small grubby place. I was fast concluding that the caller was a hoax. Then I noticed the aspect – Ben's front window looked all the way up the street to Lansdowne Primary School on Te Ore Ore Road. I dithered some more. I noticed the uncollected circulars poking out of the letterbox and set off for home.

Back in Michael Street, I left the house lights on and the van in the drive. I pulled the bike from the garage and set off for the other side of town where I had just been. I rode on the footpath with my lamp off. I had a hammer stowed up inside my jersey, its handle tucked in my belt, the cold metal part kept tapping my chest bone. I hoped I looked like a man on his way to the dairy. But I had the unsettling thought that every car that passed went out of its way to notice me.

I wasn't convinced that I would see Ben. It didn't make any sense for him to return. None whatsoever. I was back to doubting. And near the roundabout when someone I knew waved to me I almost lost heart and turned back. By now the lights were on in the houses up and down Cooper Street. I was the only one out and I pedalled slowly looking in at all the houses. No one saw me dismount. I wheeled the bike into the shadows of the drive and took out my hammer from my belt and went to the door at the side of the house. There was a small button with a light shining through. Should I press the door bell? Should I knock? Or should I just smash my way in? But then what if it wasn't Ben and I was met with laughter from the hoaxer behind the curtains across the street?

I went around to the front and peeped in the window. A man with his back half-turned was sprawled in an armchair, his long legs stretched out before him, one resting on the other. Elbows on the armrests and chin perched on a fingertip arch while he stared back at the flickering TV screen. A coffee cup on the floor beside the armchair. There was nothing else in the room. No pictures or mirrors on the walls. No carpet or book case. Just that armchair and the TV and, yeah, it was Ben.

It was Ben five years and seven months on. Suddenly I felt the weight of the hammer in my right hand and switched it to my left. I had expected to feel blind rage. Five years ago I'd have hurled myself through the window and hammered his skull to pieces. I wouldn't have thought twice about it. But I hadn't come here inflamed with rage. I had pedalled here out of curiosity – or was it out of duty to that old rage? I'm not sure I have the correct answer. Except what I saw in the window undid me completely. Ben in slippers stretched out before the telly. The bare walls and bare boards and a ruined man with a hole in the toe of his slipper. I stuck the hammer back in my belt, picked up my bike and pedalled home.

I got out the photos that night. Natalie in her gym wear, tights, ponytail, vaulting over the horse. You can't see her grinning parents standing at the side of the hall. Soaring over obstacles – that's what I was thinking at the time. Another of her at the beach standing in wet sand, a mud pie in each hand. You can't see Vivienne, but she's there just outside the frame shrieking, 'No! No!' at the child. There's a more up-to-date one of Natalie I took last year in Wellington. I had driven down to help them into their new flat. When Ben was in their lives it was always my fear that they would move off to somewhere and that I would have to pick up the scraps of my life and limp after. But the move to Wellington was of course a move to better things. A new life. The idea being to expand Natalie's horizons. The older photographs were to celebrate our hopes. Now I wish I had waited a few days for her to settle. In these photos Natalie is smiling out at her new world but the smile is paper thin. Something sadder is showing through. Something like a memory so that, all these years later, the record reveals a brave little face holding back something bitter.

I drove past Ben's again the next night. The lights were out, and I wondered if he had slipped away again. I think I was hoping that he had. Then, two days later, I saw him in town. I was coming out of New World supermarket and I saw him across the street with his nose in the window of Treasures, an antique shop and trader's. He was in long black trousers and a white open-neck office shirt. I watched him peering in the window; then he must have felt my eyes burning into his neck. He straightened up and turned around. He saw me and his lips parted. He took his hands out of his pockets. He waited – presumably expecting something – abuse, Hell to rain, me to drop my groceries and rush him, whatever. He waited, and when nothing happened he sniffed and turned and wandered off. For a man who must have realised that he had just been given back his life he didn't look that grateful.

On my way home I detoured down South Road. I've

made a point of avoiding it these past years. It's the most crushing feeling to turn up to your old life, isn't it. Even the power lines weave a memory particular to this place at another time. I see someone is finally living in Bennetts'. The grass has been mown. Curtains were hanging in the windows in that front room. On to our old house. It reeked with abandonment. Natalie's old trout windsock still flew from a long bamboo I bound to the downpipe at the side of the house. No one occupies a place forever. Places change hands. I suppose that's the lesson here. And yet, memories have a certain stickability. I was lost in thought when Ron Harris tapped on my roof. I hadn't even seen him come out of his house. 'Hello, stranger!' The red face and bottle-blue veins pressed in the window. 'Ron,' I said.

'You didn't recognise me, did you,' he said.

'Of course I recognised you.'

We shook hands and he looked across to his house.

'I said to Alice, "That's Charlie's van. I'm sure it is." She said, "No." I said, "I'm going out there and if I make a fool of myself it will at least have been worthwhile knowing for sure."'

'Well, now you know,' I said.

Ron wanted to know what I had been up to. He said he had seen me working out on the barn on Mt Holdsworth Road. 'You and that German hippie. What's his name, Jürgen . . .'

'Reuben. He's not German either,' I said, though Ron didn't look particularly persuaded.

'I gave you a toot. You had your nose in the paint.'

Ron studied me under his sunburnt eyebrows. I could see him looking for a sign that I knew what he knew.

I said, 'Are you going to say it, Ron, or shall I?'

He straightened up and looked around.

'Alice saw him in the supermarket. I said to her, "Don't be bloody ridiculous." She swore and we argued it. Then, bugger me, Charlie, I saw him the next day in Queen Street.' He lowered his face back to the window. 'It's all a long time ago,' he said.

'Sure is,' I said.

'I don't know what brought him back.'

I shook my head.

'I never liked the man,' he said then.

The front door at the Harrises' opened. 'There's Alice,' I said. She waved and I waved back at her.

Ron said, 'She'll be expecting you to come in for a cuppa.'

'Not this time.'

'What about Natalie and Viv? In good spirits?' And while I thought about what to say he slipped in, 'Alice will want to know.'

'That's all right, Ron. Vivienne's doing well. She's finished that course she was doing.'

'And the young lady?'

'She's happy,' I said.

'Good. Good. That's excellent,' he said.

'She's enrolled in a design course. That seems to be her thing at the moment.'

'I'll tell Alice,' he said.

I've never been sure which story the Harrises have heard. If they know about Natalie's baby then the only other source besides me or Vivienne would be the Suttons; and even then what Pete knew and what his parents have since found out has I hope remained secret.

I was hardly in the door at home when the phone rang. Immediately I thought it was the anonymous caller. There was no reason to believe it would be. It was just a feeling. I grabbed the phone and snapped into the receiver. 'Charlie?' said an old woman's voice. It was Alice inviting me over for dinner Tuesday week. She must have interrogated Ron after I drove off.

Vivienne rang me later that night. She said she wanted to wait until Natalie was asleep.

'Is what I hear true?' she asked.

'I take it you're talking about your old boyfriend,' I said.

'Sick,' she said. 'Why? What does he want?'

'Would you like me to go round and ask, Viv?'

She started to say something else, on a different train of thought, when she stopped.

'What?' she said. 'What's that? What did you just say? You know where he lives?'

I didn't want to mention the anonymous caller. But as I left a gap in our conversation Viv leapt ahead with her dark conclusions.

'Oh no, here we go. Charlie. Please,' she said. 'Promise me you won't do anything. Promise me.'

'I haven't, have I?'

'I want to hear you say it.'

'Say what?'

'Now you listen. You won't be any use to your daughter inside prison.'

'I'm not planning to go back,' I said.

'Shit, Charlie,' she said then. 'What's he want? What's he trying to prove?'

'You know him better than I do,' I said. 'You lived with the man.'

'That's not fair,' she said. 'Let's not get into that.'

'I'm just making the point . . .'

'I know what you're doing. Anyhow, just promise me. I want you to promise me you won't do anything silly.'

'Viv, I'm thirty-seven years old.' I don't know what made me say that, except it was the only thing I could think of that I could say convincingly at that moment.

'Promise me,' she said.

'Alice Harris rang to invite me over,' I said.

'Alice is thoughtful like that.' Then she said, 'I'm waiting.'

'Okay. Okay,' I said. 'Is that all? I want to go to bed.'

'Wait. Wait. Give me Reuben's number before you go.'

'What? So you can ring up and check on me? I'm thirty-seven years old, Viv.'

It wasn't only Vivienne, though. I felt like everyone was watching me. I felt them waiting for me to erupt. Even out at Richardsons' property, miles from anywhere, I caught Mrs Richardson sneak a long look at me from her porch. Reuben and I were converting an old barn to a sleepout. I was on the roof painting when I looked down and saw Mrs Richardson on her wooden deck. She was in her riding pants and boots, and with her two silly afghan dogs. I caught her watching me and I had an idea she was thinking and wondering to herself, What sort of man is he? What kind of person pulls another from a car and tries to bludgeon them into the next world? I had the feeling she had just caught up with old news. That's often the case out here. I sometimes think there's a moat around town for all the traffic and news that passes between it and the countryside. I dipped my paintbrush and Mrs Richardson turned indoors with her dogs.

Reuben had not said anything so far. I'm sure he had heard the news. He'd have to have been in a coma this past week not to hear. All the same, Reuben is not one to rush forward with his thoughts or concerns. He usually waits to give Providence a chance to shine, and yet, when we sat on the Richardsons' porch silently eating our sandwiches, the subject of Ben sat in the unspoken air between us.

Out of all this unpleasant business surrounding Ben and Natalie, Reuben was the best thing that happened to me. He was the tall Jesus figure I met in Rimutaka Prison. He'd done some minor cannabis thing and found himself working in the fields alongside men like myself, who weren't bad in themselves but who had done bad things. There is a difference. There were some real hard arses in there, some so young it was frightening. There was no light in their eyes. You couldn't tell what the hell they were about half the time. They sat together but weren't together. Scarier than wolves, some of them. Reuben stood out with his white face and ponytail. No tats either. He didn't invite it upon himself and there were plenty of opportunities. He took it upon himself to watch over me, to walk the straight and narrow, and, to some extent, I allowed him that role.

We got out around the same time. Then, one Sunday morning, he turned up at my door. He said he had some people he wanted me to meet. He waited for me to pull on my sneakers then we drove out to a hippie church in the countryside. We walked across long strawlike grass to a small purple church. There were women in dyed cheesecloth dresses and bare feet clutching bunches of flowers, as well as some older renegades, like Rube, with grey in their ponytails, bony-arsed in their black jeans, kids with rat tails and patterns shaved into their hair. Reuben got up there by the pulpit and rested his big blond hairy arms to welcome 'Brother Charlie'. People turned and smiled. Small kids looked up at me. The woman beside me clasped my arm and pressed. You could say I felt 'found', though to date God has proved more elusive.

The Sunday morning after Ben's return, Rube stood up there at the end of the morning's business and conducted a sermon. Raising his eyes from the book he was reading out of, he found me, innocent as a plumber, at the end of the bench at the back of the room, next to Maggie whom I normally sit with, Maggie of the lovely musk fragrance. This is what Reuben targeted me with: 'Thy rebuke hath broken his heart, he is full of heaviness: he looked for some to have pity on him, but there was no man, neither found he any, to comfort him.' I folded and unfolded my legs as Reuben read on describing Ben's lodgings in Hell. Maggie turned her head slightly and I saw the jib of her nose and her dark eye.

Afterwards I sat there until everyone filed out. I continued to sit there enjoying the quiet. I could hear the wind tearing open the fields. Then, various cars started up and left. I felt a hand touch and stroke my neck. I smelt the musk, and Maggie spoke. 'What happened to you during the week, Charlie?' I put my hand over hers. I had been due over at Maggie's the night I cycled over to kill Ben.

'No excuses, Maggie. I'm afraid I can't seem able to think one up at the moment,' I said.

She took her hand away. I think she'd rather have heard a lie. Maggie's little boy, Hope, bellowed from the door – 'I want to go home. I'm hungry!'

His mother ignored him.

'What about you, Charlie?'

'I don't know, Maggie. I was planning some things.'

38

I was staring back at the lectern, and I had an idea Maggie was frowning down at me.

'I'm hungry,' said Hope.

'In a moment, Hope.'

'But I'm hungry . . .'

'I said wait!' Then she sighed. 'All right, Charlie. I should know by now, shouldn't I. You know where I am.'

'I know, Maggie,' I said.

Reuben was waiting outside for me. He was leaning on the fender sunning himself. We watched Maggie latch the gate, and holding her little boy's hand, walk up the road to the cottage set back in the lavender. We could smell the cows in the paddock. Reuben gazed at the shaven hill that tilts back behind Maggie's; it looks like an upturned billiard table.

'I got a call from Mrs Richardson last night. She doesn't want you back on the job.'

'No. She can't be serious.'

The line in Reuben's jaw tightened. 'That's the way it is,' he said. 'I can't help what she thinks.'

'So she thinks, does she. What else did she say?'

'I'm amazed this thing has carried on as long as it has,' he said.

'You too,' I said.

He raised himself to full height and as he spoke he yawned at the same time. 'So, anyway,' he said, 'I told Mrs Richardson she'd lose me too.'

'No,' I said. Though I was glad he'd put it to Mrs Richardson, flattered, of course, that he'd put himself on the line for me. Even so, 'There's no need, Rube. Honestly. It's crazy.'

'Maybe. It's what I told her.'

'And?' I asked.

'And . . . she said she would think about it.'

I looked up the road. Maggie was at her gate, knee-high in long grass, looking back our way.

'You could do worse than that,' said Reuben.

'Maybe.'

'Well, it's your life. Whatever you decide.' Then he looked up with mischief in his face. 'Let me know, will you?'

'Dirty bastard. I'll shop you in to Beverley.'

'She wouldn't believe you,' he said.

'No. Probably not. So,' I said. I slapped the hood to send him on his way. But he wasn't finished. He looked off to the fields and drew a line with his mouth. He looked at me then looked away again.

'Aw God. Not you too. Go on then,' I said. 'Say it.'

'I'll say it just once, then no more. You'll never hear another word on it from me.'

'Go ahead. I'm getting it from so many directions I'm starting to feel dangerous.'

Reuben looked across at me.

'It's a joke,' I said.

'I imagine you know what I'm going to say.'

'I heard it all in there,' I said, and Rube looked over at the church.

'You could kill him. That's an option. But then think of the cost. Natalie loses a father.'

'Rube, believe me,' I said. 'I'm not about to kill anybody.'

He looked at me closely. He was trying to decide whether my smile was real or not.

'No. Probably not,' he said. He got in behind the wheel then. I tapped on his roof. I waited until he left and closed the farm gate to Babylon.

Near Maggie's I slowed down and thought about taking up her invitation. I like her place. I like the feel of the rooms, the timber floors, the smell of baking, and Maggie's artwork and the view from the windows. However, Babylon is on the back route between Masterton and Carterton. It looked to me like I was on my way to Swingers, a big red-painted restaurant just north and east of Carterton. For some years there was nothing as bold as a restaurant. Just paddocks. Then a woman converted a barn around the time potato wedges became fashionable. The same enterprising woman stuck a green with a flag out in a paddock and suddenly she had a well in a desert. You can rent a club and a pail of balls and head out to the driving range until your burger and wedges are ready. Swingers is where Ben used to take Natalie for 'good behaviour'.

Sunday noon. I couldn't have picked a worse time. The carpark was full and all the outside tables were taken. I sat inside in the gloom watching sparrows peck the gravel around the lunch crowd outside. Other diners heaved golf balls out to the mown field. The range is where Ben had coached her, guided Natalie's dumb arms, coached her body into a strange and uncomfortable position, spreading her fingers into an unnatural grip, and Natalie, obedient to the coach's commands, kept her head down, blocking out all distraction.

This is where it all started. Then, after a while, Ben started applying one set of instructions to another game. The little man inside him must have laughed at how easy it all was – all those times at home in South Road crawling across the living-room carpet on his hands and knees, pretending he was a train blowing steam: 'Choo woo, choo woo.' And Natalie, as a twelve-year-old will, trusting in Ben's

41

instructions. This is what he told her: 'The tunnel must not move until the train has gone in one end and out the other . . .' Natalie focusing, wanting to get it right. These are the things that came out later. At the golf range, it was Ben's short temper. She kept topping the ball, then after the ball danced a few skittish feet, Ben would roll his eyes. 'You're not listening to me, are you?' So she'd place a ball down on the tee for Arnold Palmer to show her and *whoosh*. The ball soared. She said Ben was dropping them near the flag, and while she just felt awkward Ben seemed to be full of practised, foreign movement. So, at home, whenever they played Ben's fucked-up games, she listened like she had listened at the driving range to Ben tell her that today she will be a tunnel. She must not move, not so much as a shake of a whisker, otherwise she will cause 'landslides' and 'slippages'. She must not move and he'll slip through as easy as a Popsicle. That's what he told her the first time. Eager, wanting to get it right, she learns that a tunnel must hold its breath and act witless. I'm putting my own spin on this. But I have the scene fixed in my mind, everything as Natalie described it. It used to make Viv cry and cry to hear all this, to think that she might have been parking the car or struggling in the back door with her arms filled with groceries at the very moment that Ben, at the other end of the house, was tightening his belt, pulling back the curtains, and commanding his 'tunnel' to get about and pick up the cushions. 'Cavalry's home,' he'd say.

Later, when we found out the story and there was time to consider all our parts in it, I'd say to her, 'Natalie, why the hell didn't you think to say something?' I mean, even when Ben was rubbing up against her didn't she think to act or say something? She said she just thought this is how a tunnel feels, slightly surprised and holding its questioning breath. Fucking hell, Ben did a good job on her!

'Sir? Sir?'

I looked up at a flustered young face.

'Your wedges and one tea. Table six. Sir?'

Now the older woman who had taken my order came over. She gave a warm smile and crouching by me spoke in a quiet, confidential manner.

'Sir, there's a table outside. If you would prefer . . .' As she said this I was aware of the silence of the other diners bent over their food.

'What's the matter here?' I asked.

'You were swearing, sir.'

'I was?'

The woman smiled and nodded.

'You are welcome to stay here if you prefer but I thought I should tell you.'

I bent down and put my face next to hers. 'Are you sure I was swearing? I didn't hear myself . . .'

She looked over at the other tables. She seemed to be evaluating a range of answers.

'Well,' she said, 'I don't think anyone else heard.'

'No?'

She smiled and shook her head.

'I didn't say "fuck" did I?' Her smile vanished. I had betrayed her friendship, and we were back to listening to the scrape of the knives and forks. 'It's all right,' I said. 'Outside sounds good to me.' I stood up. I went to pick up the bowl of wedges and the woman said, 'Andrea will bring it out to you, sir.'

The 'outside' table wasn't in the populated courtyard. It was at the other end of the restaurant. In fact it was the only

43

table out there, next to half a dozen plastic bags of mulch, and dozens of small pot plants still to be planted. The waitress saw me smiling.

She said, 'If you prefer and if you don't mind waiting I'm sure one of the others . . .'

'Nope. This is me,' I said.

'Just call out if you want anything else . . .'

'I will,' I said. 'Thank you, Andrea.'

I waited until she closed the door before I sat down. I didn't want anyone hearing me think aloud again.

For a long time after, I blamed Viv. Partly it was grief talking out loud and a need to pin the blame somewhere. Viv was the obvious candidate. She was the one on the spot. But, as she pointed out, this happened during the time she was holding down her desk job at the Solway. She couldn't be all places at once. She was hardly ever home and Ben could come and go as he pleased. He even left little messages on Natalie's pillow. A bit of scribble. 'Train due in at nine.' So she'd lie in bed waiting for the train to trundle up the dark hall and 'choo woo' its way into her bedroom. The first time Natalie spoke about this I thought back to all those nights when I had telephoned and there was no answer. At the time, I innocently assumed that everyone was out. Never, not in my wildest thoughts, did I ever imagine Ben in his white underwear crawling beneath the ringing phone in the hall as he made his way to my daughter's bedroom.

Some things you can't imagine, or don't want to imagine. Although, in my case, maybe I'm capable of more than I'd normally care to admit to. I remember, a little after Ben moved in with Viv, sneaking around the back of the house one night to stand under the clothesline in the dark, inspecting Ben's underwear, noting the heft of the arse, the damp sag of the crotch. This is the crazy shit you find yourself doing. Still, you don't imagine what you can't bear to imagine, and Viv and I, we burnt ourselves up thinking about where we were and what we were doing at the time Ben was calling through the dark – 'Choo woo, choo woo.'

I know where Viv was and what she was doing. As often as not she was leaning dreamily beneath the 'best employee for the month' portrait, one foot out of its shoe to scratch an itchy ankle, sneaking looks at the clock, willing the time to pass. But, whatever the hour, no matter the shift, she never happened in on anything. To start with she didn't. If I have any snitch on Viv then it's to do with what came later.

Now the door to the kitchen opened. It was the older waitress poking her face round the door.

'I wasn't swearing again, was I?'

She laughed. 'No sir, you weren't,' as if my question had no history. 'I just came out to ask if there is anything else I can bring you?'

'A burger and another tea.'

A whisker of disappointment crossed her face. I waited until she had called the order through, then I said, 'I like it out here.'

'Well, you stay out here as long as you like.'

'I think I will,' I said. Then I thought to put the woman's mind at rest. I didn't want her to worry about me, so I said, 'My daughter used to come here,' and that little disclosure seemed to transform me in her eyes.

She looked relieved. 'Oh it's a favourite with the dads as well,' she said, and I thought, That's how it must have looked to everyone. Like my little girl belonged to Ben.

'She was about twelve, thirteen. A mop of dark hair. Dark eyes. She was probably wearing a Mickey Mouse sweat top. I think it was grafted onto her.'

The woman smiled and shook her head. 'We have so many that fit that description.'

'Pretty little thing,' I said. 'You'd definitely remember her if you saw her.'

This time the woman smiled up at the sky. 'Lots of them too, sir.'

'This would have been about five years ago. Five years and seven months and more.'

'Ah, well, I wasn't here then.'

'I wasn't accusing you of anything,' I said. 'What's your name?'

'Yvonne.'

'Well, Yvonne, please don't take it the wrong way. I don't mean to accuse you . . .'

'I know you weren't. It's just that every face blurs into another. I can't remember every face . . .'

'Natalie. Her name is Natalie.'

'Natalie,' she said, trying the name out for herself. 'Natalie. It's pretty.'

She was looking over her shoulder now. I looked away to the golf balls raining down in the paddock to make her exit easier on her. I know I come across a bit blunt. Ben is smooth as soap of course. Yet I'm the dangerous one. And nothing that's happened since appears to have shifted opinion.

Later, as I was leaving, I was aware of the kitchen staff crammed into the one window to get a good look at me. My guess is the younger one, Andrea, put the word about. I was looking under the bushes at the entrance. One of the times Natalie came here with Ben she found a small bird, a thrush I think it was, by these same bushes. I suppose it must have flown against the glass and concussed itself. Anyway, they met the bird twice, the first time on their way into the restaurant when Ben almost stepped on it before lifting his heel in time like he was about to step in shit. Natalie dropped to her knees and tried to entice the bird but it moved away from her hand, glowering back over its shoulder, a proud, wounded little thing. Then, on their way out, the bird must have had a change of heart. It allowed Natalie to pick it up. After that, they couldn't be parted. Ben couldn't persuade her to put the bird back. They argued. Apparently there was a stand-off with Ben in the car and Natalie sitting on the porch step cradling the bird. She won out in the end. But she had another battle on her hands when she got home. Viv didn't want it in the house. She is terrified of birds. She can't hold them, so afraid is she of crushing them. Later that day when I got home from work there was a message on my voicemail and in the recorded background I could hear Vivienne shouting up the hall, 'Don't bother your father. He won't want a bird.' I called back in the evening but apparently I had left it too late. 'Mrs Austen' was no longer a problem.

After Swingers I decided to take a run up to Queen Elizabeth Park. It was still early afternoon and I was feeling restless. I knew I didn't want to go home. I stood under the trees watching the croquet players. Nothing more strenuous than the minute hand shifting on a clock. The same restricted movement. And for the two-hundred-and-fiftieth time I wondered what I was doing living here. Why wasn't I over the hill in the city where I could be closer to Natalie? I walked up to the skateboarding pit, then around the island

47

in the river, and took the path cutting across the green field. An older crowd was out and about, and I wished they weren't. I wished for something better to hope for. I watched them photograph one another. Some who looked like they might be walking off their lunch. Others who looked a bit sad on it like Monday might be figuring in their thoughts a day early. Some rollerbladers. Young families. Fathers who hardly looked of age pushing prams and carrying hairless babies on their backs.

Apart from the message that Natalie left on my voicemail I didn't hear of the bird again until some months later. By then it was winter (already she must have been pregnant), and on those Tuesdays when we met for our date, a few times, she asked me to pick her up outside the park gates. I'd sit in the car with the heater on waiting for her and the Sutton kid to walk out of the darkness carrying plastic bags filled with feathers.

'What have you there, sweet pea?'

'Nothing.'

'Looks like something.'

She'd button up and look over at the Sutton boy. A blow torch wouldn't have seen her part with information.

Then I might notice the Sutton kid holding his breath. A skinny runt of a kid whose shoulders pointed through his father's old rugby jersey. I never heard him speak around adults. He never raised his eyes from the ground. 'Okay, I see it's top secret.'

I didn't set eyes on Mrs Austen until that Sunday afternoon I stepped into the Bennetts' front room. I saw a bird but at that moment it was just part of the backdrop. And it wasn't until hours later, in the early hours of the new day by which time I was in a police cell, that my thoughts returned to the bird on the stand, that I realised I had seen Mrs Austen, and that all the feathers Natalie and Pete had stolen from nests in Queen Elizabeth Park were to reconstruct her.

With a bit more effort I might have made the connection between the feather-gathering and the empty house next door earlier than I did. A quick word about the Bennetts. When we first moved to South Road, Frankie and Sarah Bennett were our neighbours. They were slightly older than us, not by many years but enough for us to defer to them. They loved doing things for us. When Natalie came along, Sarah would take the baby from Viv and shoo us out the door to the pictures. Sarah was thirty-seven when she died. Too young of course. She was a good-looking woman. Handsome rather than pretty. In a black one-piece bathing suit walking for the river at the end of the road with a towel slung over her shoulder is how I prefer to remember her. Dark page-boy hair. Sunglasses. But that healthy picture was misleading; even as she laughed and flashed her white teeth, death was ticking inside her skull. One night she came over to borrow some Disprin after complaining of a headache. Frank had gone out to find an all-night pharmacy but was too long in returning and Sarah couldn't wait. She slumped at our kitchen table. Vivienne gave her a glass of water and popped two Disprin tablets. She swallowed these, then asked for two more. The headache, she said, was like a sledgehammer swinging back and forth inside her head. That night we heard the ambulance come for her. When I went out for a pee around four a.m. the lights were on over at Bennetts'. Frank must have left them on in the panic, either that or he didn't expect to be away long. Next morning I saw him as I was backing out the drive. Frank was walking home from the hospital. He looked dazed, like he might be trying to remember something as simple as his own name. He walked right by the car with his hand to his temple. I watched him take in his milk and pick up the paper off his lawn; then halfway along the garden path he knelt and put the milk down to pull up a weed. And later, much later when I found out that Sarah was dead, I remembered Frank pulling up that weed, and I wondered how he could have found room in his thoughts for such a thing.

There was Sarah's funeral. For a few months after, Frank made a brave show of continuing the way things had been. He was much too light and breezy for his own good and it all caught up with him in the end. One morning I found him sitting by his letterbox, drunk and crying. He was so drunk I had to put him to bed. The next time I saw him was the last. He must have just stepped from the shower because his hair was wet and he'd just put a comb through it. Even his smile looked tried-on as he broke the news to us that he was moving to Auckland.

After Frank, a trail of new people and cars passed in and out of the place, none of whom were interested in being our neighbours. With the last lot, we could only guess at who lived there and who was visiting. There were wild parties. Windows were smashed. I called the police one night, and a few days later we woke to find the house abandoned, the front door open, and a window at the side of the house banging on a broken sash.

There were no more inhabitants until Peter Sutton followed his pregnant cat over to Bennetts'. It was Pete who put Natalie onto the idea of making a home for Mrs Austen over at the Bennetts'. He showed Natalie through the trapdoor under the house, and they came up through a hole in the floorboards. Nine months later, Natalie showed her mother the way.

Ben had whisked Natalie and her mother out to Castle Point for the weekend. Natalie had had the baby already. That had happened three days earlier. Though no one apart from Pete knew about it. For three days and nights Natalie ran between the houses. She was getting up in the middle of the night to go over to Bennetts' to feed her baby. She couldn't have kept that up much longer. The girl must have been in a fog. How that escaped Vivienne's notice I'll never know.

Natalie must have been tempted to tell her mother. She must have wanted to; you'd have thought she was desperate to, and yet, tough little bugger that she is, she held back. She held back for the sake of her mother's happiness. Then something quite unexpected happened.

Ben decided that they needed some time away together and made arrangements for them to spend the weekend out at the coast. Only they forgot to tell Natalie about the plan. Or, if they did, in her sleepless state she soon forgot.

She woke up in the back seat of Ben's car. She saw the countryside flash by the window. The next thing she was shouting at Ben to stop the car. His shoulders rose with a sigh as if her outburst was entirely predictable and that for the moment he would tolerate it and do his best to concentrate on the road. 'Ben, please don't do this. Please, I have to go back. I have to . . .' Ben pretended he couldn't hear. 'Ben, please,' she said. Finally Ben said, 'Vivienne,' and her mother turned around and made a silent plea for peace. Anything for peace.

Several kilometres on, and this time Natalie persuades Ben to stop so she can have a pee.

This is on the road to Castle Point where there is nothing

but hills and sheep and shingle slips. Of course she's not about to squat down where Ben decides so she starts for some trees they passed further back. Vivienne said she was gone five minutes before she and Ben began to wonder what's keeping her. Ben looks up in his rear-view mirror and the next thing Viv says they're reversing up the road at speed. Ben has his window down and is driving with his head turned up the road to where Natalie has pulled over a blue Toyota heading back to town. She's running up the road to the open door of the Toyota. Now they draw even to two young guys. They hadn't made the connection between the pretty girl and the car parked up on the roadside. Now they've seen the whole story and want no part in it. They fishtail in the roadside gravel in their rush to get away.

Ben starts screaming at Natalie to get in the fucking car. He's ballistic. Off his head. 'This is the last fucking time, Vivienne. I swear to God on this.' Vivienne has to play peacemaker. She can't believe it either. She's moving in that brittle way of hers, like the next outburst will see her head explode. She can't believe what she saw with her own eyes. Of course she isn't aware that she's dealing with a young mother beside herself at leaving her baby. She has no idea about all that – a child-mother for God's sake. She snatches Natalie's wrist trying hard to hurt her as she leads her back to the car, whining about how much she has been looking forward to this weekend and now look at who has to go and spoil it.

'No second guesses required,' says Ben.

Vivienne has an idea that Natalie tried to get away again just after they arrived at the beach cottage. I know the place. It's the same cottage that Vivienne and I used to stay in when Natalie was still a baby. It's three doors past the motor camp, a big ugly Fibrolite thing, but with doors that open onto a small lawn and steps down to the beach. Anyway, they arrive and transfer some stuff from the car to the house. Vivienne had given Natalie some money to go to the beach store for milk and bread. Meanwhile she and Ben set up their director chairs. They are having a drink when they look back at each other with the same question. What the hell has happened to Natalie? She's been gone half an hour. Ben puts his drink down and without a word gets up. Viv hears him back the car out. It was a good hour before he returned, this time with Natalie. After the ugly fighting earlier Vivienne doesn't want to say anything which might ignite the situation. She doesn't want to spark anything; she takes the milk and bread from Natalie with a smile and makes a start on preparing their meal.

The first time Vivienne told me that I sat waiting to hear more. She still hadn't explained why she thought Natalie had tried to run off home.

'I thought I explained,' she said.

'No, Viv. You said she was gone for a bit.'

'Well, it must have been just a feeling,' she said.

We were still in the habit of asking each other questions to fill in spaces and answer the other's fears. These sessions hadn't yet reached the interrogatory sessions they would become. The scent of guilt wasn't on either one of us at that point.

The night passes – without incident, she said. The most she would allow was that Ben got into the wine. But that's all. Anyway, in the morning when Viv goes downstairs to put on the coffee she looks in Natalie's room to find her gone. She yells upstairs to Ben. Together they run up to the end of the beach. But that's to satisfy Viv. Ben is happy to see the back of her. He's not about to budge for anything or anyone. 'I know what's happened, Viv. I can tell you now she's hitched a lift back to town,' he says. 'Let go of her. That's my advice.'

They didn't arrive home until five o'clock. Soon as they pull up to the end of the drive Viv runs inside the house. She's ready to tear strips off Natalie. She checks all the rooms. Then she goes back outside and walks up and down the street calling out for her. She feels like she's fetching back a dog that's got loose in the neighbour's rubbish. She knocks on the door of the Harrises'. Ron is at the bowling club and Alice hasn't seen her. She is on the phone to the Suttons when Natalie walks in. 'The crisis appears to be over, Nancy.' Then she puts the phone down. She says to Natalie, 'Well then, Miss Walkabout . . .'

The toilet in the hall flushes and Ben comes out tightening his trouser belt.

'Well. Well. Well. Look what the cat dragged in.'

Viv folds her arms. She says, 'I'm still waiting to hear . . .'

'Miss Holiday Cheer,' says Ben.

'Well?' asks her mother again.

'Forget it, Vivienne. It'll be lies by the dozen,' says Ben. He heads out to the kitchen and they follow after. In the kitchen, Ben assumes the role of the injured party. He acts put out. He runs back over all they did to look for her. How they combed the beach and left messages at the motor camp and at the beach store. Until Natalie, bless her, interrupts to ask, 'Did you call the police?'

'Ben was talking,' says her mother.

'That's okay, Vivienne,' says Ben. 'That was next on my list. The police was the next stop after this.'

He opens the fridge and they watch him fish around for a beer. 'Behind the eggs,' says Viv.

Natalie starts to leave the kitchen.

'Wait,' says Vivienne. 'You're not going anywhere until I find out a few things. What I want to know, young lady, is how you got home.'

'I hitched,' she says.

'See! Wild. Untameable. What did I say, Viv? I said it would be a mistake to bring her.'

'Ben, wait, please. You can have your say in a minute. First, I want to hear from Natalie. I want you to tell me what is going on. First leaping out of cars, now this disappearing act. What is going on here?'

Natalie hardly knows where to begin. She's made a decision to tell her mother but she doesn't know how to describe the situation or where to begin or who to blame. She looks at Ben smirking, then back at her mother's folded arms. She says, 'I'll show you.'

'This'll be good,' says Ben. 'Show and tell.'

Viv though is not so dismissive, not nearly enough for Ben's liking. 'No, Vivienne, really. Come on,' he says.

'No,' says Viv. 'If that's what she wants then let's do that and see where it leads us. I don't want us to end up screaming abuse at one another. I want this to be handled in a calm and reasonable manner.'

They start off up the hall, Natalie leading the way.

'This better be good, young lady,' says her mother. Then at the door she hesitates. She looks out at the road and asks Natalie, 'Does this mean I will need shoes?'

'Nope,' she says.

But out in the street Viv starts worrying about shoes. The pavement is hot enough to fry eggs on. Then she starts to wonder where she is being taken. At the top of Bennetts' drive she says, 'Oh no. I don't think so, Natalie. This is private property.'

'It's Mrs Austen's place,' says Natalie, and her mother's heart sinks.

'Not that bloody bird,' she says. 'Not this again. Is this what this is all about? Is this what you want to show me?'

'Please, Ma,' she says. 'We're nearly there.'

And, seeing how crushed she looks, Viv motions with her hand for Natalie to continue.

'I asked if I would need shoes. I did ask,' she says.

In the Bennetts' drive, and as they draw level with the kitchen window, Ben taps on the window and raises his eyes. Viv replies with a shrug. She mouths something like, 'How the hell do I know?'

She follows Natalie around to the trapdoor at the side of the house. This is where Pete followed Orange Cat, and Natalie followed Pete, and now Viv with much less enthusiasm is considering the trail. She crouches down and peers into the dark space underneath the house. She says, 'You can forget that for starters. I'm not going in there.'

'Then I can't show you what I have to show you,' says Natalie.

'Dammit! Natalie. Damn you,' says her mother. 'Can't you just tell me?' Natalie shuts her eyes and shakes her head, and her mother says, 'This is hardly the time to be asking me for favours.' Still, Vivienne manages to poke her head through the trapdoor. She peers into the shadows. 'Are there any spiders under here?'

'Nope.'

'Dead things. I know cats choose places like these . . .'

'It's just a short way. You're almost there,' says Natalie.

'I'm the one you should be trying to please,' says her mother.

She wriggles through, complaining and bitching every inch of the way. 'I can't believe I'm doing this. You'll never get Ben under here. I can tell you that now.'

Natalie shifts the ply covering and a moment later Viv emerges in a block of dazzling daylight. For a moment her earlier fears of trespass lift. In a frivolous moment she says, 'Hello Frankie. Hello Sarah.'

Natalie is already over by the door.

'Wait. Wait. Bloody hell,' says Vivienne. She takes a moment to brush the dust off herself. In the hall she notices the walled-up heat. The house is a furnace. This is when Viv said she began to feel afraid. She took a forward step and stopped and couldn't move after that. Natalie had to come and get her. Even then at the top of the hall she refused to be led any further and peered around the door – not wanting any skeletons or other unpleasant surprises to topple down on her.

'My God,' she said, her eye sweeping the room. The same view that I would see an hour later. Mrs Austen in her gaudy costume of feathers. She remembers the bird. Viv is discovering and labelling things. Working through a trail of objects – a filthy, stained towel; now a mattress. Natalie tries to get her to step inside the room but her mother resists. 'No. No, Natalie. I think I want to stay where I am for now. Thank you.' She looks around the room again. 'Say something, Natalie. Tell me what is going on. What am I looking at? I don't like what I'm thinking. What's that you're holding, darling? What's that . . . that carton?'

Natalie pulls a rag away from the baby's face and holds the carton out to her mother.

Viv said it took her breath away. She didn't know what to say. She looked away. The thing in the carton – it made her feel sick. She says she had to force herself to look again. 'Say something, please, Natalie. I need you to say something.'

'It's a baby, Mum,' she says.

'Oh God. Yes. Yes. It is,' says Vivienne.

'Choo Woo,' says Natalie. 'That's her name.'

'Oh my God,' says Vivienne. 'Oh my God.'

'She's dead, Ma,' says Natalie then. 'I tried to get back and feed her. I tried and Ben stopped me. I tried, Ma. I did. I got here as fast as I could. Now she's dead. And it's not fair. It isn't.'

Vivienne's hands hover over the carton. She knows she should pick up the baby but she can't bring herself to. The tiny limbs will snap in her hands. She presents her hands then takes them away. She doesn't know what to think or do. Then she notices Natalie, the small pale face with its hopeful eyes, hoping that her mother won't be too mad, that she won't tell her off.

'Oh my poor baby,' says Viv. 'My poor baby.' She puts her arms around Natalie and whispers in her ear. 'Who did this to you? Who? I need to know, darling.'

'Mr Fonda,' she says.

'Who?' she asks. 'Who did you say, darling?' But as she asks the question she's making the connection. 'Oh God. Oh God,' she says, looking away to a distant wall inside her head, bouncing off thoughts, wondering how, and realising, fitting in pieces she hadn't thought of belonging to one another. Ben's treats. The meals out.

'I'm sorry, Mum. I'm so sorry. I wasn't going to tell you. I don't know what to do.'

'You've done enough,' says Viv. 'You did this? All by yourself?'

'Pete was here,' she says.

'The Sutton boy? Good God. All by yourself? My poor baby.' She pulls Natalie in to her, and stares at the far wall.

'Ben!' she says then.

They leave by the back door this time with Viv striding ahead up the drive. She doesn't notice the gravel effect on her feet. She runs up the steps into the house, and in the hall she shouts for Ben. She shouts for him and at him.

He hasn't moved from where they left him, at the table, nursing his can of beer, interested to see them back, mildly amused by the door-banging and shouting. He smiles at each one, mother and daughter, at the way they are looking at him, and something else as well, that invisible *somethingarather* that can change the air when both are in the room at the same time. I've felt it plenty of times. I'm sure Ben has too.

'So, Viv. What was it this time? Another bird's nest? An interesting feather?' Ben is hugging himself at the prospect.

'I want you out of my house.'

'Well, that's different,' says Ben. 'I wasn't expecting that.'

'Now. Right this minute. I don't want you here another second.'

Ben pops his eyes with mock surprise. He tries to find Natalie with a smile.

'You leave her alone,' says her mother, and Ben raises his hands in mock surrender. 'Just get out of my house. Get out now and nothing more will be said.'

'Whoah,' says Ben. He crosses his legs and smiles up at her. 'I'm lost, Viv. I'm totally lost on this one. I mean, you're joking, right?'

'I don't want any screaming or yelling. I just want you gone,' she says.

'I'm sorry, Viv, but I still don't get it. I thought Natalie was the bad egg here. She was, what . . .' He looks at his watch. 'Fifteen minutes ago? Two hours ago, well that was quite a different story. You should have heard your mother, Natalie. You'd be feeling a bit sick if you could have heard your mother on about you.'

'Either you leave the house or I call the cops,' says Viv, and that gets Ben's attention.

He rises to his feet and holds his hands out. 'Okay, Viv, let's stay calm, shall we.' Then he starts shaking his head. He opens the palms of his hands. 'I don't know what to say,' he says.

'I think I'll just call the cops anyway,' she says.

'All right. All right!' he says. 'Let's go back to the beginning. Information, Vivy!'

'You've been interfering with my baby,' she says.

'Interfering,' he says. Viv said he didn't miss a beat. He didn't so much as blink. In a split second he absorbed the shock of being found out and rallied his defence. He dropped a hand onto the table and looked her in the eye. 'You wouldn't mean a certain schoolgirl's infatuation, would you?' Then he starts nodding like this is something he's been holding back from telling for some time.

'No, Ben. I don't want to hear any more lies. I'm not going to look away any longer,' she says.

'Look away,' he says. 'What the hell is that supposed to mean?' He starts towards her. 'I need information, Viv.'

'Don't! Don't come any closer,' she warns him.

'I'm lost, baby. I'm all at sea here, Viv. Natalie?' He takes a step towards Natalie until Viv shouts that she will call the cops.

'I will, Ben. I'll call the cops.'

'You listen to some schoolgirl fantasy and that's it?'

'Oh God, Ben, how I wish.'

'Well, that is how I'm reading it, Viv. I haven't heard anything that contains so much as a grain of truth. And frankly, I would have thought I deserved better.'

'All right, Ben. The truth. If that's what you want.'

'It is. It is,' he says.

'I was prepared to give you an easy way out, Ben. If you left by the door I mightn't've done anything more. So long as you were gone . . .'

Ben is trying a range of different expressions on her. 'I'm sorry, Viv, but it's none the clearer.'

'All right,' she says. 'If that's what you want.' She checks with Natalie who nods. 'All right, I'll show you.'

'Hallelujah!' rejoices Ben. 'A breakthrough at last.'

They file out. In the hall Viv had the presence of mind to pick up Ben's cellphone from the hall table.

Ben's brought his can of beer with him. Outside he laughs at their Pied Piper formation, and as they enter the Bennetts' drive he says, 'I might have guessed this house would be somehow involved. What are you going to show me, ladies? A ghost? A poltergeist?' He's chuckling to himself, marvelling at the situation. 'Two hours ago we were enjoying ourselves at a certain beach house. Do you remember what we were doing, Viv?'

'Shut up!' she says. 'For once in your life . . .'

'Oh, it bites after all,' he laughs.

This time they enter the Bennetts' through the back door. Vivienne goes first. In the kitchen Ben calls out, 'Hello! Anyone home?' Then to Natalie he whispers, 'Where's the Pied Piper taking us?' And Viv snaps back at him to back off.

'It was just a question, Viv. Not a fucking missile attack.'

They carry on up to the front room. Ben stations himself at the door. They watch him take it all in. His eye arrives at Mrs Austen. 'Christ Almighty.' But the other stuff – a Coke bottle, the cough lollies, the bloody towel. His expression changes by degrees. 'So, Miss Natalie, this is where you've been hiding. The bird.' He nods at Mrs Austen's stand. 'Clever to think of that.'

'I don't want you talking to her. Anything you want to say you say to me. You got that?' says Vivienne.

'Mother fucking Hubbard,' he says.

Viv ignores the insult. She says to Natalie, 'Go ahead. Show him.'

Natalie picks up the carton and shoves it under Ben's nose.

'What the fuck is that?' he says.

'It's your baby,' says Vivienne. Then she says, 'All right, Natalie.' And she takes the carton away from Ben's stricken face.

'Vivienne, surely you don't think . . .'

But Viv puts her hands to her ears. 'No! I don't want to hear it.'

'Surely to God . . .'

'I'm not listening, Ben. I'm not . . .'

'Vivy sweet. This is crazy. Madness.'

'I said *enough*! That's why we're here in this room, Ben. I'm tired of your lies. I am sick to death of your explanations.'

'Okay, then. All right.' He takes a deep breath and looks Viv in the eye. 'I've tried to be patient. I am trying, Viv . . . But there are some things that are difficult for a mother to understand . . .'

'You poor sick bastard,' she says.

'Please don't say that, Vivienne.'

'Sick. Sick. Sick,' she says.

'I wish,' he starts to say. 'Really this is so undignified.' He closes his eyes and takes a deep breath. Perhaps the scene will disappear when he opens them. The horror will pass like some ghastly joke. Then when he opens his eyes he starts laughing. 'Really, Viv. I'm sorry. But you should see yourself. You look like a cancerous old hen.'

'Say what you like. I don't care any more,' she says.

'All right. All right. You're right. Enough. This isn't getting us anywhere. We're beating up on one another when I think what we should do is go over to the Suttons' and confront Mr and Mrs over their wayward son.'

'Ben,' says Vivienne, 'Peter Sutton is twelve years old. He's just a little boy.'

Ben starts to blink furiously. He looks around for Natalie. 'Ball's in your court, Natalie. This is becoming a serious matter. I wonder how far you're prepared to carry this little make-believe . . .'

'I haven't made up anything,' she says. 'It's all true.'

'Natalie, please . . .'

'It is . . .'

'Unbelievable,' says Ben. 'Viv, are you really going to listen to her on this?'

Then Natalie says, 'I called her Choo Woo.'

'What?' says Ben. 'What did you say?'

More meekly this time she explains: 'The baby. It's a she. I called her Choo Woo.'

'You little shit,' says Ben. He steps in Natalie's direction and as he does so Viv picked up the Coke bottle.

'No, Ben! I warned you. Stay away from her.'

'She's trying to ruin me. Us. Viv. She's trying to bugger up everything and all because of that ugly fucking thing!'

He flicked out his hand and caught the carton with the baby in it, knocking it from Natalie's grasp. Then Vivienne dropped the Coke bottle and started hammering her fists against Ben's chest. He pushed her off easily. 'Pathetic. You're all so bloody pathetic.' He walked out of there with his beer can. Viv says he stopped on the front porch to take a drink, emptied it and threw it back down the hall. She waited until he went home, then she rang me – and caught me home in Michael Street, half-listening, and half-turned to the cricket drama in the Caribbean.

# THREE

I followed the last of the ponytailed rollerbladers out the park gates and drove over to Cooper Street. There was a leafy kind of light about – not that I was concerned about being caught looking in a house window; the pensioners were all indoors. Vivienne will want to know what he looks like, how he's changed. I found him where I left him last time watching the flickering screen, in the same armchair, a dangling arm, fingertips resting on top of a beer can. I'd say he's a little greyer than when he was living in South Road. A little paunchier. A man dressed in office black and white but without a job as far as I can tell: '. . . cut out of the land of the living, for the transgression of thy people was he stricken . . .' It's just deserts in my view.

Ben broke my heart. Then he corrupted me. He led me to a very deep place in the soul that I'd prefer to have remained ignorant of, but as a result of which, when I sit with Maggie out at Babylon, I know good and evil. I know better than most out at that purple church about these duelling kingdoms. I am alive to the possibilities of good and evil cohabiting under one roof. Ben taught me that – because, isn't it true that what he did to my baby I have repeated – not in the physical sense, God save me from that, no – but in my need to know I have gone through the very same doors that Ben did?

I have pestered Natalie for information, always wanting more, wanting to drag the shaded areas of her experience into the light. 'Then what, sweetheart?' On that question the doors have creaked open to forbidden worlds. I have had to know, and knowing has turned me into what I am today. Many times as I have re-enacted beating Ben to a pulp, of the same necessity I have seduced my baby.

Dawn in the countryside is a religious event. Reuben told me that when we were in prison. The dawn is slipping by outside my side window, the fresh dew in the slabs of paddock flying past. Dawn finds a broken-down barn sagging at the knees but with a will to stay up despite everything. A painted cow. Sheep that have been dipped in white paint and which run off batteries for a limited life span. This is what Natalie saw early one morning on this same road with Ben beside her.

This is how childhood slipped from her. One night she

went to bed with thoughts for Mrs Austen. In the morning she woke to the luminous white of her mother's boyfriend's underwear.

'Did you forget?' he says to her. Twice now she has foxed him, pretending to sleep when he's come choo wooing into her room at night. Is that what he's talking about?

'Our day at the beach. This is the day,' he says.

She thinks to ask after her mother. Has he left her a note? He tells her that Vivienne has given them her blessing. But if that's the case then why are they stealing out of the house? Why is he whispering at her to hurry? *Hurry.*

They are halfway to Tinui when she remembers Mrs Austen. She turns to Ben with the thought popping out of her like a confession.

'I forgot to feed her, Ben.' And when he doesn't respond (she says he appeared to be in a deep slumber) she repeats what she just said, and this time he says, 'I heard, princess.' And he looks pissed off to have heard. He looks out his side window and shakes his head.

'I thought we had all that out. I thought the bird was over at Suttons'.'

'She is,' she says. She'd lied because Bennetts' is out of bounds and Pete's secret.

'Then I don't see what the problem is. If it's over at Suttons' Pete can feed it. True?' She has no choice but to agree. She sits back defeated, her thoughts back with Mrs Austen waiting in the plastic ice-cream container, her eyes circling at every strange noise.

Near Tinui she asked if they could stop at the garage so she could telephone Pete. She anticipated his question. She says Pete thinks he's feeding a dog. He tends to ram the food into Mrs Austen's mouth. 'Please, Ben?' she asks. Ben released his mouth as though he might be about to say something, then he changed his mind, and Natalie felt the car accelerate beneath them.

Slowly he turns her thoughts around. He breaks down her defences and turns her mind to other things.

He has promised to show her what he and Vivienne used to do, and Natalie is a willing learner. She is curious to know more, to experience that other side of her mother, that part which is always facing the other way, that part which is always eclipsed by a mother-child concern for which shadow and censorship were invented.

Think of the man we saw up on the stage – winking to his audience. Here he is turning to Natalie with a story about her mother taking off her top and driving out to the coast bare-breasted.

'No!' says Natalie. She can't believe that of her mother. She is of course over the moon and delirious at the possibility.

'She did. Absolutely. I'm telling you she did. She sat right where you are now.'

She places the palms of her hands either side of her knees on the upholstered seat.

'Here?' she asks, then looking out at the road and bare hills she wonders, 'Did anyone see her?'

'A truck,' recalls Ben, then he remembers. 'Yes! Oh yes, a farmhand. Boy, you should have seen his face!'

'Like?'

'Like he'd looked up and caught a glimpse of I don't know what. As you know, your mother is rather large in that department.'

When we heard these things Vivienne couldn't believe that the man she had invited into her home and who slept with her each night was the same person Natalie spoke of. They seemed like two different people.

Riversdale. I used to come here all the time. Then, after discovering what Ben had done to Natalie, and, more to the point, where, parts of the landscape vanished for me. Bits of Ben stuck to everywhere that I'd held to be precious, and so Riversdale was one of those places which dropped off the map. But forgetting was a stupid thing to hope for. You don't know that of course, not at the time you don't. You just keep averting your eyes and blocking your thoughts, and hoping to be diverted by something new. In my case, Babylon was that something new, and Maggie. Then, after a while, and as Rube has said often enough, time is the cure. Reason slips in its ten cents' worth. Reason says, if I give up places like Riversdale, because of the unpleasant memories they hold, then I might as well give up Natalie.

There's a nice clean look to the sea today. Long watery walls, razor-sharp at the top with the light shining through. It's not so long ago that I'd have been out there in amongst it. The reason why I'm a house painter is the sea. In the days when I was surfing, house painting seemed the only compatible occupation. You got to keep your own hours, and when you're nineteen years of age nothing is more important than being master of your own time. Then I met Vivienne. She knew she was marrying a distracted man with a gap in his front teeth, and that income would be uncertain, a point worrying to some but not to us, not when you're nineteen years old.

The black-suited surfers perching on their seahorses lay down and began scratching to make it outside a larger set. A section broke left and right just north of the motor camp on a mid-tide bar. I watched a curtain of white water chase a surfer along a wall and I seemed to remember something like joy.

I drove past the beach houses and baches, small blunt-looking dwellings, some elevated on sticks straining for more view of the ocean. I didn't see another soul and what I found to be slightly depressing must have been reassuring to a man of Ben's age driving along with a young girl in the passenger seat. I parked where they did at the end of the road. From here a sandy track weaves through clumps of speargrass and sandhills down to an empty and wild beach. Ben picked his spot well.

Natalie still didn't know what shape the day would take. She gets out of Ben's Mazda sniffing the shaded air, blinking at the white sand, wondering aloud where they are going.

'Going?' says Ben. 'We're not *going* anywhere. We're here, sunshine. We've arrived at our island.'

It must have been a merry moment. Ben locking up, packing away the cheap fizzy wine, then leading Natalie through the sandhills. 'Might as well whip your sneakers and socks off,' he tells her. 'They're no good to you here. I don't want Vivienne bitching at me about wet clothes.'

They made their way south – Natalie in the shore break, Ben on the wet sand, reminiscing, 'Viv used to love it here. She'd take off her shoes and run about in the sand. Of course she took off more than that if there was no one around.'

'No!' says Natalie – delighted and outraged. 'Not Mum.'

'Vivienne did. Sure. Why not?'

She can't picture it – that's why not. But she likes to hear these stories. She sometimes thinks of her mother as only partially complete. She knows her father won't tell her anything. I wouldn't talk privately about Viv to a child except in my fable of the woman who turned me into a chicken. But Ben is different. Ben tells her all sorts of things. Wild things she'd never have imagined of her mother, like all those times she was at school and her mother came out here with Ben, riding topless in the passenger seat of the car. Her mother is a more interesting person than she thought. She presses Ben for more information.

'Your mother,' he tells her. 'She'd walk for miles without a stitch on. We both did. A couple of desert island characters.'

'And you were Man Friday?' she says, and Ben's eyes twinkle.

'That's right, Nat. That's right. I was.'

They continue south for the sandhills and farmland, and at some point Ben tells her to keep an eye out for Vivienne's old footprints. But, footprints don't last that long, do they? She wonders at this, pondering Ben's strange comment. The noise of the sea is colossal. The faraway cries of the gulls. She looks across to Ben stomping in the sand, a thin smile under the brim of his sun hat.

At some point Natalie started to splash water at him and Ben drew back like he was ducking knives.

'Chicken shit! Chicken shit!' she yells at him, and wily Ben, grinning in mock horror says, 'Who me? Who's chicken shit?' He steps out of his trousers and catches up to her, and starts splashing water at her. 'So I'm chicken shit, eh? Is that what you think?'

'You were.'

'Grumpy,' he calls her then.

'I'm not.'

'You were.'

'Maybe.' The moment becomes dull as out of nothing-ness she remembers Mrs Austen and holds onto the thought.

'Happy?' asks Ben.

She nods.

After a while Ben has had enough of the walking. He looks behind himself calculating their distance and decides it's time he described the situation. Here it is, then. They are the survivors of a shipwreck. Ben raises an eyebrow and Natalie takes this as a signal to slip into character. So they stagger their shipwrecked selves out of the tide up the white sand past the high tide mark to a sheltered place at the bottom of a sandhill, where Ben produces a bottle of plonk. 'Yalumba. Vivienne's favourite . . .' If it's Vivienne's favourite then it must be Natalie's as well.

'Down the hatch,' says Ben.

She is surprised by the way it dries out the tongue. The weightlessness of it, like foam, but leaving a tartness which she can only get rid of by taking another mouthful.

Looking on, Ben laughs. 'Vivienne will not be pleased if I turn you into a lush.' But she knows by his tone that he is not the slightest bit concerned either.

Now she watches Ben gaze up and down the beach. He seems to be looking for something.

'Yup.'

'Yup what?'

'This is it.'

'Where?'

'Where Vivienne . . . silly . . .'

'Oh,' she says. 'Oh that!' How could she forget that. She giggles, and as another line of foam races up the beach she imagines her mother stepping through it, and realises suddenly that she has arrived at a place in her mother's past. 'We're here! We're a couple of Crusoes!' She closes her eyes. The sun is warm. She feels like she is glowing from the inside out. She says to Ben, 'I like being a Crusoe.' She inhales in a way she hopes is how her mother might have, but then, opening her eyes, she finds Ben looking at her doubtfully.

'I don't want to disappoint you but you don't quite cut it as a Crusoe figure.'

'Why not? What's the matter with me?'

'Your clothes for starters. Did you forget? We've just struggled ashore.'

'And we're shipwrecked.'

'Right,' he says. 'Okay. The thing to do is to hang our clothes out to dry. That's how Vivienne and I used to go about it. Still, that was then and this is now. Different performances.'

'Can't we play it too?'

It must have been music to Ben's ears. He must have been congratulating himself while training his eyes to bulge at the unexpectedness of Natalie's brilliant suggestion.

'Well, yes. I suppose so,' he says. And Natalie watches the idea spread to different parts of his face. 'You're right, Natalie. That's what we are here for. You're the one calling the shots.'

She takes off her Mickey Mouse sweat top and hands it to Ben.

'Garment number one,' he says. She pulls the T-shirt over her head and unsnaps her bra. 'Garment two and three . . . Garment four . . .' And so on until she is naked as a piece of driftwood. It's a wonderful feeling. The best kind of feeling. She runs down to the water.

'Look at me. I'm Vivienne!' She raises her knees in a

way she has imagined her mother doing to make fun of a marching girl. And Ben calls back, 'You're a beautiful woman, Vivienne.' She knows how happy it makes her mother to hear this, and knowing now how it feels she smiles her Vivienne smile.

Now they walk up the beach to dry themselves on a bleached log. Ben gets out the Yalumba. She is feeling skilled at this now. She takes the bottle and tips it back in her mouth, spilling some which Ben laps up like a dog with his tongue.

'Waste not, want not,' he says, and it's the funniest thing she's ever heard. They fall about laughing – Natalie at the dog-tongue feeling.

Around the next point they find themselves in a horse-shoe bay. They are all alone in the world. It is their desert island. Ben takes off his clothes. He makes a joke of it – flinging his shirt and underpants over his head. They laugh at themselves. She laughs at him – at the funny sock thing with the blind eye. Then Ben leans back and pretends to take a reading of the sun's position and decides that it's time they built a shelter.

Giggling with Yalumba Natalie asks, 'Do you think it's dangerous?'

'What?' Then he sees what she's getting at. 'Well, yes. Quite possibly . . .'

'Tigers. Snakes?'

'You know,' he begins to say, then dismisses whatever idea he had. 'No, I'd rather not speculate for now.'

They set to, gathering lengths of driftwood which Ben sorts into different lengths. The longer pieces he starts to assemble into a frame. The lengths rest into one another. The main frame he ties at the top with his belt. Then he produces a Swiss Army knife and cuts some flax for the floor.

Natalie watches him make a mattress of their clothing. It's like he's done all this before. He sits down and smiles up at her.

'Want to know something?'

'Maybe.'

'You know why people get fat?'

'Why?'

'You won't believe this. Maybe I shouldn't tell.'

'No! Tell! Tell!' She begs him.

'It's because they swallow clouds.'

'Clouds!'

'They swallow clouds. It's the absolute truth. Do you want me to show you?'

'Yes,' she says giggling. She definitely needs to know about this.

He pats the ground beside himself, beside Crusoe, and she lies down and tilts her head back. He instructs her to open her mouth wider. 'Wider!' She is reminded of the coaching voice at the driving range. Doubt and hope seesaw inside of her. Can she do it? She has to do it. 'Wider, princess. The sun has to shine like a torch down your throat. Otherwise the clouds won't know where to go. That's it. That's it,' he says. Then he tells her, 'Close your eyes unless you want to be blinded.' She closes her eyes and feels his mouth on hers. Ben's lips on hers. Then Ben blows hot desert air down her throat. She feels the cloud build and muster in her stomach, and it is a fat feeling. She is becoming bloated. Ben has made her fat! Her head starts to swim and the sky shifts from circles to rectangles. Her head is light and giggly. Her arms and legs though feel like sandbags. She could close her eyes and sleep. Or, she could float up to the sky. Float across the Tasman. Or she could do nothing in particular or she could do everything that is asked of her. Or, she might just be whatever Ben decides she is.

'Hello, Vivienne,' says the voice next to her.

Or, she might just be Vivienne. She smiles her Vivienne smile. She closes her Vivienne eyes.

Then the voice beside her says, 'May I say hello to Vivienne's young breasts? How are you and you. My, are you twins?' She laughs at Ben's put-on English butler's voice. She laughs and Ben says, 'I know what Vivienne's breasts like most of anything in this world.'

'What? What?' She's bursting to find out her mother's secrets.

'This,' he says.

And 'this' is Ben's chest fuzzing up against her, and then, she wonders through her closed eyelids, is that his mouth closing over her breast?

'My. My. My,' he says.

She forgot who she was there for a moment. She forgot she is Vivienne. She remembers to smile Vivienne's smile.


And the next? These are the details, the things that she told her mother. So I heard them secondhand. You need to know. You have to know. But then you can't forget it or put it behind you. You can't shove it in a room and lock the door. This is information that stays with you forever, clouding everything. The world is not quite the same place any more. Ben opened a door to a room I never asked to look inside. Here it is, then. Here it is.

His cheeks muzzle and dog her ribcage and she yelps. He announces a new plan and immediately she wants to know. 'What? What?'

He will paint her in tiger stripes. That is, if she wants.

Of course, she cries. 'Yes. Yes.' But with what, she wonders. 'Lie back, Vivienne,' he tells her. She feels his tongue circle her neck. Jack Frost, she thinks. Another stripe down her left side leaves her shivering and tingling, tingling all over. Next he paints a stripe down her middle. He starts between her breasts and she feels his dog tongue draw a line down her belly, around her belly button, circling there, before moving on. The stripe keeps going. Lengthening. She lifts her knees and as she does so she feels Ben's tongue slip inside her. 'God! No!' She thought it – but didn't actually cry out. She's thinking she ought to, but isn't really sure, not so certain now that this other feeling has set in, now that she is Vivienne, and Ben's tongue is darting here and there into new places for a tongue. He stripes the inside of her thighs and does a circle around her opening. Then it stops. She can feel the old track marks drying over her. She opens her eyes and there's Ben, astride her, but not touching, and there's his thing at a nagging and demanding lean. Ben too, with his angry eyes.

'Tiger it,' he whispers. 'Tiger it.' She remembers the voice at the driving range telling her off within earshot of other golfers after she topped the ball. So she does as he asks. She does so without knowing why or what next. She waits for Ben's instructions.

Now he pushes her down and gets between her legs and all the blind bends crash together. Yes. No. Yes. No. He wedges himself in my baby. She doesn't know what next, she worries that she is going to disappoint. She cries at his dumbfuck shoulder. 'It's not working. It's not!'

'Come on, Vivienne. You like this . . .'

'I'm not Vivienne. I'm not!' But it's too late to revert to Natalie. Ben isn't listening. She can feel the resolve of his body. He tells her to calm herself, to relax, to breathe slowly. As she does so he surprises her, pushing up inside and everything gives. Everything. Everything is easier now that new space has been discovered. She feels her insides grabbing at him. Now Ben is breathing next to her. Panting his dog pant. Then he collapses over her. For a long time, she said, she lay there with a dead weight on her. She was waiting patiently for the coach's voice to return. Then at last Ben decides it is morning. He sits up. She thought he looked puzzled, like he'd just woken up and found himself naked and next to her in a crude shelter.

The sea is no longer a pleasant surprise. It is numbingly cold. She kneels in it until a small wave washes up inside her. She scrubs delicately because everything feels sore and newly discovered. Ben wades out and dives into a wave. He comes up snorting, closing first one nostril then the other. She watches him for these adult moves. She watches him crouch down for a handful of wet sand. She watches the way he washes between his legs – holding himself, inspecting himself. She says they dressed in silence. Then Ben scattered the flax and kicked the driftwood frame apart, and within a minute it was like it was never there, and by the time they wandered around the point back into view of the baches and beach houses the idea of the desert island had vanished. They are back in character. She has given up Vivienne. She is back to Natalie, and Ben has shed Crusoe and all talk of tigers and snakes. She walks back to the car following old footprints. Vivienne's, she realises.

These are not pleasant things to think about. It is, however, my daughter's past, her history, and that cannot be rubbed out or started again. Still, I hate to think how many times

I've played that scene over and over in my mind; from Natalie's point of view to begin with, and then from Ben's, wondering what kind of man he is, and why that day, that hour, and what kind of hunger beat in his heart. Wondering is what leads you to commit the same crime.

I've walked further than I intended. On other occasions I've looked for Crusoe's shelter, but of course the elements have long since rearranged everything. The wind has dashed in here like a practical nurse anxious to tidy up after the obscenity. I wish there was a cleaning woman in my head. I don't mean to forget; but I would like for there to be a pause between the here and now and what happened. I'd like to have my life back.

I trudged back up the beach to the van. I drove slowly past the empty houses. What must Natalie have felt? What was she thinking? I'm sure Ben was wondering the same thing: is that a smile or frown on princess's face? Natalie didn't know what she should feel or what there was she might talk about. For a brief time she had been Vivienne. Now she was back to Natalie with a memory of a driftwood shelter and the play of shadow and light. Everything with a positive and a negative. The yeses and noes banging into one another. The *yessino* of Ben's dog's tongue. The collapsible feeling inside of her and the *yessinoes* the world expanded to after that.

Ben, of course, had to know more precisely. He kept looking between her and the road wishing she would say something – until, finally, he takes the initiative. 'Tell you what. Why don't I make a start? All I want to say is this. Our little shipwreck experience has to remain our secret. You realise that, don't you.'

'Yes, Ben,' she says.

'Our secret. No one else's.'

'I know, Ben.'

'I know you do, Princess. But I just want it understood that we don't want to hurt those closest to us, do we?'

She shook her head and bit her gums at the thought of her mother sitting on the edge of the bed staring at the morning walls. At any cost she must protect her. She must sacrifice.

It was dark before Ben got her back to Masterton. He dropped her outside the Solway. She sometimes ate there with her mother. Especially if Ben had rehearsals or was out of town and if I was also unavailable.

'Remember what I said, princess.'

'I know, Ben.'

Then, as she's getting out, Ben reaches for her wrist. 'Hey!' She thought she must have forgotten something. Then she remembers to say, 'Thanks.'

'Mates?' he asks.

'Mates,' she answers.

She watched Ben re-enter the traffic then she walked across the forecourt. She stopped outside the glass doors at the entrance. She could see the front desk to the left of the foyer. Her mother was signing in a guest. Her mother looked so unawares, and on a day when so much had happened, that she was struck by a new discovery of how apart their lives were. The guest departed and she watched the smile leave her mother's face. It was like something whipped off a table top. Alone, she looked so much more daunting. One glance from her mother and she feels that her flesh and bone will part. Everything will come out and in a blink her mother will revert to the sad figure perched on the edge of her bed inscribed in Natalie's memory from the time after her father walked out so she turns around and starts for home. She was in South Road before she remembered to think of Mrs Austen. It was already dark. The streetlights picked up the tips of the long grass in Bennetts'. The drive at the side of the house disappeared into a black hole. She looked back across the road and wondered why the lights weren't on in Suttons'. It was Pete's idea to leave the back door locked. He said a secret place shouldn't have a common entrance, and, as he pointed out, bird houses don't have doors. They have entrances. She wished she had overruled him because she knew in her heart of hearts she couldn't crawl underneath the house and go to Mrs Austen, however needy and however appalling was the thought of her with just big, dumb Benson, her teddy, for company.

The next morning, she went across to Bennetts', slid under the house, no problem, and found Mrs Austen lying on the bottom of the ice-cream container, her neck splayed awkwardly, her eyes still and wax-like, the beak half-open as if death had come in the middle of an interesting thought.

# FOUR

We enjoyed a gentle winter that year. The serious cold that threatens July and August failed to arrive. We woke to a few nasty frosts, and one or two southerly fronts shook the trees, but they came and went, and people began to look around at where they lived with a fond regard. Soon, though, a sense of foreboding crept into their thoughts. If it was this good then you could bet there would be a price to pay. Summer would be hell. Some predicted drought. Others, floods. Now we began to view with suspicion these blue days piling up as we waited for the worst to arrive.

Natalie and Pete Sutton across the street spent their days climbing the trees for feathers and pretending to live the life Mrs Austen should have had and perhaps would have but for Natalie's loss of nerve. Pete managed to talk his father round to taking Mrs Austen off to a taxidermist; after that the bird was smuggled back to Bennetts' looking fuller in body and healthier than it had in life. In the trees of Queen Elizabeth Park Natalie and Pete perched on branches talking to each other in their bird talk, and while they worked on transforming Mrs Austen back to some semblance of adulthood, Ben was doing something similar to Natalie.

During that same spell of fine house-painting weather, Natalie seemed to be sick a lot. What we failed to recognise at the time was classic morning sickness. Still, you don't make a connection like that with a twelve-year-old. Once when she came into the kitchen and the smell of Ben's fried eggs turned her stomach, she heaved on the spot. Vivienne put it down to a stomach bug. She made Natalie stay home, and from the hotel she caught Ben on his mobile and asked him to drop by the house to check on her.

Natalie was getting out of the bath when Ben waltzed in the bathroom door like it was a public entrance. She reached for a towel to cover herself up and he laughed at her modesty, averting his eyes and still managing to find her in the mirror.

'Well, hello, Vivienne. Look at you. It's Vivienne to a T. Vivienne's cheekbones. It's Vivienne made perfect.'

'Do you think so?' she says.

'Oh, no question. Absolutely no doubt.'

'So I'm Vivienne?' She's getting used to these character changes now. She smiles. She smiles back at herself in the mirror. Over her shoulder Ben raises a finger.

83

'In actual fact,' he says, 'I'm Mr Fonda calling in on Mrs Fonda.'

She's a bit slow on the uptake. She doesn't want to appear dumb, but she hasn't heard of these characters before.

Ben, however, seems aware that he has got ahead of himself, so he puts Mr and Mrs Fonda away for the moment. 'Hey,' he says, 'I just had a thought. Do you remember the first time I came round?'

'Yes.'

'Rubbish! You were fast asleep.'

'No. I remember.'

'What was Vivienne wearing?'

'A red halter-neck and tan-coloured jeans.'

'Possibly. I'd need you to show me to be sure.'

So they troop through to Vivienne's room where Natalie opens her mother's wardrobe and starts parting the dresses, tops and coats. And when she fails to find what she's after he says, 'Yes, I had an idea you were fast asleep.'

'Nope,' she says, determined to prove otherwise. She can remember everything from that gloomy time before Ben arrived in their lives. I had moved out of South Road and Natalie's mother had given up putting on a brave face. She had given up trying. Natalie remembers her mother's listlessness. And how the efforts of her friends made no impression whatsoever. Hopeless, useless advice most of it anyway, and as soon as her friends left Viv went back to mourning. She sat sunk in an armchair watching trash on TV for hours on end. She slept long hours. Some days she couldn't get out of bed to go to work. Then at last her deep unhappiness began to lift, just as everyone said it would. She joined a women's gym. She joined the 'Dinner for 6' club where she met someone from the local theatre who talked her into showing up to an audition. And there, she met Ben. Natalie remembers her mother's excitement. The shopping expeditions that followed. The clothes symbolising that moment she gave up one life for another, and started to glow again.

'The halter-neck,' she says, fishing out the garment.

But Ben is already distracted, wondering what else is in Vivienne's drawers. 'Look at these things. I haven't seen this stuff for a long, long while, let me tell you.' Then he looks up with those faint lines of apology and wishfulness. 'Mrs Fonda, would you oblige?'

'Now?'

'I was thinking some time today,' he says.

She tried on the tank top and Ben continued to go through her mother's panty drawer like an excited little boy around sweets.

'Oh yes. Yes. Yes. And hello to you,' he says to each 'old friend'. He selects the briefest, skimpiest pair and hands them to Natalie. 'Mrs Fonda, would you?' Natalie is reluctant. She'd rather not put them on. Her mother is funny about things like that. 'Oh that! Don't worry about Mother Hubbard. She won't mind,' he says. 'Besides, Mrs Fonda is an old friend of Vivienne's. And let's be realistic, Natalie. Frankly, I doubt whether Mother Hubbard could fit into these any more.'

She laughs, traitorously, and immediately covers up her mouth.

'Exactly,' says Ben.

'I wasn't laughing at Mum. I was laughing at Mother Hubbard.'

'Good for you,' he says. 'Now, let's see what we have here . . .' He selects one of Vivienne's blouses. Then he chooses a scarf. She wraps it around her head for Ben to study and decide. He holds her by the shoulders and stares into the picture he's created. 'We're almost there, love bug. Lipstick and eye shadow will do it.'

In the bathroom, with Ben looking over her shoulder, Natalie applies the same quantities she has watched her mother do on countless occasions.

'You're a woman to admire,' Ben tells her. 'Now, where would Mrs Fonda like to go?'

She hadn't thought that they would go out. Masterton's such a small place.

'I don't know, Ben.'

'What don't you know?'

'What if someone sees me?'

'But that's the whole point, Natalie.'

'I don't know, Ben.'

'Don't know, who?' he says then, his hands on his hips.

'Mr Fonda.'

'Good. Now, what don't you know?'

'I don't know if I should go out looking like this.'

'Like who? Who are we speaking of here?'

'Mrs Fonda?' she replies tentatively.

'Mrs Fonda is right. The magnificent Mrs Fonda. Now that we've cleared up that little point, where would Mrs Fonda like to go?'

'Swingers?'

'Oh, Mrs Fonda, I don't think so. I think we can do better. Somewhere more atmospheric . . .'

They get in the car, Natalie cringing in the broad daylight. She runs a nervous eye along the top of the Harrises' fence. She drops her chin in case Mrs Sutton is watching from across the street. Ben, though, doesn't have a care in the world. He makes some tuneless whistle as they reverse out to South Road.

He had some business to complete in Featherston, and as they drew into a service station he said to Natalie that she might think about preparing to revert to being Vivienne. She watches him park, hoping for more, a clue, an explanation. Something bold and mischievous is tucked inside his cheek. 'Won't be long, Vivienne,' he says as he closes the door. She has been sitting there for five minutes when out Ben's side window she notices Ben and another man, the garage owner, looking her way. They are standing up to the office window pinching the blinds apart. Ben seems to be pointing her out. Then the other man comes out. A smiling crinkly face grinning at her like he recognises her. Then he reaches in and offers his hand. 'Well, at last I get to meet the little lady. Gidday, Vivienne.' She is too shocked to say anything. Clearly the man is waiting for her to say something. His head is hanging there in the window. Natalie still can't think what to say. Then the man turns back to Ben. 'See, I told you she wouldn't know me from a brass monkey.' He drops his head back and introduces himself. 'Tommy Patterson. We've spoken on the phone several times.' He looks at her more intently, perhaps to give her another chance to recognise him. Then he says, 'Well, it's always nice to put a face to a name.'

Later, driving away, she complained to Ben. She felt so foolish and stupid not knowing who it was she was supposed to recognise.

'It wasn't fair to do that.'

'What?' he says. 'Tom wanted to meet Vivienne. Now he's met her.'

She wonders about this. She's becoming confused. She'd

better run this past Ben. 'So now I'm Vivienne. I mean, I'm still Vivienne?'

Ben looks across at her, then smiles back at the empty road. 'No, sweet pea, now you're Mrs Fonda. Vivienne was just a small cameo.'

They cut across the back of Carterton that day, past the Kennel Club. They drove with the windows down, following the zigzag road. Natalie with a pair of sunglasses that Ben had dug out of the dash, her pale chin raised, and the make-believe somehow surviving the open countryside, the sheer unrelieved green emptiness, her hair and the sunglasses and her pale skin in that fine manure smell from the paddocks.

They would have passed the church of Babylon. I don't think Maggie and Hope were in the cottage at that stage. This was more than five years ago. She might have been though. She might have been outside planting and looked up at that moment in which Ben drove by with my daughter. She might have thought it was a photograph she'd seen in a book of black-and-white celebrity shots, blinked, and smiled at the tricks played by the Wairarapa countryside.

Chester Road delivered them onto the Mt Holdsworth road, where they drove past the basket weavers and the potter's house with the red windowsills, before leaving the road and driving along a bumpy farm track for the river, finally coming to a halt in a paddock. For the moment, they sat in the car looking out at the poppies and dragonflies. 'This is it,' he said at last: the place where he had taken Vivienne on their first date.

When they get out of the car through the trees, Natalie can hear the jostling hurry of the river. She wonders if her excitement is what her mother felt the first time Ben brought her here. She wonders if this is what Mrs Fonda is supposed to feel?

They took the track down to the river. It's mostly gravel and river boulders. The winter rains would have been fetching off forty metres across the river stones. Near by, a stream of white water rushed past their feet and dropped into a deep pool flush against a grey, quarried rock face.

'Well, Mrs Fonda, what do you reckon? Is this an improvement on wedges?'

They stayed by the river. Ben showed her how to skip stones across the wide part of the river to the shade under the trees. They listened out for the thwack of the stone clipping a tree. 'There you go,' he said. 'You got one!' This was different from the golf range. Her success seemed to please him. He clutched her shoulder. 'You're a hot shot with a flat stone, I'll say that,' he said. Otherwise he talked and reminisced about the 'old days' when he and Vivienne would come here and take off their clothes and dive in the deep pool by the quarry face. I would have thought that was a cue to action. But Natalie says nothing happened. They spent the rest of the afternoon there until it was time to pick up Vivienne.

She watches Ben pick himself up and fold the blanket. There seems to be an order to all this activity. She feels like she is an item waiting to be packed up. First, Ben looks her over, and after stroking his chin decides that they had better 'recover Natalie'.

She knelt at the edge of the river, and Ben got down beside her to wash off the eye shadow and lipstick. Patches of her mother's colouring run off on a current to join the rush downstream. Since she isn't quite sure she asks Ben, 'Am I Natalie now?'

'No, you're a little green man that dropped down from the moon. Course you're bloody Natalie.'

She wonders what she said to make him so short with her. Whenever she is Mrs Fonda, she notices he is polite and patient with her.

Back at the car he tells her to take off her clothes. When she hesitated he shook his head and moved off to the boot muttering something. He gets out of the Mazda his costume bag, the one he uses for the theatre, with her jeans, T-shirt and Mickey Mouse sweat top, and holding it out to her, says, 'We don't want to confuse Mum, do we?'

That day Vivienne was left waiting on the roadside outside the Solway, her head turning both ways with the traffic flow. She was never sure from which direction Ben would turn up. It usually depended on where his appointments had taken him. So she is gazing off in the wrong direction when the Mazda rolls up and toots, making her jump back. She sees Natalie in the front, but if there was anything unusual or disturbing about that then, it quickly retreats before her relief that Ben remembered to turn up. I know Vivy still trawls back through these moments. At the time she couldn't see beyond the surface.

'Hello, you two,' she says getting in the back. 'My feet.' She removes her shoes. 'My poor, poor feet. Oh God, that's better. Yes,' she says, closing her eyes. Then she remembers to ask after Natalie. 'How's the tummy? No more sickie?'

'Christ, Vivienne. I wish you'd stop babying her. Sickie. Tummy.'

'Well, she is my baby,' says Vivienne in the back. 'Aren't you, sweet?'

Natalie looks across to Ben. She sees him close his eyes. Ben is irritated and her mother has failed to see it. It is the first time in her life that she is aware of something which has completely escaped her mother's notice. Her mother has no idea just how irritating she is to Ben.

Now that the extraordinariness of that discovery is out of the way, she seems to see it all the time. At night, the living-room door ajar, she sees her mother sit down on Ben's knee. She watches Vivienne put her hand behind Ben's neck and then rub her cheek against the top of Ben's head. What her mother can't see is plain as day to her – the shortness of Ben's neck and its twist of disgruntlement.

There are two Viviennes living under the one roof these days. One is always in the foreground and the other in the background. That winter they never seemed to be together in the same place, or, when they were, to occupy the same place. Whenever Vivienne was on her shift, Ben made Natalie wear her mother's clothes. He even parted her hair with a fringe like her mother's. It was much later after we fished out a photograph taken of Natalie that winter that we even noticed.

One night, her mother climbed into bed with her. They used to do that a lot in the old days, snuggling up, talking in the dark.

It's easier to ask difficult things when you can't see the other's face, so Natalie asks her mother, 'Do you think you and Ben will stay together?'

'Natalie! Goodness gracious. Where did that come from?' Her mother begins to laugh. 'I don't know – you are a puzzle these days. We are together. I don't know how we can be any more together than this.'

'Forever, together?'

'Well, "forever" is a long time. You can never tell. But

I will say this. The planets would have to fall out of kilter for anything to happen. I love your father. But I love Ben as well.'

It's clear then. She mustn't disturb the planets. The last thing she wants is a return to the bad old days of her mother sitting on the edge of her bed staring into nothingness. She starts to distance herself from Ben, escaping over to Bennetts' whenever she hears Ben's car turn into the drive.

Now Ben is the one feeling put out. The only time Natalie seems to be around is when Mother Hubbard is in the house. Things are not what they used to be. Things aren't what they're meant to be. He catches up with her one night coming out of the bathroom. 'Well, hello, if it isn't the phantom. I think we need to have us a little talk, Mrs Fonda. Tomorrow I'll come by the school in the lunch hour.'

The next day she waited for him. She and Pete lay on the cut grass in the drowsy sunshine. She looked up in time to see the white Mazda glide by the outside playing field. She notices the wire fence around the playing field and feels a surge in her heart as she realises that she is outside Ben's range. For once her world has been cut off from his. She lay closer to Pete, smiled at his warbling noises. She snuggled against him and sank lower in the grass and with alligator eyes watched Ben drive to the end, where he turns around. Then he comes back the other way, scanning the field, searching past the column-like teachers on lunch duty. She shut her eyes and waited until she heard the impatient exhaust of the Mazda, and felt an inward satisfaction. Control has come back to her.

After school she played with Pete down by the river. It was close on dark when she walked home through the cold pockets of air and the rich green aroma of cut grass on Pete's knees. She walked with him because he had hurt himself earlier. She watched him cross the road then she turned up her drive, and there was the Mazda at the end. She stopped and looked again and realised it was Ben. It was the back of Ben's head.

He is just sitting there staring at the garage doors. She wonders what to do here. Should she go to the front door and pretend she hasn't seen him? That might just make things worse. Knowing Ben, and realising that he has set her a trap, she knows that the only option is to oblige him. She walks down the drive kicking at the shingle. She knows better than to sneak up on him. The element of surprise must rest with Ben at all times.

'Well, well. Mrs Fonda.'

'Ben,' she said, trying to sound normal and unalarmed, 'is anything the matter?'

'Is there something the matter? That's an interesting question. Something to ponder, isn't it?' Then he says, 'Was that the Sutton kid I saw you with earlier? Holding hands?'

She is surprised. She wasn't aware of Ben earlier. But he must have been out there in the landscape somewhere. He must have seen Pete fall off his bike in the gravel at the bottom of South Road. Ben must have been down near the river. She feels a little afraid to think that he was there, so close, without her knowledge.

'Pete cut himself. I had to help him. A piece of broken glass tore through his shoe.'

But he shakes his head. 'Let's not talk about that. Christ, I don't even want to know about it. I've got a bigger subject on my mind.'

Ben pauses. He taps a two-finger beat on the steering column.

She waits – knowing what to expect.

'You saw me at lunchtime and chose to ignore me. Why?'

'I didn't see you.'

'Liar!'

'I didn't, Ben. Honest.'

'No. No. You saw me.'

She starts to deny it again and this time he raises a hand to interrupt her. 'Let's just say I'm right, okay, Natalie? Now, what I want to know is *why* . . . why you chose to ignore me.'

She doesn't answer. She doesn't know what to say. She looks up the drive. The lights have come on at Suttons'.

'Sweetie pie, I can't hear you.'

'I don't know,' she says.

'Who?'

'Ben,' she corrects herself. 'I don't know, Ben.'

'Why not, sweetheart?'

'I just don't.'

'Well, I damn well do. Driving up and down like a fuck-ing fairground bunny. How do you think I felt. Have you any idea?'

'I don't know,' she says.

Ben shakes his head and stares at the dashboard.

'I'm disappointed, Natalie.'

'I didn't see you.'

'Liar! I won't stand being lied to.'

'I don't know what to say, Ben. What do you want me to say?'

'Let's try a different tack. What have you and Mum been talking about?'

'Nothing.'

'Here we go. The other night, Natalie. Remember?'

'She was tired,' she says.

'Vivienne is always tired. I'll repeat the question. What did you talk about?'

'It was nothing. I can't remember.'

'Viv climbed into bed with you. Think back, Natalie.'

'We talked about Dad,' she says.

'Ha! Good,' he says. 'This is progress.' And when she fails to add anything more he prompts her along. 'And what did Vivienne have to say about good ole Charlie man?'

'She talked about you too.'

'Oh?'

'Just talked. Yapped,' she says.

'Yapped,' he says. 'Well, that's funny. That's what I was wanting to do with you at lunchtime, baby, and you chose to look away. Ah! Don't you do that. Don't you look away. That's better. You know what you did.' Now he laid his head back and studied his face in the rear-view mirror. 'I have to say I'm disappointed, Natalie. I thought we under-stood each other. I thought we had each other's trust. In fact . . .' He stops and turns his head. They both heard it, the front door opening. 'Is that who I think it is? Christ,' he says. 'Here comes the cavalry.'

'Natalie? Ben? Is that Ben with you, honey?'

'No, it's a fucking leprechaun. Go ahead. Answer her, Natalie.'

'Here, Ma.'

'Here, Ma,' says Ben.

'I thought I heard someone draw up and . . . For goodness sake, what are you two doing out here?'

'Pete cut his foot. I was telling Ben about it,' she says.

'Well, is he okay? Nothing serious I hope?'

'He's fine, Ma.'

'Ma,' says Ben. He rests his hands on the steering wheel and drops his head and mutters a quick instruction. 'All right. All right. Tell Mother Hubbard I'm taking you out to dinner.'

'What?'

'Don't what me. Tell her I'm taking you out to dinner.'

'Natalie? What's going on?'

She feels torn in two directions at once.

'Can't hear you,' says the voice in the window.

She shuts her eyes and calls up the driveway. 'Ben is taking me out to dinner, Ma.'

'Ma,' he says again.

It's like her mother's on the edge of something and can't bear to step closer; like she's trying to see through a murky window.

'What, now? Tonight?' she asks. 'But I made apple crumble. Tell Ben. Tell him I made his favourite.'

'Mum says she . . .'

'I know. Apple crumble. Let's go.' He switches on the ignition and turns over the motor. As she crosses around the front of the car she hears her mother call out – 'Natalie?' And Natalie can't look. The voice in her head is going, 'No, Mum. Let me go.' She can't bear to look. She doesn't want to see the look on her mother's face. But then as Ben swings out to South Road she raises her eyes to sneak a glance back at the porch. She notices that her mother has on her kitchen apron over her Solway Park uniform. She sees layers of duty, and folds of confusion and disappointment, and hands that don't know what to do with themselves.

'Applefuckingcrumble. Can you believe it?' says Ben, as they accelerate away. At the top of South Road Ben glances across to Natalie. Her head is turned away. 'You realise, don't you, that none of this would have happened had you not ignored me. That's something you want to think about.'

'Yes, Ben,' she says.

'Yes Ben is right,' he answers.

That evening they drove through town. Ben with his attention divided between the road ahead and the drab view out the side window at where his life had landed him. The discoloured two-storey buildings that appeared solid on the outside but were empty on the inside – *est 1935* anchoring them like credentials to a promise of long ago. Cardboard signs in the secondhand windows advertising small businesses that will come and go like fireflies.

I think I may have seen them that night. I haven't come out and said so to Vivienne. But I will say it now. I did see them. This was the Tuesday night I found Vivienne so upset and the evening meal gone to waste. In town I happened to see them bailed up at a set of lights. I pulled away, pretending that I hadn't seen my daughter sitting like a captive in a white Mazda. Remember, what I saw and what I was prepared to admit to having seen were mediated through other circumstances. I was feeling aggrieved.

Natalie thought they were going out to eat. Ben did say they were going out to eat. So far all they have done is drive up and down and around the same streets. She can't get her mother out of her thoughts. Her beggaring eyes. She can't think to say anything that Ben might like to hear. 'Go on, spit it out,' Ben says after a while. It's not one thing or another except that everything appears to be unhealthily linked. She tells him, 'I don't want to play Vivienne any more, or Mrs Fonda, or Choo woo or anything.'

Ben doesn't answer right away. He looks left and right like the careful motorist he is tonight. Then he scratches his ear and they drive down another block before he decides to answer.

'Well, that was quite a speech back there. Quite a speech. Unfortunately it does mean "Goodbye, Vivienne".'

'No!' she says. That's not what she meant. No, it's not, and she starts to cry. 'Please don't leave Mum.'

'Well,' he says, releasing the steering wheel. 'You're the one calling the tune, Mrs Fonda. It's in your hands.'

She sniffs through her tears. 'You said, Ben . . . You said we didn't want to hurt those closest to us. You said . . .'

'I know what I said, and that's my point. Mum's happiness. That's what we all want.'

She starts to say something else but abandons it. Her place in the scheme of things has just become clear. She must do whatever Ben asks her to do for the sake of her mother's happiness.

They must have looked like they were searching for something that night. Ben hunched over the wheel driving extra slow. In no hurry to get anywhere. Driving in circles. Down South Road to the Beltway, back up the main drag to town, around the roundabout by Queen Elizabeth Park, passing all the obvious places, the burger bars, the Chinese takeaways she thought Ben had had in mind, departing and circling back because they had nowhere to go.

# FIVE

There was talk around that time of Natalie coming to live with me. But every time Viv mentioned it Natalie kicked up a fuss. She said my place was too small. She didn't like the neighbourhood – the way the dogs rushed at her. She just wanted to stay in South Road, and when finally there was no hiding that fact from me, I was flabbergasted. She couldn't complain of the times we had together. We enjoyed each other's company. I was never one of those fathers that beat a weary track to McDonald's for a 'paid-up dad experience'. We went horse-riding. We drove out to the coast.

I showed her how to climb onto a wave with her new boogie board. Man, we enjoyed ourselves. The stuff about 'the dogs' and the distance that Michael Street was from school made no sense at all – God knows that should have been a stand-out clue. Instead, rejection got in the way, and blocked my senses. Weeks passed where I didn't hear from her or call her. I decided to let her be. If it came to the cold shoulder, then her old man could do better. What a moron. What a complete fucking moron I was. It shames me, but there you are.

For a short period she managed to avoid Ben. The task was helped by her mother's insistence that she go straight to the hotel after school. You'd have thought this insistence would have raised questions, that Ben might have taken umbrage. But nothing was said as far as I know.

Still, it wasn't long either before this new arrangement began to frustrate Ben. He caught up with her one afternoon as she was walking up the Beltway to the main road. Natalie heard the Mazda turn out of South Road. Without turning, she knew it was Ben. She closed her eyes and stopped till he came alongside the curb and called across, 'Hello, sunshine.' If she'd cared to look, she might have seen a big leery grin stretching his face from ear to ear. But she chose not to, and eyes ahead, fixed on her destination, she told him, 'I have to go, Ben. I have to go to Mum's.'

'Mum's. Do I know anyone called Mum's?'

'Vivienne,' she said.

'Oh, Big Bum. Well, Big Bum will just have to do what big bums do best, and sit and wait.' Then, as he leant over to open the side door, she took off up the road. She ran away from him!

For the rest of the week her mother's schedule saw her

at home every night. Then Ben was away on business for a few days. A week passed and she began to wonder if it was safe to conclude that she had got away with something.

Then one afternoon a younger kid came to Natalie's class with a message for her to report to the school office. Mrs Rouse, the school secretary, met her out in the corridor with the surprising news that her father was there to collect her for her appointment. Natalie followed the secretary along the hall to the administrative area, and there she found her 'father' standing outside the principal's office. She thought Ben looked very tall. He was looking up at the dux board. She looked at his neatly pressed white collar and the flash tie and saw at once his ability to convince the world that he was who he professed to be.

He smiled down at her. 'Silly goose.' Then to Mrs Rouse he says, 'Her mother and I laid a bet that she would forget her appointment.'

The school secretary laughed. 'You're wasting your time if you expect anything different at their age.'

'I expect you're right,' says Ben.

'Oh yes. Though I have to say Natalie would be one of the more responsible ones.'

This was a surprise. Natalie wonders how Mrs Rouse would ever know. Then she realises that the school secretary is playing the same game as Ben. She is simply saying what is expected of her.

'You don't have to say anything, lovey. I know what toothache is like,' she said, and Ben placed a fatherly hand on her shoulder.

'Miss Forgetful,' he said once they were outside.

Then, in the car, he says, 'Have you any idea how bad I felt when you ran away up the street? I'm disappointed.

Extremely disappointed. I mean, Natalie, did you forget what we talked about . . . what we discussed?'

She remembers the equation. They are a pyramid: each side is there to support the other.

'I'm trying,' she says.

'You're not trying. That's the problem. That's what is so very galling, Natalie.'

'I'll try. I will, Ben.'

Ben turns to look out his side window and they drive home in that slow, regretful way of his. Of course she is wondering what he has in mind. What are they doing back at South Road at this hour? Home at this hour – it carries a taint of illegality. Still, she hardly dares ask. She can't even look at him in case Ben finds something he doesn't like in her expression. They park at the end of the drive. 'Inside, princess.'

In the kitchen he glances up at the wall clock and checks with her. 'Vivy's on what?'

'Days,' she answers.

'Good. All right, we have some costume changes to make. Come along, Mrs Fonda. Let's not piss about. Clothes off, please.'

She starts to undo the buttons on her blouse but is much too slow for him. 'I don't want to be here when the cavalry charge,' he says, and he pulls her towards him and undresses her until the kitchen lino under her bare feet makes a point of her nakedness. 'I've come up with a new script. We're going to play tiger on the savanna.' That's what the brown package on the table is about then. It contains the body paints. The way Ben gets everything ready reminds Natalie of a tradesman at work. She thinks of Mr Sutton across the street, the way he spread his pliers and switches when he rewired the Sutton's house. 'Still please. That's it,' he says. 'And you can get that bullshit worry off your face. It washes off.' As he paints, she notices his eyes; they're concentrated like he's painting from a picture already formed in his head. He starts in the area of her throat. He dabs and drags the brush between her breasts and over her belly. 'One yellow stripe. Now for a blackie . . .' Alternating the stripes as he moves around her column.

Afterwards she felt like she's been dipped in a paint pot. Ben turns her round from east to west, admiring her from all vantage points. 'Oh, Mrs Fonda. You should see yourself. You make a great tigress.' She is about to roar for him when his attention is diverted to a small area he overlooked. He picks up the black brush and dabs her nipples, then he sets about painting her face black. She closes her eyes until the snails stop crawling over her.

Then it's Ben's turn. He strips off eagerly. She has to paint him black all over. Face. Lips. Eyelids. Tummy and thighs until his thing gets in the way. 'Mr It, too, sweet thing.' So she paints it black, his balls, and backside, until Ben is a black man. The African tribesman. A hunter. She is the tiger. The house is the savanna. She's supposed to find her watering hole and then lie down in the long grass and wait for the hunter to find her.

Ben can't resist taking a peep at himself in the mirror. He wants to see what he looks like cast as a black man. He takes the shaving mirror and looks fascinated at his black cock. Then he comes out to the hall already in character, bent at the knees, his head at a strange angle that he must have decided is African.

He sniffs her all over, then explains to her that he is familiarising himself with her tiger scent. Then he pats her on the bum to send her on her way. 'No, you silly bitch! On all fours.' Of course. She is the tiger. She crawls up the hall wondering where she can hide. Wishing there really was somewhere but knowing in the end there won't be. She can hear the African chanting from the kitchen – 'Thirty-five, forty, forty-five, fifty . . .' She is kneeling behind the couch when the counting stops. The floorboards begin to creak. She can see Ben's shadow, his finger-spiked hands climbing over the wall as he parts the tall savanna grass, sniffing high and low. At that moment the phone in the hall began to ring – a loud twentieth-century interruption of this centuries-old ritual; it's the first she's ever thought of the phone ringing in that sense. She can picture her mother in the hotel reception area, her puzzled face next to the phone. The technology is still not sufficiently advanced to enable her to see through the mouthpiece to these events taking place at home. But Natalie knows, can imagine her mother's face, the concern it will spread across the desk before snapping to with a smile for a passing guest. It crosses her mind that she could run away – out of the house, maybe across to Suttons'. She wonders what Mrs Sutton would make of a striped tiger bursting into her kitchen. Mr Sutton with knife and fork in hand, the Lord's prayer stuck up a nostril, and in his painfully slow and deliberate way inquiring of the tiger, 'Is that you, Natalie?'

That's what she's thinking of – Mr Sutton with his knife and fork – when fucking Ben jumps her. He dug his teeth into her shoulder until she screamed. Then he carries his 'dead prey' into the kitchen, sets her on the table, arranges her, and fucks her like he did at the beach, and God knows how many other times, mumbling his cloud crap or whatever form of nonsense it takes in the savanna. She submits in the way of the shot prey, of course, but there ticking away in the tiger's thoughts is that other consideration – her mother's happiness.

Later, they're in the bathroom taking it in turns to wash the paint off each other, when the phone rings again. Neither mentions it since they both know who it is calling. And Natalie hardly dares mention her mother at a time like this. The word 'mother' would indicate wrongdoing and she knows Ben well enough to know that he doesn't want to feel bad about anything he does, ever. So they carry on washing the paint off themselves. First, Ben removes the tiger stripes, then she washes the black man off Ben.

He draws the towel back and forth across his shoulders, pleased with himself.

'Burger King, did I hear you say?' Hoping he will surprise her in a pleasant way.

She should be at the hotel. She should have been there an hour ago. She knows who it was ringing. She knows that what she is going to say will disappoint him, but since he's had his pleasure maybe he will be more forgiving.

'I can't, Ben,' she says. 'I have to be at the hotel.'

'No, sweetness. You're supposed to say, "Why thank you, Mr Fonda. Burger and fries would please me greatly."'

Vivienne was on her way home when she saw them turn out of the South Belt in the direction of town. She was looking to cross the road when she saw the Mazda. She thought Ben was coming to collect her so she stayed put. Then the Mazda turned in the opposite direction. Natalie was in the front. Her little Highness perched next to Ben. The two of them together – that one glance at her daughter with Ben aged her. She felt her heart twist in an ugly way and turn green. For several minutes she stood in a cold wind watching after, as the late afternoon freight trucks roared by.

She turned around and went back to the hotel. In the kitchen, Stewy took one look at her. 'Vivy, what's the matter, love. Come here. Come and sit down.' He poured her a stiff drink. 'I'll have to stay at my watch, Vivy, love.'

'I don't mind, Stewy,' she said. 'I'm happy to sit here and watch. That is, if you don't mind.'

'Me! No, blimey. I find it's a flattering experience to have a good-looking woman like yourself feasting her eyes on me. Though I don't suppose it's much of a feast.'

She laughed; and Stewy, flicking a meat patty into a pan of sizzling oil, smiled at his achievement.

'What's on your mind, Vivy? Is it something you want to talk about?'

'Just a question to start with,' she said. 'What's the worst thing you've ever imagined, Stewy?'

'Imagined?'

'Well, thought of. The absolutely worst thing that has come into your thoughts and before you knew it it was there and you couldn't get rid of it.'

'Are we talking evil thoughts or just plain bad thoughts?'

'I don't know, Stewy. I'd have to think about that.'

'While you're doing that I'll flick these patties. But you go on thinking. I want you to stay,' he said.

'Thank you, Stewy. I think I will.'

She studied the womanly freckles on the backs of his chubby elbows. The thick neck. The fringe of reddish hair spilling beneath his chef's hat. The white jacket with the burnt starch marks and his grease-covered shoes. She found it impossible to imagine him away from his stainless steel cooking range. She looked at its dead reflective light and thought, 'No wonder he likes to pretend he is older, more worldly. He must never see himself as he is for that fat-smeared backdrop.' She knew from his employment record that he was the same age as her, a fact she now found distressing, especially when she took stock of his yellowing teeth and wild eyebrows. He was always flirting with her. 'When are we going to have that little drinkie, Vivienne? Just me and you, eh?' She made vague promises – all of them safely in the future. She imagined Stewy awash in alcohol and sentimentality. All chefs in her experience were sentimental. All of them outrageous flirts over their cooking ranges, all of them juggling with apparent ease the demands of flambé chicken and affairs of the heart, all of them as they would have you believe great Casanovas but for the leg irons of the stove.

She dreamily sipped her drink and answered his questions about Natalie's bird. She passed on what Natalie had told her about releasing Mrs Austen in the trees of Queen Elizabeth Park. 'I suppose it's unfair to contain something meant for the wide open space. What do you think, Stewy?'

'Viv, darling, you just described me,' he said.

'You make your own luck, Stewy. Birds don't know that.'

When she showed no sign of leaving, Stewy made her a meal. One of the waitresses snuck her in a glass of wine that a house guest had left untouched in the restaurant. Viv wondered if she was giving off some kind of distress signal. Still, she smiled at these small acts of kindness. Eventually, when Maxine who was on 'lates' came in to tell her there was a phone call for her, she asked Maxine to say she wasn't there. 'Being mysterious, are we?' asked Stewy. His back was turned; and the question didn't seek an answer, it was just an observation.

She walked home, and with the brandy and wine in her the distance felt longer. She began to feel cold halfway up South Road, by which time the alcohol had worn off and her head was full of practical thoughts.

She let herself in and walked past the front room where Ben was watching TV. She went straight to Natalie's bedroom and switched on the light.

'Get up,' she said. She wasn't loud or hysterical – too many hours had passed since she had seen them together heading up towards town – but was determined to be firm. 'You were supposed to be at the hotel. I rang three times! I want to know where you were and what you were doing.'

'I was at home.'

'I rang here three times.'

'I was sleeping.'

'You were supposed to come to the hotel, Natalie. That's the arrangement.'

'I was sleeping. I wasn't feeling well.'

Now Ben arrived in the hall. 'Vivienne,' he says, 'I thought it was the riot police. What's all the shouting about?'

Natalie can see that her mother doesn't quite know how to regard Ben, how to include him.

'I wasn't shouting, Ben. I'm talking to Natalie.' Then she says, 'I'm waiting, young lady.'

'All this shouting,' says Ben. 'Like a whirlwind swept into the house.'

'Natalie was supposed to come over to work after school. That was the arrangement.'

'Ah, gee. Oh dearie.' Ben slaps a hand against his temple. 'Blame me. My fault, Viv. I guess I'm the one at fault.

I suggested a walk and we ended up in town.'

'A walk?' asks Vivienne.

'Well, if truth be known we picked up a couple of burgers. I'm sorry, Viv. I guess this puts me in the black book.'

It's like watching a performance of something. Her mother is the angry parrot. Ben is the contrite Doberman. The two of them in the door backlit by the hall light.

'Natalie, if you had prior arrangements then no wonder your mother is angry.'

'Don't you think I have a right to be angry?'

'That's my point, Vivienne. I'm not questioning it. I'm just saying that I didn't know about it.'

Vivienne thinks about that and decides the less she says about that the better.

'Whatever,' she says. Now she directed her attention to Natalie. She says, 'I spoke to your father this evening. He wants you to spend Christmas up north with him. He thought the two of you could go camping. He mentioned a place. I forget where.'

What Vivienne missed at that moment was Ben's backward step and firm shake of his head. Natalie knows what she must say. Ben has made it clear. For the sake of her mother's happiness she pulls the duvet up under her chin, and says, 'I don't want to, Ma. I want to stay here.'

And while Vivienne is coming to terms with what she just heard, Ben lightly steps away. 'Well, maybe I'll leave you two to sort this one out.'

Vivienne waits for the living-room door to close, then she says, 'I think I need to hear you say that again just in case I think I'm going mad.'

Natalie starts to cry.

'I'm waiting,' says her mother.

She can smell Stewy's kitchen on her mother. She can feel her brandy breath.

'I don't want to, Ma. I want to stay here with you. Please?'

A week before Christmas, Ben came home with two new mountain bikes, one for himself, the other for Natalie, and announced plans for a 'Siberian adventure'. After dinner they cleared away the dishes and Ben spread a map over the table to prove that Siberia was not one of his make-believe places. It exists, or used to exist, in the folds of the hills that separate the Wairarapa Plains from the Hutt Valley. In the old days, before the current tunnel was built, shortening the journey, the train route took the 'Siberia route'. The tracks have since been pulled up and these days the Rimutaka Incline sees only mountain bikers and day hikers.

On a Saturday morning a van picked them up in Featherston. To Vivienne's pleasant surprise, there were two other families, the Harrises and the Fitzroys. Ben hadn't mentioned company. But this was just for the ride to the start of the Incline on the Hutt side of the hill.

For the trip over the hill Ben is on good behaviour. He is the life of the van – joking to Mr Harris and Mr Fitzroy about his lack of fitness. 'I may have to be stretchered out,' he says. Mr Fitzroy scratches his eyebrow and says, 'Oh, I think you're safe on this ride. A baby on a tricycle could probably manage it without too much fuss.' Vivienne is relieved to hear this. Tonight is the staff Christmas do and she's expected to be there.

There are four kids – all of them older than Natalie and all of them in the proper gear. Cycling pants. Sunglasses. Bright-coloured tunics and windbreakers. They look like cyclists. To Natalie they look like slick ferrets; she glances at them and feels fat and slow. Halfway up the winding hill road she starts to feel sick. It's months since she felt like this. She has to ask the driver to pull over which earns her a glare from Ben. But the van driver is obliging. This time she just manages to get herself out of the van in time. She scrambles over the knees of Mrs Harris, a woman with a blue headband, and with Ben holding the sliding door at arm's length she throws up on the gravel. It was quick. Explosive. Mrs Harris and Mrs Fitzroy make sympathetic noises, while Vivienne lightly puts it down to 'motion sickness', explaining to the others, 'She's hopeless in cars. Always has been right from the time she was a little girl.' A grim smile from Ben as she climbs back inside the van. She knows she has embarrassed him. His 'fattie' as he's taken to calling her lately. One of the mothers pours her a cup of water. The other kids stare at her through their alien sunglasses and Ben turns to the driver. 'I think we're okay now.'

The other kids are veterans and they speak of a country whose place names, tunnels and washouts Natalie knows nothing about. However, she was wrong to think that this would be a joint excursion. At the drop-off point it's obvious that Ben is in no hurry to get started. He checks the air pressure in their tyres. He repacks the daypack. She knows what Ben is up to. She recognises this stalling behaviour.

The Harrises and the Fitzroys set off two – and three – abreast, whereas they go in single file – Ben in the front, Natalie at the rear watching her mother riding in front of her. All her mother's uncertainty has transferred itself to the bike. Making things worse, the ground is bumpy and her front wheel keeps being knocked off course. There is the long sunny stretch beside the river. She looks up at the sun in the trees. She manages a smile despite herself. She isn't expecting to enjoy this day. After leaving the river she keeps waiting for the steep bit to arrive; and it's like the hills are holding back, or, as it would appear, the track keeps discovering a new opening in the hills, and so they go from shade to light, from close ferny banks that brush against them to great airy spaces left hanging between the track and the hills on the other side of the gully. There's no sign of the other families and they have been going an hour. Far below, the river is a flat line wriggling along on its belly. The climb must have slipped in without her noticing.

Their first break is at a place known as Creek Crossing. The bush has been cleared and grass sown. There's a shelter with some photographs of how the area used to look – two houses either side of the old railway tracks. Half the population walk beside the tracks – a girl her own age in a white dress and black lace-up boots with her parents.

'There's you and me, Nat, and I suppose that has to be Vivienne,' says Ben.

Vivienne pretends she didn't hear that. If she remembers correctly they must be close to the Siberia Tunnel. She asks Ben for the torch.

'When we need it I'll get it out,' he says.

'I just thought I would prepare.'

'We are prepared, Vivienne. I'll get it out when we need it.'

Stupidly she starts to fish in his daypack. Ben drops his bike and snatches the pack from her.

'I said I'd take care of it, Vivienne.' Then, more calmly, he says, 'Look, I know where everything is, all right. I packed the pack for that very reason.'

'I was just trying to help.'

'Good. Now you've helped.'

As it turns out her mother was right, and Natalie wonders why Ben kicked up such a fuss when after ten minutes they find themselves at the tunnel entrance. They stare through a dark corridor to a pale circle of light at the end, while her mother reads out from a notice pinned above the entrance warning people that they 'enter at their own risk'.

'If that's an issue with you, Viv, then you know the way back,' says Ben.

'It's just interesting that they would bother with that notice. I mean presumably it is there for a reason.'

'Torch,' says Ben now, holding it up for all to see.

'I just thought you'd like to know,' says Vivienne.

'Now we know,' says Ben. 'Okay, Natalie. You ride in front. I'll go in the middle with the torch. Vivienne . . .'

'I know my place,' she says.

'Oh Christ, please. Spare us the martyrdom, Viv. Look where we are, Viv, out in this splendour. In God's domain. Let's not spoil it, okay, Vivienne?'

'I was just stating a fact,' she says.

'We want the torch in safe hands, don't we?'

'I wasn't complaining,' says Vivienne.

Within a few feet of their entering the tunnel the ground fades away. It is the strangest thing. Natalie is thinking about what she will tell her friend, Pete. She's already decided that it is like riding in space. It's also obvious why it's called Siberia. The air is stunningly cold. Ben holds the torch up against the dripping ceiling and walls. The reflected walls reveal a space narrower than Vivienne expected. She says, 'It's hard to imagine a carriage even passing through here without touching the sides.' Then Natalie hears Ben behind her go, 'Choo woo' and she almost wheels out of control. 'Steady, Natalie,' comes the warning from behind. Now she hears her mother responding to Ben's choo-wooing. 'I suppose that's right. I suppose the trains were all steam. Still it makes you wonder . . .' Then Ben goes, 'Choo woo, choo woo.' Natalie can hear him chuckling at their private joke. Then a different voice. Snappish. 'Faster, Natalie. Faster.' So she pushes down on her pedals. She can't see a thing under the wheel. Her mother is drifting back. 'Ben, wait please. I can't see. Please. Wait . . .' Her mother might as well be calling out to an empty house. Natalie knows they are going much faster than her mother is comfortable with, but Ben won't let up. He snaps at her to go faster. Faster. 'Choo woo,' he goes, 'choo woo.' She looks for the torch light. It keeps bouncing off the walls then onto the ground ahead. She can hear her mother calling out to Ben to slow down. She wants to stop. She would like to but Ben is right on top of her. They will crash if she stops. Way back she hears her mother cry out, 'Bastards!' A moment later she swears wildly with fright and way up ahead the other two hear the bike frame crash into the tunnel walls.

Natalie starts to slow. She wants to stop of course. Ben hisses at her to keep going. His tone is unmistakable. She knows what it means. For the sake of her mother's happiness she must keep going. So she concentrates on the yellow beam dancing a metre ahead of her front wheel. She pedals for wherever Ben lands the beam. She can hear her mother shouting and pleading for Ben to come back. She pictures her mother sitting down in the rubble sobbing. The possibility that she may be hurt momentarily slows her down and suddenly the torch switches off. Immediately her front wheel wobbles out of control. She screams blindly, 'Ben!' Then the torch comes on and almost greedily she latches onto it. 'Choo woo,' she hears at her shoulder. She doesn't dare slow down. She pedals like she's pedalling for the next world.

Another five minutes and they come out to warm daylight. She hops off her bike and stares back into the tunnel. At the far end is the circle of light where her mother had paused to read the warning notice, but there is nothing to see in between. She can't see her mother. It is pitch black.

'Trust Vivienne,' says Ben. She watches him unstrap his helmet and is amazed at how unconcerned he appears. 'Let's face it. She was always odds-on favourite to have a prang or get lost.'

'She might be hurt,' says Natalie.

'Might be?' He laughs at that prospect. 'Not with the padding she's got. Vivy will have bounced up. Don't worry. She'll be along presently – no doubt badmouthing me, badmouthing to kingdom come. But you saw the problem, didn't you, Nat? I mean, you stop and bang, it's all over. You can't just re-mount in those conditions.'

She guesses that they are in the Wairarapa. To her left is the Siberia Washout. Rugged hills line up away to the south and east. It is mountainous and slightly scary.

'Well, goodbye, Siberia,' says Ben. He's picked up his bike; now he's fastening on the helmet.

'What about Mum?'

'She'll catch up.'

To get to the other side of the Siberia Washout they cross a dry creek bed, then wheel their bikes up a grey shingle slip to rejoin a grassy path. They freewheel a short way before Ben brakes at an overgrown track running off the main one. She wouldn't have noticed it, but Ben can spot a hairline crack in a dinner plate.

'Up here,' he says. 'We'll wait here.' She is relieved to hear that – so they will wait for her mother after all. They walk their bikes up to a small clearing. It might once have been a lookout. It has that feeling about it that induces her to remove her helmet. They can look to the beech forest on the hill across the gully. Wood pigeons of a grey colouring, lean in flight, swoop in pairs. In the direction of the downhill track they discover another picnic area where one of the other families has stopped for lunch. Natalie has an idea that it is the Harrises. She looks back across the Washout in time to see her mother stagger out of the tunnel. 'Mum,' she says. Ben has sat down on the grass to rest and stretch his legs. 'Snivelling, is she?'

'She's lying down.'

'Sounds familiar. Sounds like someone we know.'

'She could be hurt.'

'She could be lots of things.'

Natalie doesn't answer. She reaches down for her bike and as she does so Ben sits up and grabs her by the wrist.

'But I want to see if Mum is okay.'

And looking right at her he says, 'She looks all right to me.' Natalie thinks about the Harrises all squeezed in a tight bunch on a square of blanket eating their sandwiches – how far away they are from them. She lays down her handlebars and Ben nods approvingly.

'That's the girl. Let's not spoil it now. Our little adventure hasn't even begun. I brought the paints.' Then he says, 'Oh come on. Don't look at me like that, Mrs Fonda. You should know better than that.'

'But I don't feel well.' She tries to produce an 'unwell look'.

'You were unwell. That's right. Unfortunately I do

remember. But that is in the past. We have since lurched into the present. Now stop pissing wind and tell me what Cake Bottom is up to.'

Her mother is back on her feet. She's doing up her helmet. Natalie wishes she could reach across this divide and touch her mother. She wishes – and wishing makes her forget herself. She yells out to her mother. She only managed to get it out once before Ben dragged her down beside him. 'You little shit. What did you do that for? Or maybe you just forgot for the six-hundredth time – you run away from me, Mrs Fonda, and Ben is off out of here. I thought you understood this.'

'I do, Ben. I do,' she says.

'Christ. I've got to be constantly on the lookout. All the bloody time. Constantly vigilant.'

'It won't happen again. I promise.'

'I've heard that one before.'

'Honest, Ben. I didn't know I was going to do it. I didn't.'

She starts to cry then, and Ben says, 'All right. All right, Natalie. We'll call it a mistake in judgement.' She feels him take his hands away from her, the way he moves them from her sides reminding her how she did the same thing the first time she met Mrs Austen – on that occasion, unsure whether she had the bird's trust, moving her hands wider apart while ready to slap them together at any moment.

'All right,' he says. 'Shoot back up the crow's nest and report back down what you see.'

Her mother has arrived at the edge of the Washout. She looks unsure of how to proceed across. Natalie knows that if they were there with her, her mother'd be saying, 'I don't know, Ben. I don't know about this . . .' She starts across and within a few paces she drops her bike. She watches her mother pick up the bike. The sad movement in her torso. She is so full of grief she can hardly hold the bike upright. She wishes she could go to her mother.

'Can't hear you, Natalie,' says Ben.

'She's at the Washout.' Her mother keeps slipping and dropping her bike. Now Ben gets up to see for himself.

'Well, yeah. Perhaps now you can see the problem. Vivienne is not cut out for this sort of thing.'

Ben held a finger to his lips and a hand went back on Natalie's shoulder as her mother wheeled her bike along the track beneath them. They watched her continue on down the hill until, one by one, the Harrises stood up. Natalie and Ben watched Mr Harris take the bike from Vivienne and Mrs Harris put an arm round her.

'What a sad spectacle,' says Ben. 'That is not the Vivienne I met.' Then he claps his hands. 'All right,' he says, as if they had taken time out from a chore still to be completed. 'Leave the bikes here. We'll pick them up on our way back.' The only thing Ben takes is the daypack. There are no directions or instructions. She simply follows him down to the main grassy track, where, without any hesitation, Ben steps off the side of the hill. She follows after; then the two of them are sliding down the shingle scarp as though they are on skis; then at the bush line falling and grabbing at the thin manuka trunks. In quick time they find themselves crashing through the undergrowth to the river bed awash in sunshine. Ben has a small cut on his cheek, but he's smiling at where they have arrived. 'Paradise, isn't it?' he says.

They walk a short way upstream until they find a pool to Ben's liking. He lifts his T-shirt and pats his white belly. She watches him strip off. He's always so eager. Then she watches him step into the shallows, his white doughy body which these days she is more used to seeing African-coloured. He's up to his waist when he remembers her. He is disappointed to see that she is still clothed. 'Come along, Mrs Fonda,' he says.

The cool line creeps up her body. She sinks up to her shoulders. After Ben gets out she stays in the water thinking about her mother, wondering what tale she has told the Harrises. She hopes her mother has stayed with them. She hopes she hasn't gone back to look for them. In any case, their tracks are invisible.

'Mrs Fonda?' She looks up at the voice calling to her. Ben is standing on the white river stones holding up a plastic bottle of body paint.

These days she can cover him head to toe in five minutes. As usual, Mr It finds pleasure and Ben is like a small boy about 'Mr It coming out to play'.

'Today for Mrs Fonda, I think a doe. A plump doe, admittedly.' He smiles, enjoying himself, applying the light brown paint in his usual interested way. Interested in how the paint sets on her breasts and elsewhere. He paints the backs of her legs and as he does this she has a sudden urge to pee. 'All right, go on then,' he says. In the shade by the bank she squats. Ben with his hands on his hips looks the other way. When she's finished he says to her, 'Did you wash yourself?'

'It was just a pee,' she says.

'No, Natalie. Go and wash yourself.' So, for the sake of her mother's happiness she crouches down in the pool and splashes cold water over her private area.

These days she knows the drill, and without a word from Ben the young doe sets off down the creek bed. She steps

119

over the white crusted stones. She finds room in her thoughts to think, 'So this is what it feels like to go naked in the bush.' A feeling of having been 'skinned' and the light touch of air. To be free . . . Then she remembers – she is a 'doe' in flight from the 'African'. She would like to stop to take a drink from the stream but she can't because she is being pursued. She wishes she wasn't. She wishes there was some other life to drop into like one of Ben's characters. She wishes there was a door up ahead to slip through and close behind her and wait for the painted man to tiptoe past.

Up ahead a huge boulder rests in the creek. She decides to wait behind it for Ben to lope by with his African stride. Every so often a stone turns. She strains to hear more. Then the silence returns her to the dull thudding of her heart and the greaseproof sound of water emptying into a nearby pool. A white cloud crosses its surface. It is so wonderfully peaceful that a deer might well wander out. Ben, though, in his crafty African way can sniff out the thoughts of a deer. She doesn't even hear his approach. She doesn't know anything of his presence until a hand from behind closes over her mouth. Another hand lifts her and slams her down onto the creek bed. Her knees on the unforgiving stones. Ben's grunting in her ear. He has some wet mush he's sticking between her legs. 'Ben?' she says. 'Ben?' She is suddenly afraid. Everything is happening more quickly than usual. She is squelchy in his fingertips. She feels him slip inside and mutter his achievement in her ear, 'Yes, yes, yes . . .' Ben enjoying himself to the end. Her knees are hurting with his weight pressing down upon her. She closes her eyes and waits for him to finish; she thinks of the Harrises, the perfect square of their picnic blanket, the concerned way with which Mr Harris rose to greet her mother. Behaviour which in her own life she remembers as something that happened in the past. She waits until Ben gasps and rolls off her.

Now there is just this to get through – this period after, when Ben sits up from his full-of-himself state.

'Natalie. Baby . . .' He is surprised to find her crying. Then he looks up from under his black skin surprised at where they are and what they've done. Or at how, as sometimes it is, they came to be the way they are – Natalie in the deer-coloured paint, and himself in this African skin. Then a fresh surprise. 'Your knees are bleeding . . .' He wets his finger and rubs out part of the blood trickling between the knee and shin. 'Baby . . . please don't. Please don't cry. What is it?'

She says, 'Please don't leave Mum.'

'You silly bean,' he says. 'Of course I won't . . .'

'I want to see my dad,' she tells him then. 'I want to . . .'

'Please, Natalie, honey. Not that. Please don't ask for that. Not yet.' Then he fireman-lifts her and carries her, his wounded deer, back to where their clothes are. And like all the other times – even out here among the manuka, in this place people call 'nature' – the air is thick with guilt and Ben's regret.

It's another hour before they catch up to the others. Her mother is with the Fitzroys and Harrises. All of them are waiting in a paddock at the bottom of the hill. Bikes laid on their sides, spokes and chrome gleaming in the sun, the black velcro vests and cycling pants, white legs sprawled sleepily over the grass. She sees her mother labour to her feet. She seems to be favouring one leg, or at least she's making a point that she has a sore leg. Now Mr Harris and Mrs Fitzroy, the quieter woman in the van, stand up and shield their eyes.

Ben moves to the front and Natalie tucks in behind, happy to be out of sight, and determined to keep her front wheel in Ben's groove. Copy Ben's moves – that's the thing to do, she thinks. At the bottom of the hill, Ben dismounts and carelessly lets go of his bike. He pulls off his helmet and drops it to the ground. It's like he's just run through a burning building to reach her mother. 'Vivy. Thank God. We were up in the Washout. We saw you. Natalie did. She called out.' And on cue, she says, 'I called out real loud.' And Ben laughs, 'God knows, your head must have been away with the fairies, Viv.' Natalie is watchful of the others. She's trying to assess how Ben's explanation is going down. But Ben pays them not the slightest attention. Her mother is his only concern. 'I know, Vivienne. I know what you're going to say. You don't have to tell me. A party is not supposed to split up in the bush. But we saw a deer, Viv. A big beautiful thing at the top of the Washout. We just had to climb up there for a closer look.'

Natalie watches her mother consider this. She has a feeling her mother had planned for something different.

'What Washout, Ben?' she asks.

'Well, there's only the one, Viv. The Siberia,' he says, and Ben at last acknowledges the Harrises and Fitzroys. 'You should have seen it. A big hind it was.'

Mr Fitzroy singles out one of his kids. 'Meg, that'll be that whodacky you saw.'

'Whodacky? What whodacky?' somebody asks.

'Deer shit,' says Ben quickly. He's crouching down to inspect her mother's knee. 'Vivy. Vivy. What happened here, hon?'

'The tunnel.' She starts to say, 'You didn't wait . . . You . . .'

'The deer, Viv. We were waiting for you. Then we saw the deer. We thought we'd catch you up.' He stands up. She turns away as he tries to touch her cheek.

Then Mr Harris clears his throat and nods at Natalie's scraped knees.

'You've been in a few wars, I see.'

'I'm all right,' she says, and her mother pulls a strand of hair away from her face to look for herself. She doesn't like her mother looking too closely, doesn't want her thoughts plucked from her head like fruit from a bowl. She glances away and says, 'I'm all right.'

'You might be, but your knees aren't,' says Mr Harris.

'My knees are still me,' she says.

'Natalie,' says her mother.

Mr Harris smiles. 'I think you should get something on them all the same.'

'They're fine as is.'

Mr Harris laughs. 'All right, I know when I'm beat. You must be made of the same stubborn stuff as your mother. She didn't want a bandage on her leg either.'

It was a twenty-minute ride through manuka to the carpark. The sun was out, the bush showing off its silver. Under different circumstances Vivienne might have found it pretty. But she's feeling shattered. She can't bring herself to look at her daughter. She listens to the others, their giddy talk; the scoutmaster fellow, Mr Fitzroy, going on about how lucky they were to live in a country like this. Back in the tunnel she had found herself in some other country that was entirely new to her. She was as cold as she had ever been, cold, lonely, sick at heart, and everything was pitch black. It was too dark to see how bad her knee was and, in any case, she didn't care about a bit of broken skin. The real hurt was in a much deeper place. They had left her behind. Her own daughter and Ben. She felt sure they had heard her cries for help, they must have, she thought, because she could hear the rattle of their bike frames and that ridiculous 'Choo wooing' nonsense of Ben's. The two of them, she thought, and how often that phrase surprised her, the way they fell silent whenever she came into the house, that disturbingly grown-up way Natalie sat in the front seat with Ben. It was too grown-up for comfort. It made her wonder. It made her think. In the tunnel it had come to her, ghastly and bewildering, what the two of them meant, and it so shamed her she stood up suddenly as if to distance herself from the thought. She had taken a big cleansing breath and, fixing her eyes on the small circle of light, had walked calmly from the tunnel. She'd done so without hurry, proud of herself, the way she stepped out without knowing where each foot would land. And then, to arrive at that amazing view. She felt like a pioneer who upon reaching a hilltop gazes upon the newly discovered plain. And that's when she thought, 'I will leave Ben.' She would leave Ben. It was so extraordinary that she had lain down and laughed out loud. She thought of it now, with the bush robin flitting across her handlebars, and the voices close behind. I will get rid of him.

At the carpark the van driver took her bike and she limped to the door. Ben wedged in beside her. He put his hand on her knee and calmly she picked it off, and when he tried to tease a different attitude out of her she folded her arms and concentrated on the view passing the window. 'Vivy, Vivy . . .' he said. She ignored him. It was early evening. The farmland lit up in dark yellows. She started to think about the Christmas party, and after changing from the van and exchanging farewells with the Fitzroys and Harrises they drove through Greytown and Carterton without a word.

At home there was a restlessness in the house which for once, knowing that she was responsible for it, gave her pleasure. She coated her sunburnt neck with roll-on tan. She sprayed between her breasts. She caught herself smiling in the mirror. She had already moved on from Ben. She was moving on to the next thing. She chose the plum dress with the plunging neckline. She enjoyed the effect it had, the spontaneous way Ben stood up from the couch. 'Viv, you look a treat . . .' He offered to run her down to the hotel. She told him there was no need. She was being independent from now on.

They came out to the porch to see her off, Ben and Natalie. The two of them. This time it didn't bother her. She was determined that she wouldn't look back but as she got in the back of the taxi she couldn't resist. She was pleased she did. She thought they looked confused, Ben with his agitated hands buried deep in his pockets, and Natalie? Solemn, tired, she thought.

The party was in one of the hotel's conference rooms. Vivienne looked in from the doorway. Rhonda Morton had come in on her day off to hang up the decorations. There was a scent of pine. Ah yes, the Christmas tree. Everyone was there – all the restaurant staff, the room staff and even one or two from higher stations: Mr Hogan, the restaurant manager, a small, critical man widely feared by all. But this was the staff party and Sharon, a blonde boisterous waitress who sometimes got into trouble for over-fraternising with the guests, hauled him out to the dance floor and everyone cheered.

'There you are!' It was Stewy, beaming under his Christmas hat. 'You look beautiful tonight, Vivienne.'

'And you too,' she said. 'You don't look too bad yourself, Stewy.' It was the first time she had seen him out of his blue check trousers and greasy shoes. He had on a white cheese-cloth shirt. She hadn't seen one of those for years. Stewy's was unbuttoned to a flat, hairless chest.

'You're a wonderful liar, Viv. I suspect I look like some-thing that's been boiled and left in a pot to drain.'

She started to laugh. She had to put a hand to her mouth. 'Stewy!' she said.

'See,' he said. 'I know the truth when it's looking me in the eye. I'll get you a drinkie, Viv.'

He came back with a glass in each hand swaying to the music coming from the tape deck. So, Stewy was a dancer. That was a surprise.

'Vivy?' He held out her hand and she let him guide her through the crowd to the dancing area by the tape deck. They danced to 'Just an Old-fashioned Love Song'. Then 'Street Fighting Man', and Stewy held his breath until he was red in the face and twisted at the shoulders with short piston-like jabs. Then 'Norwegian Wood', and Stewy reeled back on his heels and closed his eyes and mouthed the words, 'I once had a girl or should I say she once had me.' He opened his eyes and they blurted out laughing at each other. Then later, much later in the evening, with everyone pissy-eyed, drinking drinks they didn't want or need, by now plain exhausted, she closed her eyes on Stewy's shoulder while Stewy sang softly in her ear, like it was just for her, something that he might have written specially – 'Wednesday morning at five o'clock as the day begins . . . Meeting a man from the motor trade . . .' She'd forgotten how it went. It had been so long. She thought she might as well take the first step. 'Stewy, why don't we move on . . .'

He lived on the east side of town, the oldest part near the railway station. It was a tiny cottage, with an overgrown garden out front. She thought the song had gone out of him. She noticed in the taxi that Stewy had fallen quiet, perhaps distracted by the task ahead of him.

Now he couldn't find the key in his pocket. Then he couldn't fit the key to the door. 'I must be pissed,' he said. Then he slipped the catch and sang, 'Here we go . . .' as the door opened to the glorious chorus at the Scottish Rangers ground: 'Here we go, Here we go, Here we go.' He turned on the hall lights, then the lights in the front room, holding the door for her, and on the walls were photograph after photograph of football teams. Well, just the one team. 'Champions in 73 and 74. Archibald and Co,' says Stewy, his proud little stomach bulging beneath the photographs. The colours had faded. The players wore their hair long. She thought they looked like young hippies in football socks and shorts. She'd forgotten how people looked back then; she was surprised how long ago it felt, and suddenly she felt old, too old for this. She collapsed onto the couch and closed her eyes.

'So what can Stewy get for you, Viv, love?' She opened her eyes to a plump little bar man rubbing his hands.

'Water please, Stewy.'

He pretended to look disappointed. 'Not a touch of Scotch?'

'If you think I should,' she said to please him.

'I do, Viv. I do.'

He returned with their glasses, humming, 'Here we go, Here we go, Here we go . . .' She took her glass. 'Turn down the lights shall I?'

'If you like, Stewy.'

It wasn't completely dark. The light was on in the hall. They sipped their drinks, then she thought she might as well make a start. She put her glass down and reached over and touched Stewy's cheek. In the dark she heard him cough. Then he moved closer. 'Vivy,' he said, and he moved to kiss her with his dry lips.

'Just a sec, Stewy.' She stood up and tried to reach around for her zipper. 'Stewy, help me, please.' She felt the zip crawl down her back and she smiled thinking of Stewy's pleasure. In no hurry, she thought. That was always a good sign. She climbed out of her dress then unhooked her bra, and Stewy stood back, glass in hand. 'My God, you're a splendid-looking woman, Vivienne. A handful too.'

'You can touch me, Stewy.'

'I was thinking I would,' he said.

She closed her eyes and felt his hands over her breasts. His shallow investigative breath against her cheek and eyelids. She felt him standing primly by until she began to feel like a shrine.

'Here,' she said. 'Let's get these off.' Stewy stood at attention like a small boy while she unbuttoned his shirt. She started to unbelt his trousers but Stewy said he would do that and he turned his back. She went and sat on the couch. She watched him step out of his underwear. She noted his ginger pubic hair and a funny little knob that looked like it was stuck on, a fridge magnet, she claims, reminding her of a miniature Tower of London, say, rather than of anything that had grown out of Stewy.

'Do you have a bed, Stewy?'

'Yes, of course. Sorry, Viv.' And he began to pick up his

clothes. Then she changed her mind. She didn't want to make any more discoveries.

'No, don't worry, Stewy. The couch is fine. I was just wondering.'

'You sure, Viv?'

'I'm sure, Stewy.' She lay down and spread herself. Stewy put his clothes down. Then he stared at her, the length of her. She could see him wondering where to start. 'Here,' she said, and she patted the space on the couch beside her. 'There's room for us both.'

Stewy sat on the edge of the couch gazing back at the portraits of his beloved Scottish Rangers. He shook his head. He said, 'I never thought you'd consider me, Viv. I can't believe you're here.'

She reached up and brought his face to hers and kissed him. 'Well, I'm here, Stewy.' She reached down for the miniature Tower of London and Stewy coughed. Then he coughed again, this time apologetically. 'Why don't you lie on top, Stewy. Would you like that?'

'Yes I would,' he said, and he stood up while she moved onto the small of her back and spread herself. Then he lowered himself like he thought he might break something. She spread her legs and rubbed against him until he began to stir. Stewy, teeth bared, clung on. It was starting to come right after all. She raised her hips and brought her heels down on the backs of his legs, and at once she felt Stewy shrink inside her as if she had pulled off a move that was a bit elaborate for him. She thought of Ben then and felt her own interest. Ben with his eager cock. It was no good. Stewy rolled off her and sat up on the edge of the couch.

'Sorry about that, Viv. I must have knocked back a few tonight.'

She sat up and without saying anything took the miniature Tower in her hand; it felt sticky and limp like its mind was elsewhere. Then Stewy coughed again. 'Actually, Viv, I wouldn't bother. I'm happy. Really. Don't you worry about Stewy.' She sat back against the couch and closed her eyes. For the first time in hours, since the end of the bike ride earlier in the day, she was aware of her knee hurting. 'How about a nightcap, Viv?'

'No, Stewy, I don't think so.'

'Go on. A small drop of Drambuie?'

'No,' she said. 'I'm on the desk tomorrow morning.'

'Then, I'll make you a Christmas cake. Just for you. Viv's Christmas cake with Stewy's special icing.'

She smiled at his kindness. 'That would be nice, Stewy. I'd like that.'

'You like marzipan?'

'I love marzipan,' she said. She saw how happy he was, and his thoughts leaping ahead to the morning when he would stand over his mixing bowls in his blue check trousers and greasy shoes. She saw how much he wanted to please her, and she began to cry. Suddenly she knew she wouldn't be leaving Ben after all. She didn't want cakes.

'What's the matter, love. Did I say something wrong?'

'No, Stewy. You're a good man. A kind, kind person,' she said, and Stewy smiled at the knowledge between them that kindness wasn't enough.

'That's all right, Vivy. You're still my favourite girl.'

'And you're my favourite man,' she said.

# SIX

For a while we fought each other over what we thought we knew or didn't know. Since Vivienne had most of the information, she was assigned the passive, guilty role of answering my questions. I think she threw in Stewy's miniature Tower of London as a sacrificial piece to satisfy my hunger for detail, something to cheer me up with. There are certain places in Natalie's story that we have backed away from. There are questions in my own mind that I haven't yet asked; and but for Ben's sudden and unexpected return I might not have pursued them.

When I got back from Riversdale I cleared the messages. One from Rube. He's spoken to Mrs Richardson and she's given me the okay to come back on the job. Rube sounded like I should be pleased to hear that. A message from Maggie. An invite to her place for dinner. 'I miss you,' she said, and signed off with three unanswered kisses. I'm going to have to disappoint her. I've already said yes to the Harrises on that night. Scattered in between these messages Vivienne had called three times asking me to get in touch. I smiled into the receiver, thinking, 'I can do better than that, Vivienne.'

Wellington is only an hour and a bit away, but the trip always feels longer. Hills have to be crossed, a different geography entered into, and the city and harbour never fail to surprise – and in such a way that it hardly seems believable that only eighty minutes separates its lights and bars from the dark fields and barn owls of the Wairarapa. Viv and Natalie live in Northland, so I always take the Hawkestone Street exit off the motorway, and no matter the hour I'm left with the same feeling, that I've crossed a boundary. My van and overalls suddenly feel out of place, I pass shops I couldn't possibly enter, Pasta, Antiques, Tinakori Bistro, a fancy wine bar with young faces crowding the window, faces who don't know of another life or that bad things lie ahead of them – these are not the faces you see out at Babylon either, and I'm pleased, relieved that Natalie has come to live amongst these people; with luck their good fortune will rub off on her and she'll give up staring at bare hillsides and bouncing back into bad memories. That is my hope anyway.

Between leaving home and arriving outside Viv's house in Farm Road I haven't given Ben a single thought, which is miraculous in itself. But that changes the moment Vivienne answers the door. Ben is our shared baggage, the source of our grief. We share a daughter, but mostly we share a terrible guilt. After all these years those are the two things we are left with, and the moment she opens the door there are no hallos or beg-your-pardons, and it's clear as day what's been preying on her mind.

'Charlie! Where've you been?'

'At the beach.'

'The beach.' It's like I've mentioned a code word and her eyes tilt up at me with all that story we share. There are dark crescents beneath her eyes, repositories of grief that her dark counsellor's suit cannot parry away. When she sits down with her 'victims' they must gaze across a desk and realise at that instant that she is one of them, and it can't be long after that that they realise that it is her own grief that she is counselling in them.

'I rang,' she says. 'I rang three times.'

'And here I am.'

In the hall she saw me glance up the stairs.

'Natalie's at the gym,' she said. Then the timer on the stove rang and we both looked towards the kitchen.

'You aren't expecting someone over, Viv?' I asked.

'Who would that be?' she said, as if it was a wild thought. I don't think it would have occurred to me to ask but for the oven timer. I can't remember the last time I used the oven. I use the heating rings but never the guts of the thing – and if I ever do in the future I imagine the occasion will be to mark something special.

Out in the kitchen Viv picked up a knife and began to slice a cauliflower in vertical strips. I hadn't seen that before. In South Road it would have been unthinkable.

'I rang Reuben, Charlie. He said he hadn't seen you today.'

'Not if I was out at the beach, Viv.'

'He sounded a wee bit surprised.' She waited for me to gallop in with an explanation and when I didn't she went on slicing and chopping. She said, 'Anyway, he was worried you'd go and do something.'

'Who was worried? I don't think you're talking about Rube. Not the Rube man I know,' I said.

'No. Maybe,' she says. Chop, chop she went on her board.

'Viv. Turn around a mo,' I said, and I raised my hands. 'Here I am,' I said.

'I have to pick Natalie up in twenty minutes. I need to get this on now . . .' Then her head sat back on her shoulders. She looked at her reflection in the window then turned around. 'All right,' she said. 'Tell me if you've seen him, Charlie.'

'Have I seen him? That's a laugh. I'd have to be blind to miss him. He's parading himself around town looking pretty bloody pleased with himself. You certainly know how to pick 'em.'

She thought about that, whether or not she would answer, then went back to her chopping board.

'Any idea where he's living?'

'Over by the hospital.'

She stopped chopping and turned around and looked at me closely.

'That's what I hear,' I said.

'Tell the truth. You've paid him a visit, haven't you?' She waited. Slowly she began to shake her head, 'Christ, Charlie.'

'I haven't spoken to the man and that's the honest-to-God truth.'

She wiped her hands on the front of her apron and came and sat down at the table opposite. She didn't say anything while she studied me. Then she picked one of a dozen questions darting behind her dark eyes.

'So. Are you sure it's him?'

'It's him. Unmistakably him. The Harrises saw him. Rube's seen him. I've seen him. He's even seen me see him.'

I thought Viv was maybe trying to picture him. Then she got up and went back to the bench.

'It's just a casserole, Charlie. If you'd rung to say . . .'

'I wasn't expecting anything, Viv.'

She slid the vegetables off the board into a casserole dish. Then she thought of something that needed an immediate answer.

She said, 'I can't remember if you like pineapple or not?'

'I do.'

'Good,' she said. When she opened the oven a warm draught reached me at the table. She shovelled the dish in there and closed the door. She straightened, and wiped her hands, and avoided my eyes. She said, 'When you didn't answer, I thought maybe you were out at that woman's house.'

'What woman would that be, Vivy?'

'The one with those church people.'

'They're not church people.'

'Well, whatever. Babylon.' She went on wiping down the bench. 'Maggie,' she said next. 'That's her name, isn't it? Well?' She laughed at my bashfulness. 'God, Charlie. I can't believe you thought I wouldn't know. You never really leave a place. You should know that.'

'Reuben?'

'Among others.' Then she came over and stood beside me. She reached down and took my hand in hers. 'Promise me, Charlie. Promise me you won't do anything.'

'I'm here, aren't I?' I said. 'What about Natalie?'

'What about her?'

'Does she know?'

She looked away to the door and shook her head.

'Are you sure?'

'I haven't said anything, if that's what you mean.'

She got up from the table and untied her apron. 'I've turned the timer on to thirty-five minutes. Though I'm sure I'll be back before then.'

I stood up from the table and took out my van keys. 'Let me go, eh Viv. It'll be a nice surprise for her.'

For some reason she was reluctant.

'It's no bother, Charlie.'

'I know it's not. But I want to, Viv.'

She thought about it. 'All right. But I'll ring her to let her know to expect you.' She untied the apron and threw it on the table. For some reason she went upstairs to call the gym and leave a message. I don't know why she didn't use the downstairs phone. I waited until her feet ran up to the top of the stairs then went out to the hall to look over the photographs of Natalie that Vivienne has had handsomely framed. I started with the photo taken just after their coming down here, of Natalie sitting on the sea wall in Oriental Bay. She still has a glazed look that doesn't sit properly on a thirteen-year-old's face. I'm surprised that Viv even stuck it up there. There are happier ones of her horse-riding out at Ohariu Valley. She's starting to smile again, and I find myself smiling back, as if I'm catching up with what I have missed in real life. She's laughing for her birthday photos – fourteen, fifteen, sixteen. For her seventeenth birthday Viv took her off to Rarotonga – there she is with a lei around her neck, weighing a coconut in her hand, a conch shell to her ear. There are photos of her holding up her School Cert results, of her first day at polytech. Every milestone Viv has pounced on. But the point of them seems to revolve around Vivienne's need for reassurance that she's done the right thing. The photos are proof of that.

Viv called down the stairs. 'It's the Les Mills gym. Up from James Smith's corner. You might not recognise it. James Smith's is no longer . . .'

'I'll recognise it.'

'Go up the stairs and meet her by the door. Make sure you do that, Charlie. There's all kinds of creeps hanging around the mall at night.'

I parked in lower Cuba Street and walked up to the mall. The gym was easy to find. I could hear the boom boom of the music down in the mall. I sat down on a bench and waited. After a while the music stopped and soon after the gym people started to trail out of the building. Young women, mostly, with flushed faces. Some with coats over their leotards. Others with gym bags. They walked by like proud herons. The last of them disappeared into the night and I stood around for another five minutes wondering what had happened to Natalie.

I went through the door the young women had come out of and, at the top of the stairs on the first floor landing, I found Natalie standing behind a glass door. The glass partition made her look like she was in quarantine, and then I realised that this would be a rule instilled by her mother, asking her to stay upstairs behind the glass until she arrived.

She tried to look surprised, even though her mother had already phoned.

She hugged me. 'Mum didn't say you were coming down.'

'She didn't know either,' I said.

Then she said, 'Why are you looking at me like that?'

'You look a bit pale, honey. Are you feeling all right?'

'Oh God!' she said. 'Already! How long have you been here? You and Mum are as bad as each other. You should have been a pool attendant.'

'What's a swimming pool attendant got to do with anything?'

'I don't know. You're always watching, I guess. So, here you are.'

'Here I am,' I said.

'Have you come down for anything special? To paint a house or something?'

'They can't afford my rates down here, Natalie. You should know that.' She laughed. Then I said, 'You're my special reason, honey.'

We left the mall and walked down to where I parked the van.

'Your mother thinks unsavoury types hang around this neighbourhood. I haven't seen anyone, have you?'

'No,' she said. Then she giggled. 'Only you.'

When I opened the passenger door for her I noticed that she looked in the back before getting in. The door tends to stick, so I closed it for her. Then, in the time it took me to walk around the front and get in my side, behind the wheel, Natalie's mood changed. She sounded sharper when she asked me, 'Ben's back, isn't he?' I wrestled with the handbrake and looked in my side mirror to reverse. Some goat had jammed his car in behind to my bumper. She said, 'I'm not a baby, Dad.'

'Yep,' I said, 'he's back.'

She grunted. 'Thought so.'

'Why's that, baby? Did your mother say something?' And when she didn't answer, I said, 'I'm not out to score points, I'm just asking.'

'Nope,' she said.

'What then?'

'Just the way she's been acting.'

'Like?'

'Like . . . I dunno. You know what she's like.'

'Yeah.'

'Always doing things for me.'

'Oh God. Isn't that a terrible thing. She loves you, that's why she does them.'

She fell quiet and I said, 'Don't you worry, sweetheart.'

'I'm not,' she said.

'Good. That's important. Not to worry.'

'Is that what those church people say?'

'Two guesses who you've been talking to,' I said.

After that she didn't say anything until I was parking behind Vivienne's car.

'Is that why you came down here? To protect me or something?'

'Eh, a big lump like you!'

She looked across at me. I thought she was looking and expecting to find something.

'I never think about him,' she said.

'Not ever?'

She shook her head.

'Really?'

139

She turned away and looked over at her house. Vivienne had turned on the lights in the upstairs window. It really was a picture. Just above, virtually over the house, hung a harvest moon waiting for someone to stand behind that window to admire it.

'There is something I'd like to know, Natalie.' I waited until she made a little noise of assent. 'Well,' I said, 'when you do happen to think of Ben, when you actually remember him, what is it you think of, what do you remember?'

She drew her lips tight, creating dimples of annoyance either side of her mouth.

'I told you already,' she said.

'Well, I suppose I'm still asking.'

She looked annoyed, affronted, and went to get out.

'Natalie,' I said, and the tone held her there.

'I don't know why you have to know these things,' she said.

'Because I have to. I have to know, sweetheart. Because you are my daughter.'

I saw her eyes slope down. I saw her slip into old thoughts. 'I don't know,' she said. 'I guess all sorts of things.'

'Are they . . . I mean are some of the thoughts good?'

'Some.'

'And bad?'

'Dad,' she said. 'I don't think about him that much. Honest. I don't.'

'I'm just asking . . . I just want to be sure.'

'But I've told you everything. I told you everything ages ago.'

'Well, I guess that's the problem, honey. Frankly, I don't feel like I do know everything.'

'Like?'

140

'Well, certain things. I can't say what because I don't know what. That's why I'm asking.'

'It's him, isn't it,' she said. 'You ask all these questions all the time and yet you're the one who thinks about Ben.'

'That's not true, Natalie,' I said. 'I never think about him. I'm simply asking because I'm your father and I should know.'

'Well, why don't you ask Mum then?' She folded her arms and turned away. We were both looking up at her lit window as if that was the only safe place to look.

'Maybe,' I said. 'Maybe I will.'

'Good. So can I get out now?' Without waiting for me to reply she reached for the door.

'Wait!' I said, grabbing her arm. 'Just *wait*.' She looked at the hand holding her. 'I'm not holding you. You're free to go. I just have this one question.'

She nodded, and I released her arm.

'Thank you. Right,' I said. 'That time you left your mother with Ben at the beach. How did you get back to Masterton, Natalie?'

She looked up the street. She looked different from the girl with the flushed cheekbones who had got in the van just ten minutes before. She looked full of knowledge.

'Take your time, honey,' I said.

She shook her head, and as she did so the streetlight caught one side of her face and I saw her cheek wet with tears.

'Let me say something that may help you get started,' I said. 'Something happened out at the beach house didn't it. Something between your mother and you.'

She shook her head, and this time when she reached for the door handle I didn't try to stop her. I said, 'I'll find out

141

eventually. One way or another I will.' She left the door open and ran for the steps by the letterbox. She looked like she was fleeing someone. Here we go, I thought. Her mother will be onto me with a vengeance. I picked up her gym bag and closed the gate on its latch. The front door was open. I closed that too, and found Natalie in the kitchen, her mother's arms around her. Vivienne raised her chin and the old switchblades from years back flashed in her eyes. Gently she pushed Natalie away.

'What did you do to her?'

'Do?' I said. 'I didn't *do* anything, Vivienne.'

'Look at your daughter. Look at what you've done, Charlie.'

'I asked her a question,' I said.

'What sort of question is it that reduces your daughter to tears. Look at her, Charlie.'

'I'm all right, Mum. I'm okay now. Honest,' she said.

But Vivienne wasn't listening.

'I knew it was a mistake. I should have gone and got her myself. I should have known something like this would happen.'

'There you go. Same old music, Viv. Same old horseshit.'

'I don't want that language in my house,' she said.

'Stop it. Stop it. Both of you!' We both looked at Natalie. She had her hands plastered over her ears. 'Please,' she said. 'I don't want you arguing over me. Just stop it.'

Her mother went to touch her. 'I'm sorry. I'm so sorry. I didn't mean to upset you.' Natalie slipped out of reach. She held up her hands. 'I'm okay, Mum. I'm all right.'

'Let me give you a hug,' said her mother then. She just didn't seem to hear what Natalie was saying and I just had to intervene. I couldn't shut up. I said to her, 'You don't see it, do you, Viv. You don't see yourself as you're doing it. Even now. Natalie's the one upset. You're the one wanting reassurance that it's not your fault.'

'And what's that supposed to mean?' she snapped.

Immediately I wished I hadn't said it. I said to Natalie, 'I'm sorry, honey.'

'Charlie!' her mother demanded.

'Vivienne, you know full well what I mean.'

I said to Natalie, 'I'm sorry, honey. I didn't mean to upset you.' I held my arms open to her and she backed away. She shook her head at us both and ran out of the kitchen. We heard her feet on the stairs, and Vivienne and I stared at each other with all the old hatreds flaring and ready, and in the wings, the chariots of shame that race in after a mess like the one we'd just created.

'Well,' she asked, 'are you happy now?'

'This is not what I came down here for, Viv. This is not why I'm here.'

'Why did you, then?' She folded her arms and stared at me.

'Oh no you don't,' I said. 'You're the one leaving messages of panic around the place.'

She closed her eyes, then inhaled and exhaled in that way that used to annoy the hell out of me, as if she was trying to say how reasonable she was determined to be in the face of a maelstrom of shit flying at her from all directions.

'Charlie, Charlie,' she said. 'Listen to us. Let's not say anything for a minute. Let's just hold our breath and then we'll start again, shall we?'

I sat down at the kitchen table and waited for the minute to wind up. I couldn't look at Vivienne. I just couldn't bring myself to. I could hear the taps running upstairs, then the shower. The oven timer rang and Vivienne took out the casserole and placed it on the table.

'We can still make this a pleasant evening,' she said.

'Is that a minute?' I asked.

'Charlie, look at me a second. Go on.' I raised my eyes but it was the hardest thing. 'Do you really hate me so much?' she asked.

'I don't hate you. That's ridiculous.' I started to get up.

'No, stay where you are and listen to me for a moment,' she said. 'You have to put this Ben episode behind you. You really have to try and make the effort. Don't those Babylon people preach forgiveness?'

'They don't preach,' I said.

'Talk, then, or whatever it is that they do. The point is, don't they believe in forgiveness?'

'Talking is never the same as doing, Vivienne. You should know that.'

'And what does that mean?'

'I'm not getting at you. I'm just saying what they believe.'

The shower turned off upstairs and Vivienne raised her eyes to the ceiling.

'She's a brittle little thing.'

'Not that brittle, Viv. Not so . . . I mean, does she have a boyfriend?'

Vivienne looked surprised.

'Well, she is eighteen years old. After all. I mean, hell, why wouldn't she?'

'There is no young man that I'm aware of,' she said.

'That's because you're always around cutting them off at the pass.'

'That's ridiculous.'

'You're smothering her, Viv. It's as plain as day.'

She looked at me with wonder. She said, 'Can you not say something, anything, nice? Or did you just come here to argue?'

'Look at the clothes you wear,' I said. 'You and Natalie wear the same clothes. Or haven't you noticed?'

'Plenty of mothers and daughters do that.'

'It's not healthy, Vivienne.'

'Plenty of mothers do . . . Younger mothers . . .' She turned and wiped away a tear. 'Oh God, Charlie. I don't want to argue any more.' She went and stationed herself at the window and looked out. She said, 'I had almost forgotten him, Charlie. I'd almost put him out of my life.'

'No, Viv. Don't let him get to you. Don't let it happen,' I said. I got up and hugged her. She shook her head against my chest – a little movement full of resistance.

'We can't forgive each other, can we, Charlie?'

'Don't say anything, Vivienne. For the moment let's try silence and see what happens.'

Natalie came downstairs to join us. Both her mother and I tried to make up for earlier. I got her onto her design course at the polytech. She talked of Macs and cool colour lasers. To my ears it's a different language and I could only nod and look interested. Still, it got us through the meal. Though once, when Natalie shoved the casserole meat to one side of her plate, Viv couldn't help herself. She said, 'Natalie, you're looking a bit pale, sweet. That's a sign you need iron.'

'I don't feel like I need *iron*,' she said. 'I feel fine. I just don't feel like meat.' She stabbed a cube of potato onto her fork. She followed this up with a cube of carrot.

Afterwards I helped Viv with the dishes. Just the two of us like that – it almost felt like old times. I suspect the same thought occurred to Viv because she said, 'You can sleep in my bed if you like, Charlie. It seems silly for you to sleep down here.'

I didn't answer as quickly as I might have. The truth is I was giving it my full consideration. Then I noticed I had embarrassed Viv with my silence. Her cheeks blushed. She said, 'I suppose the church woman wouldn't think much of that idea.'

'Probably not,' I said. 'The couch will do me, Viv.' I gave her a kiss on the cheek.

She stood there with her hands in the dishwater, a rind of suds halfway up her forearm, then for whatever reason she said, 'Suddenly I feel old.'

'Thirty-seven's hardly old. It can't be if I'm it,' I said. She smiled as if it was a kind thing that I had said. Then I had a different thought. 'There's no one sniffing about is there, Viv?'

She laughed as if that was an outrageous suggestion. 'I think I scare them away,' she said.

'No! No way. I don't believe that.'

'Not that I'm looking,' she said.

'Well, that's right. Why would you? A fine woman like yourself.'

'Do you think so?' She stopped rinsing for a moment and turned to face me.

'I know so,' I said. 'I know so, Vivy.'

For a moment there Ben loosened his grip on our hearts and thoughts. For a moment there it was just me and Viv. There was no history between us. No hurting. Just one of us with a teatowel and the other leaning on her hands deep in dishwater wondering if something that had been dropped long ago could be recovered.

In the night I heard footsteps on the stairs. The door to the sitting room where I was on the couch creaked and a voice poked a hole in the dark to ask if I was awake.

'Natalie?' I sat up and pulled the bedding around me. 'What time is it?'

'Two twenty-six,' she said.

I groaned, and she started to apologise.

'I thought you might be awake,' she said.

'Well, if I was I wasn't doing anything.'

'Dad,' she sighed, and I felt her smile in the dark. She moved silently through the dark and parked herself at one end of the couch. She had on her dressing gown. Her voice had none of that sleepy quality. I had a feeling she'd been up a while. I asked her if she wanted the light on.

'Nope,' she said.

'A cup of tea?'

'Nope.'

'Well, in that case, I'm all ears.'

'I was thinking what you asked me in the van. I think I can tell you. I might not be able to at another time but right now I think I can.'

'Sounds good to me,' I said.

'Do you know something?' she began. 'You never ask me about my baby, Dad. Never. Not once that I can recall.'

'Sweetheart,' I said. I reached across for her and again she held me off.

'No, I don't want any more hugs. I just want you to listen. I was a mother for four days and nights. I had a baby. She was mine and I killed her.'

'That's crazy. No. You didn't kill her, Natalie. No one's blaming you for the heat in that house.'

'I am,' she said. 'I could have saved her. I had a chance to. She was so sweet. So little. I should have tried harder to get back to her.'

'You did what you could, honey. At the time you did. You're just beating up on yourself.'

She looked at me then like I was the naive one, the unknowing one.

'If I tell you I tell you only this once,' she said.

'I can live with that,' I said.

'And you're not to tell Mum. Promise me?'

I reached over and touched her shoulder lightly. 'I'm here now, Natalie.' And she nodded. At the end of the couch she leant forward with her elbows on her knees and thought what she would say and where to begin. In the past it had had to be dragged out of her, like pulling teeth, nagging her to the point of tears. Doors were slammed. Patience and temper ran in short supply. Information was something to use against the other. But this evening it's different. For once I'm not asking. For once I'm hearing what she has to say. I'm not fishing or extracting. But if some things don't change it's this artery near the heart that every so often stops pumping, and Natalie has to interrupt her story to ask if I'm all right.

'I'm listening, baby . . .'

'Do you want me to continue?'

'I was just thinking about what you said, honey. I'm listening . . .' And we head back to that weekend she woke up in the car halfway to Castle Point, and her efforts to get back to Masterton, home to her baby lying in a carton over at Bennetts'.

# SEVEN

She is amazed at the number of sentries posted in the adult world. As she left the beach house to walk up the road a man in brass-coloured overalls stood up by a bed of marigolds. It was the same man from whom Ben had picked up the cottage key half an hour earlier. Natalie pretends he is still kneeling on the grass next to the marigolds. She raises her chin that little bit more. Whereas Mr Uttley is moved by different things. He sees a young girl clutching a twenty-dollar bill in her hand obviously heading in the wrong direction and calls out, 'Shop's the other way.' She already knows that but pretends that it's news. 'You won't find much that way,' he says, and it's true that the road turning up the hill doesn't promise any instant reward. Masterton is another eighty kilometres. Mr Uttley fished in his pocket and gave her a sweet that she thought he had been saving for such an occasion as this.

'Thanks. I'm just walking,' she told him.

She's anxious to get on her way. Ben will soon come after her. There's nothing more certain.

'Just a walk,' she says again to Mr Uttley, and she sets off up the road.

For the next two hundred metres she's aware that she's in his view. Every so often she looks behind and waves and the gardener, still where she left him, inclines his head. She can't think what she said or did to alarm him. Around the next bend the road enters the hill and she almost races for that blind spot out of Mr Uttley's view.

It's one o'clock on a Saturday afternoon. Most of the traffic coming out to the beach has already arrived and won't be leaving for another three or four hours. She's almost reached the top of the hill without a single car passing either way. Despite the heat of the sun and the heat bouncing off the tarseal she feels like she is sweating more heavily than usual and when she looks down she sees two big wet spots on her T-shirt. Her breasts are leaking. This has never happened before. Her body used to be perfectly sealed. She looks about the scattered farmland, then, after checking the road, she raises her shirt to make sure she isn't leaking away her insides. Of course it's her milk, and that sets her thinking about Choo Woo. She pictures her little hands stroking the air above the carton in Mrs Austen's room at Bennetts' and lengthens her stride. She wishes she could run but she can't;

she's still hurting between her legs, and whenever she hurries she feels as though she is coming apart at the seams.

At last, a car. And it's coming from the beach. She can hear it straining up the hill. She can't see back that far because of the bend in the road and there's no time to duck below the roadside and hide as Ben comes leisurely into view. He's not in the same hurry that he was when she was about to get into that other car heading back to Masterton. He slows right down and pulls over. He winks and smiles. And when she shows no inclination to get in he reaches over to open the door for her and pats the seat beside himself. 'In you get, Mrs Fonda. I've got the air conditioning on.' The cool air is deliciously soothing, and after she closes the door Ben says, 'That's the spirit. It's amazing how much more reasonable you are away from your mother.' She leaves the remark alone, thinking to let Ben have his say. Let him have his fun.

They drive off in the same direction, over the hill into view of Mataikona and the jagged coastline north, and with Ben apparently in no hurry, deep in thought.

'Ben, where are we going?' she asks him. He stirs, and looks bleary-eyed at the stunning views.

'Where are we going? That's what I was going to ask you. Your good mother, your trusting mother I should say, sent you down to the shop. The shop – well, as you probably recall – lies in the other direction.'

'Oh,' she says.

'"Oh doh soh loh" or "oh what a bloody nuisance I am"?'

'Sorry,' she says.

'Me too,' he says.

Ben's indignation just sails past her. She has only one thing in mind. There's only room in her thoughts for Choo

Woo. At least they are headed in the right direction – perhaps if she asks nicely, sweetly, perhaps he will let her out and pretend he never saw her. 'Let me out, Ben. Just this once? Please?' He doesn't appear to have heard. Then she thinks, what if Mrs Fonda were to ask, and this time she says, 'Let me go and I'll do anything you like. Anything.'

Without any warning Ben hit the brakes and they slid in the roadside gravel to a halt. The air conditioning made a roaring noise and Ben clutched the wheel and glowered out at the road. 'Please don't ever talk to me like that, again. God, girl. What the hell do you think I am. Just what do you think . . . as if I would be interested in *anything* or would do *anything*. As if, like I'm some fucking Johnny in a dark alley.'

'I just want to go home. I have to, Ben. Why won't you believe me . . .'

'Because it's like listening to a record,' he says. 'It's like hearing the same fucking track over and fucking over.' At that moment he caught a glimpse of his red face in the rear-view mirror and the situation became appallingly clear to him. 'God,' he says. 'Once upon a time we would be having us a ball. Once we would be high-jinksing and there'd be none of this unpleasantness. What's happened here, Natalie?'

'I just want to go home,' she tells him.

'Okay. I'm not going to be provoked. I refuse to. All right.' Then he forces a smile, and says to her, 'Look at us, Natalie. Look at these two rhinos clashing heads on the side of the road. What's the matter with us? Why aren't we with the rest of the population?'

They drive back over the hill and as they come down to the beach settlement the gardener in the brass-coloured overalls looks up from his bed of marigolds and rises to his feet. Ben waves across to him and the gardener raises his weeding fork in reply. 'Did he tell you?' she asks him. At first Ben doesn't answer. He shifts his gaze to the side window then near the shops back to the road before he says, 'Well, naturally he was concerned.'

They drive on to the store where she goes in to buy what she was supposed to return with. She wonders what he will tell her mother. But she needn't have worried. Ben takes care of that. 'She's a chip off the old block, Vivienne. Guess who I caught jawing with her mates from school. Clean forgot what we sent her out to do.'

Later, she watched her mother and Ben wander off down the beach together. She remembered another time when she and her mother had walked along the same stretch of beach. On that occasion her mother had asked her what she thought of the idea of Ben coming to live with them. She hadn't felt one way or another about it. Ben was fun and so she guessed if he came to live in the same house there would be more fun. She waited until they were beyond the motor camp then she went inside to call Pete's house. She thought that Pete could go across the road and take care of Choo Woo until she got back. He had taken care of the orange cat's litter.

Mrs Sutton answers. She says Pete is out with his dad scavenging garage sales across town in search of classic Coke bottles.

'I'll get him to call soon as he gets in,' promises Mrs Sutton.

She gives Mrs Sutton the Castle Point number, and only after she put the phone down did she realise her mistake. She had it in her head that Pete would walk in the door in the next minute. She even stood by the phone ready to pick it up. But Pete doesn't call until after seven, by which time she and her mother, and Ben, are sitting down to dinner, and when the phone goes she feels her cheeks redden. She starts to get up but Ben motions her down again. He wipes his mouth with a paper napkin and gets up from his plate of sliced ham and tomato. When Ben lifts the receiver he catches her eyes and sets his mouth in that line of annoyance. He says to the caller, 'She's eating her dinner right now,' and puts the phone down. 'I can't escape that kid,' he says, returning to the table.

'Who, Ben?' asks Vivienne.

They have to wait while Ben crams a fork loaded with ham into his mouth. 'Birdbrain,' he says. Then he is struck by a different thought. 'Wait a minute, how did he get this number?'

Now her mother and Ben stare across the table at her.

'That's a toll,' says her mother.

'Oh God save me,' says Ben. 'Don't tell me you made a toll call for the sake of one of those silly bloody birdshit conversations. If it is . . . I don't want to know.' And he makes a show of placing his hands over his ears and shaking the thought from his head.

'Ben,' says her mother, reaching across to him, 'let me handle it, please.'

'You know, Viv. You must have heard them. Cheep. Cheep. Tweet. Tweet.'

'Well, young lady?' asks her mother.

'I forgot something,' she says. 'I forgot to tell Pete something.'

'Well, couldn't it wait? I mean, here we are out at the beach. I want to get on with forgetting about home. This is what this holiday is all about.'

'I'm all for that,' says Ben. 'Absolutely. More wine, Vivy?'

Natalie doesn't know what to do. She watches her mother place a hand over her wine glass and Ben laughs at her self-restraint.

'One of these days you're going to let yourself go and I'd love to be around when it happens.'

Ben was intent on drinking that evening. When he finished the wine they opened for dinner he opened another bottle and took it and his glass out to the lawn to sit in a white plastic chair facing the sea. He stayed out there until the last of the beach was swallowed up in the dark. He was quite ready for that, for the day to depart; still, at least they will have a decent run at the evening. 'Charades,' he thinks then. 'We'll play charades.' He stands up with the thought and shouts the idea back through the sliding doors. 'Charades!'

Natalie looks up from an old pile of *National Geographics.*

'Charades,' he says again, in case they missed it the first time.

Vivienne is drying the dishes, and, as Ben steps inside beaming at the prospect, she says, 'Do we have to, Ben?'

'We don't have to do anything, Viv,' he says. 'We can sit in our gardens till the flowers rot if that's what you want.'

'I suppose I'm just not very good at those charade things,' she says.

'Natalie? I know you have certain talents in that area,' he says.

'I'm reading,' she says, then Ben takes a step across to her and rips the magazine from her hands.

'Was reading,' he says. Then he starts flicking through the spread on Antarctica that she was reading. 'What a godforsaken place. Christ, look at it.' Then he tosses the magazine on the pile and speaks up. 'Come on then. Who's first? Nat? Viv? Before I call on volunteers. Viv, will you give up the bloody dishes for a moment.'

Natalie watches to see what her mother will do. She is smiling grimly, clinging onto her good humour. She switches on the kettle then asks Ben, 'Are you ready for that cuppa now?'

'No, I bloody aren't. I want to play charades,' he says.

Vivienne smiles at her difficult house guest. 'Well, we could go for a walk. Is that the sea I can hear?'

'Charades, Vivienne,' he says.

'Ben, I told you. I'm no good at that sort of thing.'

'Well, of course not, Vivienne. What do you expect? You won't ever succeed at something if you keep on telling yourself you can't do it. You act like you're weighed down with lead in your pack. You'd think I was asking you to trudge across the Gobi Desert.'

Viv smiles down at the kitchen floor. She knows he's partly right in what he said. She just wishes he wouldn't drink so much.

'Charades gives you the chance to be someone else, and that's actually the point, Viv. The point behind the exercise if you like. Charades gives you the chance to say yes where normally you might say no. It's a liberating thing . . .'

'I know,' she says. 'I know what you say is true.' She smiles at the floor between them.

'Viv, are you with me?'

'Ben, I'd rather not.'

'For fuck's sake, Vivienne. It's so tedious being yourself all the bloody time.'

'I'm going to make some tea,' she says.

'Boring, Miss Solway.' Then he looks at Natalie and he says, 'I know you're with me, aren't you, Natalie?'

Is she? She looks up at Ben and wonders if his nod was intended to be a command. 'I don't mind,' she says.

'See! Hear that, Viv? Your own daughter's a starter. At least she's got some gas in the tank.'

Natalie watches her mother smile as she pours the tea; she might be smiling at the thought of herself playing charades. Ben sees it too, and senses a chink in her resistance. 'Come on, Vivienne. It'll give you the chance to play someone you aren't. It'll free you up.' Her mother is still weighing up the challenge. She might be looking down from the end of a high diving board. Then she looks down and closes her eyes and shakes her head.

'Disappointing, Viv. Very disappointing.'

Then her mother looks up and sticks her hands on her hips and says to Ben, 'Who said anything about not playing?'

'Well, well,' says Ben. 'Wonders never cease.'

Vivienne tosses the teatowel over the dish rack and comes out to the living area. She places her hands back on her hips and looks Ben in the eye. 'Who's first?'

Ben looks around. He still has a glass in his hand. Things are shifting along more quickly than he had bargained for. 'Where's that *National Geo.* Flick it over here, Nat.'

The magazine is open at the spread on Captain Scott's fatal South Pole expedition. Ben holds it before him like a lay preacher. He rocks on his feet, closes his eyes and tilts his head back. 'Okay. It's coming to me. Here it is. Here's the script. Is everyone on their toes?' Natalie gets up and folds her arms beside her mother.

'All right,' says Ben. 'I'll be Captain Scott. You can be Oates, Natalie. Viv, you can be one of the troopers . . .' Her mother starts to pout, so Ben says, 'All right, save us. Let me have another look.' He snaps his fingers for the magazine.

Then he scans the columns until he picks up a name. 'Here it is. Bowers, Viv. That'll be you.'

'Bowers,' says Vivienne, trying out the name for herself, assessing it for hidden value.

They receive their instructions from Ben out on the lawn. They watch as he lies down on the sandy grass and wraps his arms around himself, instantly moving into character, making his teeth chatter. He is barefoot in jeans and an old sweatshirt with Alpha Theatre lettering faded over his chest. Otherwise it is Captain Scott, unshaven, with the dead eyes of a floor rug, looking up and appealing to each of them. 'Oates. Bowers.'

'Yes,' Natalie answers mechanically.

'Yes, Captain,' says her mother to show that she is on the ball.

And Ben raises his head to look past his feet. 'There's a blizzard raging. Our best chance is for you both to cuddle up to me.'

Already Natalie can sense her mother is about to drop out of the game. Ben must have sensed her hesitation as well.

'Bowers,' he says to her. 'It's our only chance. We have to make ourselves a bundle of warmth.'

Still, her mother is not that keen. The game is not taking the shape she thought it would. She unfolds her arms and gets down beside Ben.

'Oates?' he says.

Natalie follows suit and lies down beside her mother even though she knows that this is not what Captain Scott had in mind. Still, there's nothing he can do about it without his slipping out of character.

The moon sits above the sea. A cluster of stars balances

overhead. Natalie's thoughts turn to Choo Woo lying in the dark at Mrs Austen's. She wriggles closer to her mother. She goes to rest her head on her shoulder but her mother turns away. Ever since the ride over the Rimutaka Incline before Christmas her mother has not been able to touch her or look her properly in the eye. It requires Captain Scott to speak up before she remembers that she is Oates and, as she tells herself, Oates would not know anyone called Choo Woo. With that convenient discovery she decides to enter into Oates more fully. Since she can do nothing to help her baby she might as well take refuge in another character.

The complaining noises are from Captain Scott. His frostbitten feet are troubling him. Vivienne rubs his shoulder, his thigh. She arrives at Ben's frostbitten feet and nervously looks over to see what Natalie is doing; she wants to please, to do the right thing.

'Mr Oates, I believe you were going to say something?'

'Was I?' asks Natalie, before Ben, in a tired and slightly exasperated voice, reminds her of the plot.

'We are three famous British polar explorers . . .'

She remembers now. She remembers the bold text from *National Geographic*. She scrambles up and announces, 'I am just going outside. I may be some time.'

She has started for inside the house before Ben calls her back with another stage direction.

'The beach, Oates. Terra firma articus.'

She drops down the three wooden steps onto the sand. She is not clear about which direction to take. She thinks back to what she read in *National Geographic* about the next act in the fateful expedition. She hangs about in the shadows listening to Ben put the various pieces in place, and a final order for her mother: 'Oates has gone for a while. I think

I had better check. You keep an eye on the dogs.'

'What dogs, Ben?'

'Vivienne, please. *The* dogs.'

'Oh,' she says. Then she asks, 'How long do I have to stay out here?'

'Out here? Viv, for God's sake, pay attention. You're inside the tent.' Then he reverts to his theatrical captain's voice: 'No point risking more lives than necessary.'

Natalie can see him at the edge of the lawn peering into the darkness of the beach. His thin, reedy voice calls out to her: 'Oates? Oates? Where are you?' Natalie isn't sure whether Oates is expected to reply. In the *National Geographic* article Oates was never seen again, so she moves off in the direction of the lighthouse on the point. She keeps to the high part of the beach and the reflected light of the baches. In one lit window she sees some kids her own age, their heads bent over a board game. They are kneeling on chairs and reaching for a bowl of chippies.

'Oates? Are you there?'

His voice sounded full of mischief. Should she call back? Or should she remain true to Oates? She decides to keep moving but doesn't do so with any real conviction.

'Oates!' There was a definite edge to Ben's voice that time. So she answers back, 'Is that you, Captain Scott?'

At the sight of the drunken figure stumbling towards her she doesn't feel so much like Oates as the prey from their other games. There is no difference between Oates and the deer character. She is the polar cap. The distant hill. The point of all of this.

'Captain Scott?' she asks, with an innocence that sounds foolish even to Ben's ears.

'No, it's Father fucking Christmas.' And just like that

the character of Captain Scott disappears into the night. She can never keep up with his character changes. Once again she wonders what happened between Captain Scott calling out for Oates in the snow storm and the arrival of Mr Fonda a few minutes later. She watches Ben check behind him. Then she hears him lower his zip. She smells his winey breath and feels his stomach rub up against her. 'Bowers is back at camp,' he says. She feels like she is locked up in a small room with Ben. The world is this small room to which Ben holds the key. 'I don't want to die out in this frozen terra without a last gasp of pleasure.' She knows what to do. She knows what Ben likes. She drops to her knees in the sand, Ben's hands on her shoulders. A few seconds later she hears her mother calling out for them – 'Hello! Oates! Captain Scott? Where are you?' She takes her mouth away and Ben swears under his breath. His hand drops back on to her head. She can't believe he would want her to continue – 'Ben, it's Mum!'

'Hallelujah. The cavalry's arrived.'

'Oates? Is that you?'

'Over here, Bowers,' says Ben.

He does up his jeans and Natalie gets to her feet – the curtain dropping at the moment of her mother's arrival.

'You found Oates,' her mother says to Ben.

'Safe and sound,' says Ben. 'We're rewriting history.'

'Well,' she asks, 'what now?'

'Back to base,' says Ben.

'Watch out for crevasses,' says her mother.

They trudge back to the house – Ben sullen for what Bowers interrupted. Her mother, though, Natalie has noticed, is upbeat and chirpy. She's come through the game well. She's kept in Bower's character for the most part. She's succeeded where she thought she would fail.

Back at 'base' Ben grumpily surveys the lawn, hands on hips, wondering what he can salvage from this South Pole situation. Natalie stands with her mother watching him think, and scratch his belly beneath his sweatshirt. He starts to shiver, then he clutches his hands to his chest. Her mother is not used to these quick character changes and sketches. 'Ben?' she asks. 'Are you all right?' Ben ignores her. Captain Scott, however, answers with talk of morphine and opium pills that are at their disposal should the cold become unbearable. And Natalie knows by the bright way of his talk that Ben has something in mind and that these new lines are scaffolding to get them into a new situation.

They watch Ben lower himself to the ground and pat the area either side of himself. 'This time I'll be the meat in the sandwich. Bowers, close the tent flaps.' Natalie watches her mother happily kneel to zip up the tent entrance. With her mother's back turned Ben looks up at her and slaps the ground the other side of himself. 'You're over here, Oates.' Then he says, 'My God, it's cold. Hurry, Bowers. Hurry.' He complains of his feet, his frostbitten feet.

Natalie discovers her mother up on an elbow peering over the top of Ben. It comes as a shock to realise that her mother doesn't know what to do. She is actually looking to take a lead from her. So Natalie moves down to Ben's frostbitten feet, her mother following after. She takes the left foot, her mother the other, and they work at restoring Ben's blood flow. His feet feel sandpapery from walking in the sand. Her mother blows hot air over the Arctic explorer's feet.

Now Ben starts complaining of his hands. His frostbitten fingers. So they leave his feet and repeat the exercise with his hands, huffing and blowing. Natalie looks across at her mother. She is bent over her work, rubbing the captain's hands like she's rubbing dirt off the potatoes under a cold tap at home. It occurs to her that her mother doesn't understand the point of the game. She actually thinks it has to do with Captain Scott's frostbite. Her mother's unknowingness is almost childlike.

Now Ben shifts more fully on to his side to face Natalie. His teeth are chattering. 'Oates. Bowers.' He calls them together – the two sides of the sandwich – to press up against him, Vivienne against his back, his belly pressed in against Natalie, so that neither can see what the other is doing. They are together but without the knowledge of the other. Then she feels Ben reach for her hand and guide it down to where she discovers Ben's cock waiting in the doorway. For her mother's benefit he remains Captain Scott with his teeth chattering. But there comes a moment when he shifts his position, just slightly, a brief moment when Oates and Bowers find themselves facing each other over the top of his head. Only it's not Bowers any longer. It's her mother, and Natalie can tell that in her mother's eyes she has stopped being Oates. They regard each other the way they used to in the mirror, when each reflected the past and future. Now, to their mutual astonishment, the gap has closed, and there are tears running down her mother's face. Even though she has glimpsed something which in her wildest dreams she never expected, she doesn't make a sound. She doesn't utter so much as a syllable. The awful discovery is there in her eyes, a vocabulary sunk to such a depth that there is no question of it being raised for fear of what it might do to their world.

'Mum?' whispers Natalie. It is such a small word to carry

so much responsibility. 'Mum?' she says, and her mother closes her eyes like a child hoping that what she can't see won't exist. A sob rose from her, one she could no longer suppress, and Ben, alert as ever to changes in the atmosphere, turns his head slightly with the old order: 'Stay closer to me, Bowers. Press up against me. That's right.'

Her mother drops from view. Though Natalie can hear her sobbing. Still, Mr Fonda won't let her stop. Whenever she pauses his hand closes over her wrist. For the sake of her mother's happiness they must press on. Ben pays no notice to her mother crying into the floor of their tent. Mr Fonda has relieved Captain Scott of command and nothing can get in the way of Mr Fonda, ever. Finally he raises himself and she feels his squirt. A wave draws up the beach and Ben makes a throat-clearing noise. Then, quickly, he pushes everything back inside his trousers and rolls onto his back. He must have heard Vivienne, of course; now he has to acknowledge her, he has to say something which will make everything seem right. Gazing up at the night sky he finds a message there. 'We've only got each other,' he says. 'We would all do well to remember that.'

Natalie gets up. Mr Fonda has had his pleasure. There's no longer any point in staying in character – the skit is over. Her mother is lying face down on her stomach, her face hidden from the world. Nothing is said, because no words can adequately paper over the cracks in their little world.

And later, because there is always a later, Natalie lies in bed with the light out listening to Ben whistling and busying himself in the kitchen. She listens to the sound of the crockery in the sink, to the noise of clutter and forgetfulness. 'Afterwards' is what he does best. The mopping up. After Mr Fonda takes up his bowler hat and departs the stage this is the best time to be around Ben, and Natalie can sense her mother's discovery of a lighter mood. She recognises all the sounds. Ben's one-sided banter. And now this. His clownish effort to make her mother dance to the Joe Cocker tune he's whistling and the half-remembered lyrics mumbled on her shoulder. The noises of Ben's shame which she knows from experience but which are all new to her mother. She can hear her mother trying to push him off.

'No, Ben, I don't want to. We have to talk.'

'That is what we're doing, love bug.'

'I mean a serious talk.'

'Vivy. Viv. It's late. The birds are in their nests.'

'I know it's late, Ben. But I want you to tell me what happened tonight. I want to hear it from you before I say anything else.'

'Well, Viv, there's no mystery. We played a game. I was Scott. You were Bowers. Nats was Oates.'

Natalie can almost hear the clockwork of her mother's thoughts. 'So. It was just a game. Nothing happened?'

'Oh yes! We were freezing our nuts off, remember, Vivy?' And from her bedroom Natalie hears Ben set his teeth to chattering. 'I think I know what the problem is. You have to know when to step out of character. Viv, listen. You know what I think? I think you're still locked away inside Bowers. Look at you. You're as pale as ice. Look at you. You're shaking. Come here. Come to Ben. Let Ben warm you up.'

'No, I'm perfectly all right.'

'Vivy. I said the blizzard's over with. We were just playing. Now we're not. Now we're home on the range. We're out of the blizzard.'

Someone switches on the jug, then Natalie hears Ben ask, 'Herbal or gumboot?'

'Viv?' he says a moment later.

'Peppermint,' her mother answers. Peppermint. And with that one word Natalie feels her mother has conceded something. Just a word, a flavour, up to then. Now it means something else. It means her mother has forgiven Ben. It means she is all alone.

Sunday morning, Natalie woke with Choo Woo in her thoughts. She woke up with the feeling that this would be the day by which she would be judged forever. She slipped out of bed and out of the house to what at that hour was a silvery world, the air sharpish. She stood outside the Castle Point store rubbing warmth back into her bare arms. She watched a few surfers awaken from their surfboards and pull themselves over a wave. A man trailing three dogs on leashes walked at the water's edge. She watched the sun climb out of the ocean and shine in the windows of the baches along the beach road. She surprised the storekeeper when he opened his doors at seven thirty. He asked if she wanted anything – milk, bread, a newspaper? – and looked at her strangely when she said she didn't need anything. 'I'm waiting for someone,' she explained, which in essence was true. She was waiting for a lift back to Masterton to feed her baby.

The hour changed. Now small children left the shop with ice-block juice running down their chins. They were shouted at by stern-looking women from the motor camp, their fleshy arms filled with the bread which they had ordered the previous afternoon. Natalie watched this traffic and began to worry that Ben wouldn't be far away. Soon he'd turn up for his papers.

So far only two cars have drawn up to the pumps. A

farmer with a barking dog in the back of his ute. He told her where he was headed. It wasn't a place she'd ever heard and it didn't have the ring of town about it. She declined that offer. Then she asked two women if they were headed back to town. One answered yes and the other no. They drove off, the one who had said no with an unpleasant backward glance as she reached around for her seatbelt.

At last she recognised a face.

'Mr Patterson!' The man in the fishing cap turned from the pump. It was definitely him, the Featherston garage owner. Tom Patterson. She walked over to him. 'Remember me?' His wrinkled eyes peered into hers. 'I was with Ben that day. Ben Strang? Kleenz Industrial Towels?' Then she remembers and realises what the problem is. 'You probably don't remember. I was Vivienne.'

'Yes,' he says.

'Only I'm not Vivienne any more. I'm Natalie. Her daughter. My mother is Vivienne. People say we look alike.'

'Yes, maybe,' says the garage owner. Natalie can see him hunting back through his memory for the day.

She asks him if he's headed back home, and before he can decline she says, 'I'm only going as far as Masterton.' She watches him scratch his chin. She knows what he's thinking – he's thinking of ways to say no.

'How old are you?'

'Fifteen.'

'Nope,' he says. 'Still too young. I'd want your mother's permission.' Then he says, 'Did you say Ben is out here at the beach? I'd listen to him. One or the other.'

She started to cry, and the colourless eyes of Tom Patterson drifted back to her request.

'Masterton?' he says, and, thinking that at last she has

won, she starts towards the car door.

'Whoah,' says the garage-man. Then he gazes up the road, front and behind, like he's afraid of having been seen talking to her. 'I'd like to. Honest I would. But I'm sorry. Whatever it is that's so urgent I'm sure it can wait. That's my advice. It's all I can help you with.' He places the hose nozzle back on the pump, and seeing she is still there when he turns around, he asks her, 'Who did you say you were?'

'Natalie,' she answers.

'Natalie. That's a pretty name,' he says. 'I'm sorry, Natalie. I can't help.'

There was a pay phone by the door. She thought she'd try Suttons' again. She got Pete's mother and she didn't know where Pete was. 'He got up after breakfast and left the house. It's like having a boarder around the house. He comes and goes and doesn't say where or what.' But that was reason for hope too, she thought. Maybe Pete was over at Mrs Austen's. She hung up, and turned around to find a combi van had taken the place of the garage owner.

Three boys were crammed in to the front. She approached the one nearest the window wearing Dirty Dog shades. She asks him if they are headed back to town.

'Could be,' says Dog Shades.

'Will you take me?'

'If you fuck me,' he says, and the other two, his mates, pretend to feel shame and disgust; they drop their faces into their hands.

'Christ, Warren . . .'

'Gross, man . . .'

The one in shades laughs at his friends. Then when he turns back he looks surprised to find her still there.

'Who's the driver?' asks Natalie.

'He is,' says Dog Shades, hooking his thumb across to the one with curly brown hair and an earring in his ear.

'I'll fuck him,' she says.

'Holy mother! Did you hear that. Whooeee!' Then Dog Shades looks at her doubly hard and reports back. 'She's serious!' Then he reaches over the back to open the sliding door. When he looks back she's still standing there. 'Well, are ya or aren't ya?'

Natalie looks across at the driver. 'I said I would fuck him – not you or your friend.'

'So?'

'So get out,' she says.

'Go on. Get your arses out,' says the driver.

Dog Shades and the middle one climb out and skip away to the pump where they assess her.

'She's a carney,' says the quiet one.

'Hey, Phil!' yells Dog Shades. 'You'll go to jail for this. She's a carney!'

'Eat shit!' says the driver. Then he says to Natalie, 'Are you in or out?'

She climbed in and closed the door after. She looked down at the two boys standing where she was just a minute ago.

'I'm Phil,' says the driver.

'I don't care who you are or what your name is,' she says.

'Christ, hope you don't bite my cock off,' he says.

His mates laugh and slap their sides. They crowd the side window. 'She's definitely jail bait,' says the quiet one again.

Natalie winds the window up. She turns to the driver. 'Are we going or what?'

'We're gone. We're out of here,' he says.

Soon as they move off, he says to her, 'I've never done anything like this in my life. I swear, nothing like this has ever happened to me.'

Near the motor camp she happened to glance across to the house behind the stone wall. She looked up at the sleepy windows. The rusted fences around the cemetery plots slip by. She ducked down in case Mr Uttley should see her. When she comes up the driver is looking at her with new suspicion. 'What's this? What are you doing down there? Bloody hell,' he says. 'You better not be a runaway.' Immediately the thought causes him to take his foot off the accelerator pedal and Natalie feels the van slow down under them. They're not even where Ben caught up to her yesterday.

She says, 'It's my girlfriend's birthday party. I'm supposed to be there. It's a surprise.'

The driver doesn't take his eyes off her.

'Watch the road,' she says.

'I know where I'm going,' he says. She can see that he's still assessing what she told him. 'What's your girlfriend's name?'

'Trudy,' she says.

'Rudey Trudy,' he says, shifting his eyes back to the road.

'That's what everyone says,' she answers.

They haven't stopped, that's the main thing. Though she wishes he would speed up. Now the driver looks at her. He nods at the damp spots over her front. 'You're sweating.'

She doesn't know what to say about that, so she ignores him.

'I don't want to get into any trouble over this.'

'I told you,' she says.

'I know. Rudey Trudy.' Then he says, 'You're not on anything I hope?'

'No.'

'Just a thought,' he says.

'I just want to get home. To Trude's.'

'Rudey Trudy's,' he says, and he chops down a gear to take on the hill. 'Here we come.'

They drove on until near the pub the driver was visited by another thought.

'How do I know you'll keep to your side of the bargain?'

'You don't,' she says. She said it way too quickly, and immediately the van slowed and the driver began searching for a place to pull over.

'That's what I thought. You're full of shit. I should have known. I should just throw you out here.'

'Tinui,' she says then. 'That's halfway. We'll do it there.'

'Promise?'

'That's what I said.'

They drove on without pause after that. She thought about her conversation with Mrs Sutton and wondered if Pete was across the road at Mrs Austen's. He'll know what to do and her baby will be safe.

'You're smiling at something,' says the driver. 'That's a good sign. Do you like surfing?'

'Yep.'

'Ever done it?'

'Nope.'

The boy laughed. 'You haven't lived. Know what a tube is? I bet you don't.'

'No,' she says.

'Heaven is what it is.'

Nearer to Tinui the sidelong glances returned. The driver kept waiting for her to change her mind. She said nothing to put his mind at rest. But then, as the pub came into view and after she pointed to the road ahead and told him to keep going straight he brightened up. They took another turn-off and found themselves on a narrow country road. They drove by two grass tennis courts, the farmers bent-kneed in white shorts and white office shirts and big floppy hats. A man sitting in an umpire's chair gave a merry wave. She thought the driver might have a place in mind but it never seemed to arrive so she took over and told him to pull over to a gravelly area on a wide bend. He cut the engine and for a moment they sat there listening to the leaves of the floodbank poplars rustling in a warm wind that blew up the valley. She'd already been up four hours. She saw where the sun was sitting in the sky and felt new panic.

'Come on, then. I don't have much time,' she says to the driver. She climbs over the back and starts clearing away wetsuits. Then she lies down and waits for the boy. She needs to get this over and done quick as possible. But the boy is fumbling with his tape box. She says, 'I don't want any music.' She can't imagine what gave him that idea. And glancing up at the van's ceiling has brought her back to the baby's position in the world. She spreads her fingers and flutters them above her chest. She turns her head left and then right. She wonders what her baby could have gained from its brief venture in the world so far.

The boy appears surprised to find her so ready and willing. There's nothing for him to do. She's hoisted her dress up around her hips. She closes her eyes and waits for the boy to lower himself. All she can think is for him to hurry. That's what she's expecting. Instead she feels his hands on her swollen breasts and she cries out. She had no idea they would be so sore. The boy draws back. 'What did I do? What?'

She sits up and looks for herself. They're leaking. Choo Woo's meal is leaking out of her. She mops up one side then the other with the tail of her dress. The boy looks on with a horrified face.

'It's just milk,' she says.

'Milk!'

'For my baby,' she says. Besides Pete, the boy is the only other person in the world to know.

'Holy shit,' he says. 'Holy shit.' He looks out the window then down at her, at her breasts, then down below. And she recognises the whole sequence – the regret for the situation he's found himself in, one part wanting no further involvement, the other, the male part, unable to stop. She knows from Ben how the world is divided.

'Go on, then. Hurry up if you're going to do it.'

So he lowers himself and as he does so she turns her head away. She doesn't want his kisses.

'Christ,' he says. 'What made you?'

Now the boy rolls on top and gropes around until everything finds its place. But that hurts too and she has to push him off. She's still sore where Choo Woo tore herself out. And the boy sits up red-faced with complaint. She knows what to do. 'Pretend I'm a tiger,' she tells the boy. He looks on dumbfounded as she shows him what a tiger can do. Soon as he has had his squirt she detaches herself and climbs over the front; she winds down the window and spits it out on the roadside. There's a water bottle on the floor. She picks that up and rinses her mouth and spits that out the window. She is aware of the boy sitting crumpled against the wall of his van with a wounded look, wondering how she could have detached herself so fast.

'Can we go now?' she asks him. When the boy turns his

head away, like someone refusing sympathy, she reminds him of their arrangement. And when he failed to respond to that she leant on the van horn. Up the road a hawk ravaging a carcass looked up.

'All right, fucking hell, I'm coming. I'm coming,' says the boy. He pulls up his jeans and crawls into the driver's seat.

'Hurry. Just hurry,' she tells him.

The tennis players look up with their pleasant faces and wave. The boy looks back at them like he didn't see them. Then he turns to her with something he just remembered.

'A baby?' he says. 'How old are you?'

'Thirteen. Nearly fourteen.'

'Oh God, I'm dead. I knew it. I knew it!'

'It doesn't matter,' she says.

'Thirteen,' he says. 'I'd never have guessed. You look older. Much older. You look sixteen.'

'I don't care,' she says.

'I know. But I'm just saying . . .'

'I'm not planning to tell anyone.'

'Really?' asks the boy.

'I don't care,' she says. 'Can't this thing go any faster?'

'What made you?' he says, shaking his head at her and the road.

'Faster,' she says.

'I am. I am. Man. This is the wildest thing that has ever happened to me. I swear to God.' For the rest of the way he kept looking at her, shaking his head, and she knew what that was about: wishing he wasn't in this situation, wishing that he didn't know what she had told him. Then, as they came over the last hill and the flat tops of Masterton shimmered in the grey heat, he started getting nervous again.

174

'You won't tell anyone, right? You did promise.'

'I didn't promise,' she says. 'I said I don't care.'

Then he says, 'Don't you want to ask me anything?'

She can't think what. 'Nope,' she says. But then something does cross her mind and when she turns her head he knows what's coming next. 'I know. Faster. Faster.'

In South Road, they slow down. She looks back at the sleepy-eyed cottages, their muslin cloth fringes and geranium-coloured cheeks. Their simple unhurriedness is maddening. The whole way down the street her hand is on the doorhandle ready to jump out. Her eyes dart across to Mrs Austen's as they pass the drive. She's told the boy to drop her a few houses on. She doesn't want him trailing her back here one day. The boy looks across to the house they are parked outside.

'It looks a quiet affair,' he says. 'Trudy's, I mean.' She'd forgotten that story. She shrugs; she doesn't need it any longer, and so she doesn't answer. She gets out of the van. The boy is looking at her with wonder. 'Don't you want to see me again?' he asks her. She doesn't answer that either. She points him off in the direction of the South Belt. 'That takes you back to town. Take the heavy vehicle detour. You'll come to a roundabout. Go right at the garage. You'll know where you are then.' The way the boy is looking at her makes her wonder if he took any of that in. She says, 'You can go back to your friends now.'

She waits until the van turns right at the bottom of South Road, then she does a quick check of the windows nearest to see who might have noticed. The whole neighbourhood is dead; nothing is moving for the heat.

When she opens the back door, the trapped heat takes her breath away. Pete calls from the other end of the house,

'Natalie? Is that you?' and she thinks, 'Yes. Yes. Yes.' For once her hopes have come to something. For once . . . She runs up the hall. In the front room Pete is crouched over the carton. He's holding the eye dropper he used to feed Mrs Austen with. At his feet is a saucer filled with Mrs Austen's old mix of milk, water, and breadcrumbs. Pete's face is flushed from the heat and sheer helplessness. He looks up at her. He says, 'I didn't know what else to do. You should have been here, Natalie. You shouldn't leave your baby.'

'I know that, Pete. I know all that.' She pulled off her T-shirt and sat down on the mattress, her back to the wall. Then she held out her hands. 'Give her here, Pete. Give her to me. I know what to do.' For the last forty-eight hours she's been waiting for this moment. Now she's here, ready, it's not what she thought it would be. She watches him put down the eye dropper and pick up the carton. His eyes are downcast in that disapproving way he's inherited from his mother. She takes the carton from him and looks down at the tiny shrivelled creature. 'She's not moving. Why aren't her eyes open? Her mouth's all . . . and her eyes.'

'She's dead,' says Pete.

'No,' she says. 'She can't be.' Not after what she went through to get here. She can't be dead. She can't possibly be.

'She's dead, Natalie.'

'Stop saying that!' she says.

'I tried to give her some of Mrs Austen's mush this morning. She cried a bit then stopped. I thought she was sleeping.'

'Please don't die,' she says to the baby. She tries to move its eyelids.

'You should have been here, Natalie. A mother is

176

supposed to be with her baby.' Then he says, 'I knew this would happen . . .'

She is only half-listening to Pete. She looks down at her baby, her tiny arms and legs folded on one another. She thinks of an elderly person asleep on a riverbank in the sun. It pleased her to think that; she thought perhaps that's what being dead is.

'I knew we should have told somebody,' says Pete.

She wonders if Choo Woo ever opened her eyes and saw the world she was born into. She wonders if she saw her. Or Pete. Or Mrs Austen. She lifts her out of the carton. She's so light. She hardly weighs anything. Light as candyfloss. She's so tiny and her breast is so big and clumsy next to her. She tries to run a droplet of milk into her mouth but it just runs across the baby's cheek.

She hears Pete say, 'I don't know what to do.' When she looks up she sees that he is crying. She doesn't feel she has it inside her to say anything comforting to Pete. She can't tell him anything that will make him feel better. But since she's just noticed the heat again she asks him to open the windows.

He brushes away his tears and sniffs angrily at her. 'You didn't want me to open the windows, remember, Natalie? You said somebody would hear her crying. You thought Ben would hear.'

'I'm sorry, Pete,' she says. 'It's not your fault.'

'I tried, Natalie. I did my best. You should have been here. You should have. A proper mother is supposed to know these things.'

She doesn't answer him. She doesn't care that she doesn't say anything. And Pete's words don't matter to her. He's just scared and his words are nothing more than a nervous sweat.

Now she can feel her milk, useless milk running out of her, leaking and dribbling. She can't take her eyes off her baby.

'I tried, Pete. I did,' she says.

'Yeah,' he says. 'Where were you?'

'Castle Point.'

'The beach,' he says. 'You were at the beach?'

'You know I was. You rang me, remember? That's what I wanted to tell you but Ben got to the phone first and I couldn't.' But she knows what he's thinking. He's thinking of the two worlds lying side by side: the beach and its bright sun umbrellas and her poor baby lying in this room.

'Natalie?' The change in Pete's voice forces her to look up. Suddenly he looks so young and boylike. The face hasn't changed from the one she knew in the treetops of Queen Elizabeth Park. She almost expects him to cheep cheep up at her. Instead he says to her, 'I don't want to be the only other person who knows this.'

She knows what he's getting at, that he's even right. But who can she possibly tell? She thinks of her mother as she saw her last night, her crushed look as she looked over Ben's shoulder. She thinks of the news she has still to tell her.

# EIGHT

I decided to leave the house before Vivienne came down the stairs. One look at me and she would know her day was changed. I couldn't face her. I'd say something hurtful which I'd later regret. Natalie didn't try to persuade me to stay. She watched me fold up the duvet Vivienne had given me. She asked me what I was working on and I told her. But whatever we said seemed both trifling and effortful. After pulling on my shoes – and I laboured over that exercise, not wishing to be seen to be too brisk or out to distance myself from what I'd just heard – I stood up; and Natalie bounced up from the couch. This was the sensible course – the only course of action, really – and it didn't need to be said to be understood by us both. Though there was a moment after I opened the front door, when the crisp air rushed inside, and, automatically, we both turned and looked up the stairs.

'She won't be down for another hour,' said Natalie.

I nodded up the stairs. I thought of her getting ready to go out to prison to talk to some useless piece of filth who has fucked up someone's life. That she is paid to stick kind words inside his barren head is just mindblowingly incredible to me. We have learnt not to discuss her job any more.

As usual, my departure suffered for want of the right parting note. We shuffled around each other at the door.

'Have you got enough money, sweetheart?'

'I don't want any money,' she said.

'Anything at all. You have only to ask. You know that, don't you. You make sure you ask.'

She looked at me with a completely different thought. She said, 'Mum was talking about you the other day.'

'I bet that was illuminating.'

'She said when she first met you you were always joking. She said you used to make her laugh.'

'And now?'

'I don't know. It was just something she thought of.' Then she said, 'She cares about you.'

'Well, Natalie, I care about your mum too.'

She thought about that for a moment. I could see her wondering if I really meant it. 'Dad, you won't tell her about . . .'

'No. I won't tell her.'

There was one other thing she wished to say. She said, 'I

don't think about Ben. He doesn't feature. I only told you because you asked.'

'I understand,' I said.

'It's just history. Gone,' she said.

But that was the problem, wasn't it. Everything Natalie had told me was still fresh. It was as if I had just peeped over Ben's shoulder and seen what Viv had seen more than five years before. All that time didn't make the slightest bit of difference.

I had a clear run over the hill. There wasn't much in the way of traffic at that hour, which was fortunate as I drove without any sense of what I was driving through. The Rimutaka Hill road is full of twists and razorback corners, but I seemed to come through without any memory of having made the turns.

In Featherston there were some wood fires burning. A kind of whitish cathedral light searched through the cloud and found the farmland all wet and untidy looking. Everything half grasped at this hour, half put away, half brought out. The wooden crucifixes at the side of the road that tell you you are entering the Wairarapa.

At the service station I slowed down to stare at the overalled figure opening the pumps and dragging his heavy feet across the forecourt, his grey eyebrows bristling beneath a black beanie, and I felt sure that I recognised him, that it was Mr Patterson. He put down a watering can and looked up. I had a good reason for staring at him, and to be polite I might have had to get up and walk across and explain that I was the father of the girl he'd been so wary of giving a lift to. It seemed such a lot to explain when all I really wanted to do was to stop and stare at him, and think, 'I know who you are. I know what happened that morning.' I didn't blame him, but I did want to keep looking at him. Because that's the thing about information: What do you do with it? Where can you hide it? Mr Patterson shifted his hands to his hips and I decided to push on.

That little scene between Captain Scott, Oates and Bowers, and Vivienne's moment of discovery. It surprises me that she didn't say anything. God knows how she managed to rein in her emotion. I don't know how the hell she could have just lain there and said nothing. I never will understand that. I mean I have an idea of why she might have wanted to, but actually going through with it is another thing. It's not natural. I'm sure something in her must have died, some delicate fretwork of belief and hope must have collapsed, and, of course, I know what her spoiling of Natalie is all about. She's been trying ever since to make up for that moment in which she said nothing and did nothing.

South of Masterton, I followed the northbound trucks around the Chapel Road detour and relentlessly made my way along Lansdowne Road. I thought I would just pop round for a look. I'd known it since I left Natalie at the door. I'd known I wouldn't be able to do anything that day if I didn't do this first. I drove up Ben's quiet pensioners' crescent. There were no cars about and every house appeared to be wrapped in fog. I parked outside Ben's and got out of the van.

I went to the door at the side of the house and knocked loudly. I had a sense of Ben in those slippers I'd seen him in, standing like a ruined man in a distant corner of the house, his shoulders hunched and eyes raised to the ceiling. I knocked a couple more times – I knew he was in there. I tried his door but he had locked *that*. I gave it a decent rattling. Let him know I was onto him. But these were just games I was playing even if I didn't admit as much to myself at the time. The blind rage of Dannevirke wasn't there. Maybe I was older. Maybe that was it. I don't think I was any more forgiving, but for reasons I still don't understand I was slower to act. I stared at the rippled glass pane. He could have been on the other side and I wouldn't have known.

There was another window at the end of the house. It was cheap see-through glass that revealed nothing more than a bare room. The door was closed and I bet Ben had never been in there except to close the door. I had an idea that Ben had dragged all his furnishings to some central point in the house.

Around the back the grass was long. A bathtowel hung stiffly from the clothesline. The whole place looked as empty and abandoned as Bennetts' had once, and I thought it would be like Ben to give that impression – there, but not there, looking on but part of the landscape too.

I hammered on the back door. This time I heard steps approach then veer off. I moved to the next set of windows, and these had curtains. Ben hadn't bothered to draw them back. I gave the glass a tap. I tried my knuckles next. There was a heavy rock holding down the lid of the dustbin by the door. I was thinking about what I might do with that when I heard him call back through the curtains, 'What do you want?' It was the first I'd heard him speak since Dannevirke, and I was mesmerised. I couldn't begin to put a number on the bullying conversations I'd imagined I'd one day have with Ben, and none of them went like this one. 'What do you want?' he'd asked. For a moment I wondered if he'd mistaken me for the paperboy or Mormons. Though the way he said 'you' it was clear he knew who was outside his window. The second time he asked the same question he sounded closer to the window and I was lost for words picturing him on the other side of those curtains. I didn't know what to say or what to do. I wasn't quite primed. I guess that's the answer. At least I had the wit not to say anything. I kept my mouth shut. I've seen a flat sea lie right up to the edge of a storm. I've seen it plenty of times; and it's the only explanation I can think to give for my passive behaviour.

As I was leaving I saw Ben's neighbour. A woman with a cat in her arms looked out her window across the yard at me. She was on the phone to someone telling them what she was seeing and the cat was reporting up to her. I waved to her, and she took the phone away from her ear and stared.

I went home and no sooner had I stepped in the door than I felt myself at a loose end. I was tired but I didn't want to be there. I rang Reuben's house. Beverley answered to say I had missed Rube by a few minutes. She said he'd gone out to Richardsons' – which is what I'd expected.

'Annoyed, is he, Bev?'

'He did wonder where you got to, Charlie. If he's a bit short try and be patient with him. We just got the long-range forecast. There's a big front on the way. Lambing's just started and you know what Reuben is like – he hates to lose a single lamb. They say it's already snowing, south.'

'Well, I'll be around to help. Rube knows that,' I said.

'Thanks, Charlie. He knows that and he appreciates it. It's just the mood he's in. Don't take any notice, Charlie.'

I made some coffee and toast. Then I drove out to Richardsons'. The moment the big stately wooden house showed through the trees I felt defeated. Work was the last thing I felt like. On another day I might have turned around and driven home. But I really wanted to see Rube.

I crept up the drive and parked in front of Mrs Richardson's Pajero. I switched the motor off and I looked across the lawn to the barn where Rube was working. I could see him struggling to hold a sheet of Gib he was fixing to the side of the barn. He had his shoulder pressed against the sheet while he drilled a hole. He could have waited ten more seconds. He must have heard me draw up. But Rube was out to make a point. He stuck his toe underneath the Gib and lowered it to the floor. Then he wiped his forehead with his sleeve.

'Hell. He's back,' he said.

'It's only Tuesday,' I said.

'That means you missed Monday,' he said. He crouched down to change his drill. He was keeping his face to himself in that hard-arse way of his.

'I should have known,' I said. 'Okay, I'm sorry.' And when he didn't go for that I asked him if he was ready for me to start on the roof. 'There's a patch of rust on the far side. I'll replace that. Otherwise I think it'll brush up pretty good.' Rube went on fussing with his drill. Then he said, 'Have you been round to see him yet?'

'So that's what this is about,' I said.

'It's just a question,' he said. 'Well?' he asked. 'Have you made a jerk of yourself yet?'

'Why would I do that, Rube?'

He stopped and laid down the drill then, and looked up at me. 'How many reasons do you want?'

'Beverley said you'd be like this.' He ignored that, and went on waiting for me to satisfy him. I said, 'No, Rube, I haven't spoken with the man.'

'So you've seen him, then?'

'Once. Twice. What do you expect?'

'That's why I'm asking,' he said. 'I'm asking because that's exactly the dumb thing I'd expect you to do.'

'Thanks very much, Rube. Thank you for your interest. Now do you want me to start on the fucking roof or not?'

Rube nodded at the ground and thought about what he was hearing.

'I don't know, Charlie.' And of course it wasn't anything that he didn't know. Rather, these were just words with which to fill in his disappointment. 'You're going to have to give the man up some time. You can't go on like this.'

At that moment a door opened over at the Richardson house. Rube turned his head then stood up like he'd been caught out doing something he shouldn't have. It was Mrs Richardson and her daughter. They stood on the porch, staring at my van.

'Give me your keys, Charlie. I'll shift the van for her.'

But Mrs Richardson gave him no chance. She got in her Pajero and sat on her horn to get our attention.

'The keys, Charlie. Give them . . .'

'I've got it, Rube.'

I was on my way over to the van when Mrs Richardson gave her horn another burst. If she'd turned her head she would have seen that I was halfway across the lawn. If she'd been patient I'd have moved the van in a few seconds and she would have been free to get on her snotty-arsed way. I stopped and changed course. Mrs Richardson sat behind the wheel, her eyes staring straight ahead as if she was caught in traffic. I tapped on the roof above her door. Even then she had to think about it. Was that someone tapping on my roof? 'Hello, Mrs Richardson,' I said. I gave a pleasant wave.

Finally she turned her head. She pressed a button and the window began to wind down. I felt the warm air of the fan heater on my face and smelt the rich upholstery. I felt like I was part of that outside world which a woman like Mrs Richardson might ordinarily hire someone to deal with. I felt like I was a piece of windblown litter snagged on her rose bushes.

'Mrs Richardson, I don't want you to take this personally, but I was just across the lawn. You didn't have to toot,' I said. 'I happened to be talking to Reuben about something very important. Did you not see?'

Mrs Richardson composed herself, then she spoke slowly and very deliberately. 'I am very sorry for interrupting your discussion and tooting the horn. But I have an appointment in town at nine forty-five and Holly's already late for school . . . Now, if you don't mind, your van is blocking our way.' Her daughter gawked at me from the back seat. Her daughter's rangy muscle-less legs in brown hosiery reminded me of Natalie. The old Natalie.

'Holly, isn't it?' I said.

She tried to find her mother's face in the rear-view mirror.

'I used to have a daughter like you. How old are you?'

'Thirteen,' she said.

'Really? That's how old my girl was.'

'Unbelievable,' said Mrs Richardson. 'Look. I said I was sorry. I'll say it once more. Sorry. There. Now can I please drop my daughter off at school?'

Rube called across the lawn and Mrs Richardson looked up. She managed a thin smile – and I guessed Rube was on his way over.

'Can I let you in on a little secret, Mrs Richardson?' For the first time she looked at me like she was interested to hear what I had to say. 'I wished I killed that man. I wished I'd spread his brains on the road.' Her eyes opened wide, and I went on. 'I know you know who I'm talking about. You can't imagine a feeling like that, can you? But I'm here to tell you that it could happen to you and that you could find yourself wanting to kill someone.'

Reuben pulled me away from the window. He apologised to Mrs Richardson and out of her earshot hissed at me, 'Move your fucking van before we lose the job.'

'That's what I was about to do, Rube. That's what I was on my way to doing.'

'Please,' he said then.

'Sure, Rube.'

He closed his eyes and gave me a patient nod.

I got in the van. There were plenty of places for me to pull over but I decided to follow the drive around the lawn. Then I heard Reuben call out. I saw him coming across the lawn. I slowed down for him and he tore at the doorhandle.

'Looks to me like you're walking off the job.'

'I'm moving the fucking van, Rube, just like you asked me.'

'She just told me what you said.'

I looked away to the road through the trees.

'Hey! I need this job, Charlie. Do you know what that means? I need this job.'

'Then go and kiss her arse,' I said.

For the second time in as many minutes he thought about having a lash at me. He looked behind and, seeing I was holding her up once more, he said, 'Move your van.' He slammed the door shut and belted the side of the van. I drove to the main entrance off the road and pulled over. As Mrs Richardson swept past some stones flew against my door, and I thought, 'Screw you, Reuben,' and followed after Mrs Richardson out to the State Highway.

I ate at the Harrises' that night. I wasn't very bright company. It didn't matter to Ron and Alice. They took my bleak mood as a personal challenge to cheer me up. They thought that talk of old times might do it, so they talked about the little girl they had known next door. They talked of a time when Viv and Natalie and I were still together and there was harmony under the roof.

'You came round one time to borrow the mower . . .'

'You looked so young, and with that gorgeous wee baby,' added Alice.

'You were too embarrassed to admit that you didn't own a mower,' laughed Ron. He said, 'You didn't know I knew, did you?'

'No, Ron.' I felt the uneasiness of my smile. I was too tired for this, much too tired.

Then Alice remembered that she had something to show me. She got up and produced an old Polaroid of Natalie. The photo had been sitting ready on the sideboard. The Harrises had planned the evening carefully. She popped it onto the table cloth beside my bowl of ice-cream, and I saw Natalie as I used to see her from the front window, upside down on the end of a rope tied to the tree out front. 'Cloud-walking,' she called it. She was only eight and already she was showing me the unexpected, because I remember once looking up at the sky and thinking that what she said was true, that the sky was, as she said, nothing but white puddles.

Now Ron went searching for something. We waited by our empty bowls and Alice smiled once, apologetically I thought, while he looked about the room trying to remember where he'd placed his surprise. He shuffled some magazines in the rack beneath the TV until he found what he was after. He put on his reading glasses and studied the photo in his hand.

'She's a good deal older here,' he said.

The photo had been taken in the driveway next door – at least that was my impression, judging by the looks of the eastern sky lifting away over the shoulders of Natalie and her mother. They were posing with their bikes together (for the purposes of the photo), but their apartness was just as obvious. It was there in the tilt of their shoulders, the angle of their eyes, the hurt that each had worked up in the other. Something else about the photo didn't feel or look quite right. As soon as I ran a finger along a broken edge I realised the problem. Ron removed his glasses. He looked over to Alice who nodded.

'We scissored him out, Charlie,' he said. 'I never really took to the man.'

'Well, we didn't know him like we knew you,' said Alice.

'You can't know a bullshit artist,' said Ron. 'That's the whole point. You never know who or what you're talking to or with. I thought that the first time I laid eyes on him.'

Alice drew our attention back to the photo. 'Look, Natalie has on those denim dungarees. That's how I still think of her.'

'I imagine young Peter Sutton can't be too far away, either,' said Ron. 'I imagine he's hovering in the background. Those two were thick as thieves.'

'Don't laugh, Charlie, but once there was a time when I thought Pete and Natalie would end up marrying. It sometimes happens that way.' Alice stood by the table smiling at the thought. Then she saw me and Ron staring at her. 'Oh, it's just one of those things that crosses your mind at the time. I expect she's quite the young lady these days.'

The subject of Ben didn't come up again until I was leaving. I thanked Alice. It was kind of her to have me over, and although I could not have known what the future held I didn't think that I would ever see them again. I thought that perhaps Alice knew this. She kissed my cheek. Then she thought she would hug me as well. Ron came outside. It was cold and he was only in shirtsleeves.

'For God's sake, Ron, go inside the house.'

He ignored that and laid a hand against the driver's door. 'That anonymous caller, Charlie. Any ideas?'

'Who the hell knows,' I said.

'He didn't call back?'

'Well, I don't know if he did or not. He might have. But if he did he didn't leave a message.'

He looked at me from around the corner of his face. He said, 'I've never asked and I'm not necessarily asking now. But I'm assuming something happened. That Ben did something . . .' And when I didn't answer, he said, 'Well, that's what I've heard said. Anyway, it's just talk.' His angry-looking eyebrows squared up on me. 'You look awful, Charlie. I hope you don't mind my saying that. It makes me think you're burdening yourself. Work's good, is it?'

'More than I can handle right now,' I said.

'You and . . .'

'The German fellow.'

He laughed and took his hand away from the door. I thought I was free to go but now he wished to draw my attention to Bennetts'. 'There's a young family in there now. The Williamses. He's got the lights shop in town.' Bennetts' looked the same as ever – sunk in darkness. 'They're away right now. Up in Hamilton. Sandy – that's the woman – her family's from there. I'm collecting their mail and papers for them this week.'

The same abandonment that had afflicted Bennetts' after Sarah's death had shifted to our house. He caught me staring and said, 'I saw someone sniffing about there the other day. Alice worries that a gang will move in. I told her it wouldn't happen.' Ron looked to see what I thought.

'That's right,' I said. 'It's not their kind of neighbourhood. I'm getting in the van now, Ron. It's too bloody cold out here.'

He wheeled around and looked up at the enormous night.

'There's an ugly front on the way. It was on the news.' He dropped his gaze and said, 'Hell, look at you. You're out on your feet. Go home and get some sleep.'

Good advice. Unfortunately, I couldn't face going home. Michael Street didn't feel like home any more. It held no more attachment for me than a campsite. I came out of the South Belt and headed into the countryside. I drove with the windows down to wake me up. It wasn't so cold away from Ron's place. I looked up at the night cloud. Everything looked stationary; no sign of the front that had put Rube on edge. As soon as I pulled up outside Maggie's I saw the curtain shift in the front window, and by the time I wandered up the path the door was wide open. Maggie was pleased to see me.

'Hope,' she said. 'Look who's here.' The boy looked up from his toy truck. 'Say hello to Charlie.'

The pale nocturnal-looking thing kept his head down. 'Hiya, Hope,' I said.

He kept his head down and didn't say anything.

'It's rude not to be welcoming, Hope,' said his mother.

'He's all right, Maggie.'

'No,' she said. 'He has to learn.'

'He's just warming up. He'll come around, won't you, Hope?' The boy's head sank lower to his truck.

I pulled up the chair by the fire and looked around the room and thought I couldn't live here. I'd drive her nuts with my mess. Maggie's is like being inside a house truck or church. The stained glass and polished floors give that impression. But there is something else besides the scented soaps she sells at a craft shop in Carterton; there is this feeling of reverence, a love of everything she comes into contact with. I just happened to be lucky enough to find myself on a pew alongside her that first time that Rube dragged me out to Babylon. There was a low fire in the grate and then I noticed the sexy anklet she was wearing, and for the first time I felt pleased to be where the day had dropped me.

'I'd just about given up on you,' she said.

'I got your calls, Maggie. I'm sorry about that. I was over visiting with Natalie then I was working with Rube . . .'

'I was beginning to feel like a desperate woman,' she said.

I reached out and drew her to me for a hug. I wasn't about to mention the Harrises – they belong to my old life and she doesn't like me talking about that.

'I didn't think you'd turn up,' she said.

'Well, I'm here, aren't I. I am here, at least I think I am. Hope, come here and pinch my arm. Tell me if I'm here or not.' He smiled privately and his mother laughed; then Hope looked up, happy, I thought, to hear his mother laugh.

Maggie wanted to finish up in the kitchen, so I got down

on the floor to play with her boy. We built a garage out of blocks and he parked his wooden truck in it. We crawled about the floor until it began to feel like a familiar pattern. It began to feel like the game of somebody else I knew and as soon as that thought sank in I heaved myself into a chair and found my glass.

'Charlie won't play with me any more,' the boy told his mother.

'He's played out, Hope. That's why.'

Soon enough it was the boy's bedtime. He disappeared and then came out again to say goodnight. He sat his bony arse on my knee, which I didn't like, and the thought occurred to me that there must be thousands of kids like Hope all over the country reaching out to strangers, and that Natalie must have been like that once.

After she got Hope off to bed Maggie came and took his place on my knee and that felt right; that felt a lot better.

'I spoke to Bev earlier.'

'And?' I said.

'Nothing. She just wondered how you were. I said, "How would I know? He's avoiding me."'

'Well, for starters, that's not true, is it?'

'That's what it feels like.'

'I can't help if you shiver or feel hot either,' I said. 'Anyway, what else? Did she mention my falling out with Rube?'

'No.' She looked at me with concern. 'What happened, Charlie?'

'Nothing that would make me feel very proud to tell you about, Maggie.'

'Well, you could try me.'

'I don't think I will.'

'Sometimes it can make you feel better . . .'

'It won't.' Then I said, 'So what else did Bev have to say?'

'Just that storm she's worried about. It's already snowing down south.'

'Happens every year. I don't know why everyone pretends to be surprised.'

'You look beat, Charlie,' she said then. 'You look like something drove over the top of you.' She traced my mouth with her fingertip. Then she stood up and took my hand.

Early in the night the boy came into his mother's bedroom. I was lying on my back wide awake. Ben was at the centre of my universe. I was thinking of what I might have said earlier in the day when he spoke to me through the curtains. What a wit I am when it doesn't count. I was thinking of all the brilliant things I might have said when I saw Hope in the doorway clutching his teddy bear. My own wakefulness had kept Maggie awake, and without lifting her head from the pillow she called across to her boy.

'Come here, Hope. Come into bed.'

He stood in the doorway – it was like his mother hadn't spoken – his face whiter than the moon. He clung onto his teddy bear.

'Did you have a bad dream, Hope? Come to bed. Come and snuggle up. That's the boy.'

Then the three of us lay awake. His leg touched mine once and after that I worked the duvet in between us. I still couldn't get to sleep. I couldn't stop wondering what the boy must think of this and what he'd think in the future when he cast his mind back to this moment, trying to remember who the stranger was in bed with his mother. After a while Maggie climbed over her boy and popped herself in between, and started to stroke my thigh.

'Christ, Maggie. Not like this. Not with your boy in bed with you.'

I swung my feet onto the cold floor.

'Charlie? No, Charlie, come back to bed.'

I got my things and went out to dress by the fire. Maggie came out in her T-shirt with that single word on it – EXPRESS. She watched me pull on my socks.

'It's a bit early to be getting off for work, isn't it?'

'There's no work. Mrs Richardson found out I was a lunatic.'

'Charlie, come back to bed,' she said then.

'I'm sorry, Maggie. I can't do this.'

'Can't do what?' She came over and rubbed herself against my shoulder. 'Can't do what?' she said.

'Don't, okay, Maggie? I'm going home.'

'Don't what?' she said.

I said, 'I can't be that boy's father, Maggie.' I felt the mother in her instantly rise up and the space spread between us. She bit her lip and stared at the floor by her bare feet. 'So,' she said. 'Why didn't you say?'

'I am. That's what I'm doing,' I said.

'Why all this time, Charlie?' She raised her eyes and stared at me. But I didn't have an answer. The guilty never do.

At the door she let me hug her but she didn't hug back.

'You go inside now, Maggie,' I said.

She folded her arms and looked up at the night. She took a deep breath. Then, when she looked at me, I thought she looked like she had made up her mind about something.

'I have needs too, Charlie. You know that.'

'Of course. I know that,' I said.

196

'Are you sure?' she said. 'Are you really sure? I need someone who can be with Hope and like him and do things with him.'

'I don't disagree. Only that person can't be me.'

'He adores you,' she said.

'Maggie. Come on.'

'No. He does. Absolutely, he adores you,' she said.

'I'm not his old man,' I said, and she scoffed out loud.

'Charlie, he can't even remember what his father looks like.' Then she said, 'I can't believe what I'm hearing. I feel like something else is going on here.'

'Nothing else is going on here. I can't be what I'm not and I'm not going to pretend. I'm going now, Maggie. You go back inside.'

She followed me out as far as the stock bars at the top of her drive.

'Here's your problem, Charlie, and it's not me or Hope. You just can't let go of the past.'

'Bullshit,' I said.

'It's not just what I think either.' Then she said, 'I bet you're thinking of him now. Right this second. It wouldn't surprise . . .'

'Who's *him*?'

'Come on, Charlie. You know who I'm talking about.'

'He's back in town, Maggie. Can you blame me?'

'No,' she said.

'No. That's right. Now it's the middle of the night and I really don't want to argue this shit. Goodnight, Maggie.'

She looked at me as if she was carefully weighing something up in her thoughts. She shook her head. She said, 'No. I don't think I want that awfulness hanging over me. I don't want any of that. I don't want my life contaminated by your past.' Then she said, 'There's a little boy lying in my bed.' And all of a sudden she started to cry. I reached out for her and she pulled back. 'I'm just disappointed is all, Charlie. Just very disappointed. Go,' she said.

Halfway back to town my foot came off the accelerator. I dawdled with the idea of turning round and driving back to Maggie's and asking for her forgiveness. Then I had a different, cautioning thought. Everything would be teary and huggy, I'd end up making promises which I couldn't possibly keep. All we'd be doing was postponing the unpleasantness for another day. I carried on into town.

It was after midnight. The Colonel's was brightly lit, like a hospital ward, with no one in it. I bought a basket of chicken and potato with gravy and drove around the empty streets eating off my lap. A few hamburger bars were open. A bunch of hoons crowded the new kebab place I'd heard Rube speak of. I drove back the other way and found myself back in South Road. Near Bennetts' I slowed right down, still with the chicken, mashed potato and gravy in my lap, and looked across at the house with all the history stored inside it. The Williamses were newcomers. They'd had no time to make an impression and at that moment I thought of it as as much Mrs Austen's house or Choo Woo's house, the place where Natalie gave birth, where Choo Woo was born; and as I was making those connections I was getting out of the van, I was moving down the drive, once again I was looking for a way inside my daughter's past.

I tapped in the window to the wash house, opened the latch, and hauled myself through. I couldn't see much. But I was loathe to switch on the kitchen light. I left the fridge door open instead. There was a pleasing smell of new carpet in the hall. I made my way to the front room, and, groping like a blind man, grabbed a handful of curtain and pulled it across the window. Then I switched on a standing lamp. Everything had changed of course. A TV sat in the corner where Mrs Austen's perch had once stood; the painted tree had been wallpapered over. A nice-looking tartan couch took care of the far wall, but if I looked hard enough the tartan couch disappeared behind the filthy mattress where my baby lay. From the photograph of the Williamses on the wall I realised why Ron Harris had mentioned them – their youthfulness must have reminded him of me and Viv in another life. The husband had a friendly smiling face, a dark moustache. His snowy-haired toddlers sat on plastic trikes. Their mother in denim overalls hadn't yet shaken off the effects of pregnancy. Mum and Dad and the kids are smiling for the camera. Smiling at their bright future. And at that moment I felt as sad and doomed as I have ever felt for seeing what had been lost and what could never be recovered. Viv and I would never be able to overlook what had happened. I know as much from painting houses – no amount of overcoat you slap on can stop the undercoat and ultimately the original grain showing through. Who doesn't know that, and yet, at the same time, who doesn't think they're preparing something for life when they do it.

I took out the photo of Natalie, the one Ron had given me, and compared its torn edge and damaged-looking people to the one on the mantelpiece. The most obvious thing struck me now. In this photo, my thirteen-year-old daughter is pregnant.

I shoved the photo back in my pocket and walked along the hall to the bedroom facing our old kitchen window. Mrs Austen's as it was then, and where Natalie had given birth. I sat down on one of the kid's beds and stared into darkness. Mobiles hung down from the ceiling. A clown's face stared back from the wall. I couldn't picture it – a child giving birth in here. I lifted my feet onto the bed and laid my head back on a soft pillow. Finally I was following Ron Harris's advice. I stared up at a mobile of train carriages. I had one ugly thought, then I must have nodded off.

# NINE

In town people pretended to have the farmers' concerns at heart. The bad weather was to the forefront of every conversation. In the Lotto shop where I'd gone to pick up a paper I heard someone say that somewhere down south the storm had dropped a hillside house into the sea. Everyone looked out the door at that moment as if expecting a scene of havoc. An ice-cream wrapper lay perfectly still on the footpath. A lone seagull flew inland in an otherwise perfectly still sky. It was possible to believe that the storm was just a figment of our imagination, until someone said, 'Well, it's inevitable, isn't it.'

Something else happened that morning that was to change the course of the day for me. I saw Ben. He was so close I could have reached out and touched him. It was in the supermarket. We passed each other in the cereals aisle; Ben in that tall way of his, the faraway gaze dismissing everything beneath it. He might have been thinking about the next item on his shopping list. I'm sure he saw me. He would have seen me and thought nothing more of it. I stopped and looked back as he continued for the frozen foods section. I carried on for the check-out counter. I waited across the street for him. After five minutes he came out of the supermarket and walked to a Toyota stationwagon parked up the street. The way he walked, the groceries in his arms, the raised boot on the Toyota. Ben seemed to have his life back in motion. He didn't look like he was preoccupied with the same things I was, and how was that, how could it be? He looked like a man without any memory. As he was getting in the car he looked across the road. Again, he saw me but there was no recognition. I had an idea that he thought of himself as being in the clear now. What troubled me was that I'd allowed him that privilege. We hadn't exchanged a single word and yet I had this feeling he'd walked over the top of me.

I went home and didn't know what to do with myself. There was no one to call, no one I hadn't already broken up with that I wanted to talk to. Then I remembered Pete Sutton. Earlier, awake in the Williams child's bed, I heard the doors open and close across the street. I'd listened to his van cough and fart its way up South Road. Now, back in Michael Street, hours later, I was thinking, Pete was there. Natalie had company at her birth. Pete was there.

I ran out to the car and drove to the yard. As I got out of

the car I was reminded that the tip was nearby. The air shifted with a rancid smell. Windblown paper scraps had flown and stuck against the fence right around the yard. Piles of glass were everywhere – green and brown mottled light, and a low stench of flat beer. An older version of the thin, secretive boy I'd known came out of the office. Pete still had no blood in his face, but he'd learnt to look straight ahead of himself. He pulled off his leather gloves, and as I started to introduce myself he cut me short. 'I know who you are,' he said. An Alsatian saw something in me it didn't like. It rose and made a threatening sound. 'That's Tristram. She won't bite unless I say.'

We gazed at each other for a moment.

'So, was I right?' he asked.

I was a bit slow on the uptake.

'Mr Strang. Was he where I said?'

Good God, I thought. The dog started to bark then and Pete turned and told it to shut up. The dog sat down, chastened, and the phone in the office started to ring. Pete turned his head and waited until it stopped.

'I know who that is,' he said.

Somewhat unnecessarily I said, 'It was you, Pete, who rang the other day?'

'I was twelve when I last saw him. But I don't think I'll ever forget him. One day he'll die and I'll be at his funeral. I'll look forward to that day. Go ahead,' he said then. 'Ask me whatever. I'll tell you the best I can.'

We went inside his cluttered office. The phone didn't ring again and I spent the rest of the afternoon with Pete. He went back to those days when he and Natalie pretended they were birds and climbed the trees in Queen Elizabeth Park. He reminded me of things I had forgotten. We spoke about Natalie. If I'm not mistaken I think Pete is still soft on her. I said he should call her. He laughed. He knew I was just being polite. 'She's in Wellington now,' and the mere mention of that place summed up the ground that couldn't be breached. At one point he stood up from his desk and said he had something he wanted to show me. Pete locked up the yard and we bundled into his van. We ended up down by the river. He got out and looked around the fennel and broom. The river was running moderately fast beneath the bank. He looked south to a long black line. 'The front's almost here,' he said. I thought it was still half a day off. He switched his attention to the scrub. 'Nothing's changed,' he said, and I followed him along a track to where a grown man had once driven two kids scared witless deep into the gorse.

That night I went after Ben. I'd had enough. I didn't care any more about what might happen. I wasn't thinking, 'What if I do this . . . ?' I didn't care. I drove up his drive like it was my own and I swept in his back door for that room with the closed curtains, and that's where I found him, standing in white underpants and a white singlet – wearing reading glasses which until that moment I hadn't known him to need. It was just a little mental note: Ben's wearing glasses these days. Otherwise I didn't hesitate. I have to say that the sight of me didn't rock him the way I had hoped or imagined it would. He didn't say anything. His eyes popped and his mouth shifted with an unspoken word. I hit him twice. The first blow caught him beneath his left eye. The second blow glanced off his left cheek. They were not blows to knock him off his feet – but he sat down on the floor as if that was what he thought he should do. I didn't think that he was hurting so I kicked him in the guts and that buckled him up and took all the air out of him.

'Christ,' he said. 'Christ almighty.' He rolled over onto his side and I watched him get his breath back. He coughed into his hand and started to sit up again. When he thought he was recovered he reached for his reading glasses. My foot got there ahead of his hand and I ground them under. Ben closed his eyes as if to say that that was unnecessary. Then he looked up at me. 'What do you want?' he asked. I didn't know what I wanted. I was there because I had to be. I was kicking the shit out of him because what else could I do? When I didn't answer he started to pick himself up. 'Still the same old Charlie,' he said under his breath. He started to pick the broken bits of glass out of the carpet. 'You know, Charlie, there's really no excuse. These days you can get professional help . . . It's no longer acceptable . . .' The rest of what he intended to say will forever remain a mystery. I bent down and grabbed the back of his head and stuffed his mouth with the corner of the vanity.

He shook free and staggered back to the bed squawking 'Fuck! Fuck!' He stuck his fingers in his mouth, then held them before his eyes – the blood horrifying to him. 'Fuck! You broke my teeth. I'm swallowing bits of broken teeth.' He started to panic – coughing from the back of his throat and gagging. He spat up some blood in his hand. He waved his hand at the vanity. I opened the top drawer and found him a handkerchief. 'Thank you,' he said. He stuffed the handkerchief in his mouth and lightly patted his lips. 'Oh God,' he said. 'Oh God.' He lay back on his bed, his head on his pillow, and closed his eyes. He turned on his side and groaned.

I thought I'd go through his drawers. Don't ask me what

I was looking for. I pulled out the drawers emptying everything – socks, underwear, a few shirts. Ben didn't own much in the world any more. He pulled the bloody rag out of his mouth to say, 'You won't find any money in there if that's what you're after.'

I looked at his big, soft frame and felt it come over me again. 'There is nothing in the world you can give me,' I said. 'Nothing. You understand?'

Now he raised himself onto his elbow and stared at me defiantly. 'I know. You'd like to kill me, wouldn't you, Charlie.'

'Why, Ben? Why do you think I'd want to do that?'

For the first time he looked uncertain. He laid his head back down on his pillow. 'I wouldn't hurt Natalie,' he said quietly. Intimately. I thought he had a picture of her in his head. He wasn't staring up at the ceiling, I realised, he was referring to that picture inside his head.

I said, 'I don't want you to use her name. Ever.' I thought if he said it again I'd have to smash him to a pulp to reach in and retrieve my baby.

'That's what this is about, isn't it?' he asked.

And just a wee bit too casually for my liking he dropped his head over the edge of the bed to look for something which clearly wasn't where he thought it was. He must have believed he'd seen off the worst of what he had coming.

'Get up,' I said.

He stayed put, wondering about my intentions.

'I'm not going to hit you. Get up.'

As he rolled his legs off the bed and stood up a trickle of blood ran from his mouth.

'I'd like a glass of water,' he said.

'I don't give a fuck what you want. Now go out to the

206

van,' I said. He didn't move. He stood there trying to read me. I didn't feel like telling him what I had in mind. He started looking around for some clothes to put on.

'As you are,' I said.

'No,' he said. 'No. No. No. I can't go outside like this.'

I could see him eyeing his trousers folded at the end of his bed.

'Let me put those on at least.' He was half a second from reaching for them.

'Pick them up and I'll break your nose.'

'A pair of fucking pants, Charlie, that's all I'm asking.'

'Up to you,' I said.

He looked at me and decided he could do without the trousers.

'A jersey then,' he said. 'Let me find a sweat top.'

I lost my patience then. I grabbed him and shoved him out the door.

Outside he hugged his arms about himself. He looked ridiculous and I hoped that he knew that. At the back of the cat woman's house the lights were on. There was a movement in her window as we were getting in the van. Ben didn't appear to notice. He sat in the van shaking with his hands on his bare knees, his bloody mouth gaping back at the garage. He held his jaw in his hand to speak.

'Where are we going, Charlie?'

'You'll see when we get there.'

Nine o'clock at night, a week night in Masterton, there was no one about to see a man with a bloody mouth gaping out the window.

The moment I turned into South Road, Ben groaned. 'Christ,' he said. He closed his eyes and leant against his door. He didn't open them until we had turned into

Bennetts' drive. 'What are we doing here, Charlie?'

'Looks to me like we're driving to the end of the drive and now I'm switching off the lights.' I told him to stay in the van while I got out to rummage in the Williamses' garage. I couldn't see to find what I was after. I had to get Ben to reach over and switch on the van's headlights, then in the far corner of the garage I saw what I was after, the pick and shovel. I ordered him out, and Ben complained of the cold and hugged his sides as I led him round to the vegetable patch behind the garage.

'Now what?'

'Now you dig.' I passed him the shovel and he took it in his hands and stared at it.

'It's a shovel, Ben. It's what we dig with. It's what we bury things with.'

'Bury what? What are you getting at?'

'Your baby, Ben.'

He raised the shovel then held it across himself, and I took a cautionary step back. 'Go ahead,' I said. 'You use that thing on me and I promise I'll bury you with it. Think about it, Ben.'

He answered with a grunt. He lowered the spade and laid the nose on the bed and experimented with placing his bare foot on the shoulder of the blade. The soil was already broken. The Williamses must have turned it over ready for spring planting.

I was in a police cell when Vivienne helped Natalie to bury her baby. Viv thought that the turned soil of a vegetable patch wouldn't arouse suspicion. It was after coming to see me that night in the cells when she was so practical-minded that she buried the baby. Apparently, she had dug, while Natalie looked on holding her baby in a small box. She'd asked Natalie if she wanted anything special said. 'We're not a religious family but how about this. "God have mercy on her soul."' Natalie said, 'All right,' but when the time came to hand over the box she wouldn't release her baby and Viv had to do some swift talking. She knelt by this same plot comforting her. 'Something bad happened that was none of your doing. Things just got out of control. But now, sweetheart, now we have to move on. We have to.'

Ben had been digging for twenty minutes. He was almost up to his waist. Once or twice I thought I could smell clay. I'd have been surprised if Viv dug that far down. I got him out and started him in another place, and when he grumbled I reminded him of what this was all about. 'We're looking for your daughter, Ben.'

He muttered something that I didn't catch. 'What?' I said. He looked defiantly back. 'I said, "I don't have a daughter."' He threw the nose of the spade carelessly into the ground. 'I couldn't do a thing like that.' He viewed the idea with distaste. In his wide eyes, a dark smear of contempt for the person who had done this.

'What's her name, Ben? Tell me your baby's name.'

'This is a sick exercise. Sick,' he said.

'Nope. That's not the answer,' I said. 'Go on. Say it. Say that baby's name.'

He went on digging like he hadn't heard; happy to dig now.

'What's that? I can't hear you.'

He kept digging away with his head down.

'You're a cruel bastard,' he said.

'No. Wrong again. The answer is "Choo Woo". Go on. Say it after me.'

'Fuck you,' he said, and he went on digging.

This time he only went down three feet before his shovel hit the lid of Viv's wooden sewing box. He let the shovel roll out of his hands. 'I don't want to do this. Please don't ask this of me. Charlie, don't make me . . .'

'I'm not making you do anything. You did it all on your own . . .' I wasn't through when a beam from a torch found my face. Then I heard Ron Harris at the end of it. 'Who's there?'

'Over here, Ron.'

'Charlie? Is that you?'

Then his beam moved off me and picked up a man in white underpants.

'What the hell have you got there?' asked Ron. Ben was hiding behind his hand. Then he must have thought, What's the point, because he dropped his hand and looked over at Ron. Ron said, 'Well, well, well.' He spent a moment moving his torch beam up and down Ben until he was satisfied it was who he thought it was, then he went back to shining the torch on his face. 'There's a nasty-looking injury,' he said.

There was a pause where no one said anything. Ron was waiting for the explanation he might well have felt himself entitled to hear.

'We won't be long, Ron,' I said finally.

Ron flicked his torch off, then he flicked it on again and landed the beam over at the back of the Williamses' house.

'I saw glass earlier. I said to Alice, "I'd better come over and look around."'

'That was me,' I said, but I didn't have anything more to add at that moment.

Ron was silent for a bit, hoping for more no doubt. Then he said, 'Well, I suppose I should feel relieved. I feel responsible and I'd hate the Williamses to be burgled or for anything to happen on my watch.'

'I'll make sure it's fixed,' I said.

'No, no. I'd rather do it myself,' he said. 'No offence, Charlie. But leave it to me. I'll scoot over to Jamieson's in the morning.'

Ron flicked the torch off. Then he must have thought he'd like one more look at the man in the white underpants holding the shovel. 'I'm sure there's an explanation,' he said.

'There is, Ron, and one of these days you'll hear about it,' I said.

'Before I die, I hope,' he said.

'That's a promise,' I said.

The dark returned. We listened to Ron's feet on the drive. Then Ben went back to work. After a few minutes he reported back. 'It's here. You've made your point.'

'Lift it up,' I said.

He flung the shovel aside and knelt down. He lifted the box out of the hole and set it down at my feet.

'Open it,' I said.

'I don't need to open it. I said I believe what you said.'

'What did I say?'

Ben was on his knees. Now he leant onto his hands and on all fours hung his head.

'Come on, Charlie,' he said.

'What's that, Ben?'

'I said I believe it.'

'Believe what?'

'Christ!' he said. 'What's the matter with you?'

'I just want to hear you say it.'

'I'm not going to raise the lid. I'm not going to desecrate the dead. I absolutely refuse to do it.'

'It's your daughter, Ben. You're a father. You're somebody's dad. How does it feel?'

He shook his head.

'What? I can't hear you, man.'

His eyes held the ground still. He shook his head. He was a stubborn bastard.

'What's your daughter's name? Go on. Say it!' I grabbed the shovel and held it over him. 'Say it!'

Instead, he turned his head and looked up at me. His eyes were soft, compliant. 'Go ahead,' he said then. 'Do it, Charlie. I don't care. I hate Mr Fonda.'

'What?' I said.

'Mr Fonda, Charlie, he's who did this.' He nodded. 'Go ahead,' he said. 'Please,' he whispered.

When he realised that nothing was going to happen to him, that he would live, he got up and I dropped the shovel at my side. I watched him brush the dirt off his knees and hands. He began complaining of the cold again so I told him to wait in the van. I covered up Choo Woo. I put the shovel back in the garage. When I got back in the van Ben was slumped against the door. He was no longer hugging himself, but his head was turned away. He didn't want to look at me.

'I don't know why you had to come back here,' I said.

'It's where I live,' he said. Then he straightened up and looked across at me. He had to hold his mouth together again. 'It's my home,' he said. 'There's nowhere else.'

I don't know what possessed me to think of this but at the top of South Road I asked him, 'Do you ever read the Bible?'

We were stalled at the intersection while a huge removal van carrying someone's furniture south trundled by. Ben stared right through it. 'The Bible, man,' I said. He shook his head and mumbled about his mouth hurting, so I went ahead and recited: 'He was despised and rejected of men, a man of sorrows and acquainted with grief.' I let that sink in, then I said, 'That just about describes you, doesn't it?'

He turned away and looked out his window.

'Isaiah 113,' I said.

Maybe he's since looked it up. I like to think he has. There's no way of knowing, of course. After that night, he disappeared from our lives. I dropped him off in town. I hadn't planned to; but then nothing about the night had been planned. At a set of lights I told him to get out. I didn't want him near me. I didn't want him to breathe the same air as I did. I told him to get out of the van; and for the first time since he got into the van he looked across with genuine interest. 'Just open the door and get the fuck out,' I said. I hadn't taken my eyes off the road. I didn't want to look at him. I didn't want to see him ever again. I thought he wanted to say something – and that still remains my impression. He must have realised that I was giving him his life back. The door closed after him. Like a grateful hitchhiker he left the van, and the lights turned green.

I went home and slept. I slept the sleep of the dead. People still talk about the force of the southerly that arrived early that morning but I missed it, missed the wham of the first icy blast which, as I heard later, knocked a kid off his bike into the path of an oncoming car. I just woke up to the shrill wind and the rain pounding the roof and windows. I showered and dressed and ran out to the van under the blackest skies I have ever seen. Along the South Belt I saw the airport windsock wrapped around a farm fence.

Somewhere else I nearly got stuck in mud trying to get around a tree that had fallen across the road. On the back road to Gladstone I could barely see for the long trails of rain, some a mile long, raking the farmland and pushing back my wipers. Where the road tucked into the hillside it wasn't so wild. Most of the wind was collected by an old pine forest and some very big trunks were moving about like washing on a clothesline.

Out at Rube's the turkeys and pheasants went about business as usual. The wind swept off the hill at the back and the moment the smoke left the chimney it was snatched away. I thought it would be warm inside. Beverley would have a rack of muffins cooling on a bench. I didn't go in the gate though. I sat out on the road with the motor running.

Most of the Babylon crowd were there. I recognised their vehicles – their sides airbrushed with dolphins, centaurs, sunflowers, and hopeful sunsets of the kind not seen around here. In the grey light the black denim-clad figures spread out over the hill; some bent over into the wind, others cradling newborn lambs in sacks hurrying them to the big green barn I had helped Rube build the previous summer. There were a lot of dead lambs, some only hours old, daubed against the hillside. I watched the scene from the road and felt no inclination to get out and help. I think I recognised the potential that the moment held; I think I knew that I had reached a crossroads of sorts. I could get out of the van and help Rube or I could stay on this road and keep going. Something else happened at that moment which was to help me on my way. I saw Maggie on the verandah of Rube and Bev's house. She stood under the stoop, her shoulders hunched even though the roof overhead was catching the rain. Her wonderful hair was plastered against her red cheeks.

She pulled some of it away, which is when her eye caught mine, and her neck appeared to lengthen. There was too much bad weather between us for a meaningful word or gesture. She picked up a sack from the pile by the door and headed back out into that appalling wind. She stopped to look back once, and I shan't forget that look. One moment she'd been looking at me, the next she was walking away, and by the time she stopped to look back I had turned into a stranger. That's the last I saw of her. I put the van into gear, and continued in the direction of Gladstone. Further south the weather broke, and as I came over a crest the sun lit the umbrella spread of poplars bunched in a valley. While I'm not given to superstition, I thought there might be something in that – for the moment I was prepared to suspend judgement and launch forward with hope.

# TEN

Things have changed. Oh yes! I have become the 'other' in my daughter's life. I am always there in the background. Often she cannot see me, but something will cause her to stop and detach herself from a group of friends entering a picture theatre. Something like memory has reached out and touched her shoulder. She used to say that Ben left a trace of himself in the house on South Road. The air was changed from his having been there. As I step back into a doorway she looks up the street, casting for something she sensed, the way she used to check behind herself looking for Ben, whenever she was with Pete. She is at the back of the magazine shop poring over titles; she is in a dress shop or behind a window trying on her new life – that frown, for example – I like its independent quality. She has learnt to judge the world. I'm there as she leaves the gym. I stand in the shadows and watch her button up her jacket; the way she frowns back at the hour. I don't live with her or her mother but I live nearby. We sometimes have a meal together. We do it for the sake of something which we've almost lost sight of. We are still a family. We are still holding onto a thread of what that means, even though each of us still can't get over what we know of the other. From my point of view, I much prefer to look on from the edges of Natalie's world. In a crowded picture theatre she can't see me several rows back. She and her friends tilt their faces back at the big screen; but to me the thrill is the changing expression on my daughter's face – the thrall, the wonder, the passing emotions that I have missed in her life lived so far. The laughter – yes! She laughs and tears come to my eyes. She is laughing with the entire picture theatre and I am silently crying out – Yes! Yes! Despite everything that has happened she is finding ways to rejoin the world. But I know the dangers, and I don't forget them.

As soon as I knew that Wellington was going to be my home, I drove back to Masterton to tidy up my affairs. I had to sell the house and make arrangements to shift my furnishings such as they were. I was there a week. I kept away from Ben. In the evenings I pined for Maggie, but knew in my bones that I couldn't be what she reasonably wanted for Hope. I made a point of staying away from the Babylon crowd, and avoided Rube and Beverley. That stormy day I stopped outside the farm and looked in, I realised what it was I was leaving behind. Rube and Bev take in broken people like others take in orphaned or injured animals to raise as their own. I don't need that pampering, or to be watched over, any more. And Rube, it's fair to say, probably doesn't want to hear about the ugly past.

A couple of times, however, I drove down to the Waingawa River, to the same place I went to that day with Pete Sutton before I went after Ben. I bumped along the river track and I remembered what Pete told me. This is the missing part in my daughter's ordeal. This is the part which made it so easy to wrap Ben's jaw around the corner of the vanity. It's what takes the humanity out of you and turns you savage.


Mid-January. It was hot as Hades. A big anticyclone sat over the country. Everyone in the Wairarapa slept with their doors and windows open to catch the slightest shimmer of air. The tin roofs along South Road cracked. The tar on the roads melted. Across the Beltway towards the river, herds of sheep on the paddocks opposite the aerodrome huddled in shadows and watched the grass turn brown and die. Pete and Natalie spent every minute of the day down here by the river.

There's a pool that Pete showed me. It lay buried in the spring flow. But in the summer that I speak of it was surrounded by shingle and quick-growing fennel. Pete was dipping his head in the water and rolling his eyes up the way he had observed birds to do. He was pretending he was Mrs Austen; lifting wings and shivering all over, and Natalie was sitting on the bank watching, calling to him, 'Cheep cheep' and Pete answering, 'Tweet tweet', when they heard the snatched breath of the car coming off the tarseal on to the river gravel. They froze, and Pete felt the bird character clip its wings and fly out his throat as they listened to the weeds claw at the underbelly of the car. The engine died and in the buzzing heat they heard the crack-knuckled sound of a door opening. Downriver, they could see the disturbed dust settling back over the scrub. Natalie held a finger to her lips for silence, and Pete squeezed his eyes shut, then they heard him call out – 'Natalie?' Like he was politely inquiring. He doesn't want to make a fuss. But then they hear the scrub snapping and Ben, surprisingly near, change his tone. 'Mrs Fonda, I hope you're not hiding from me.'

Pete asks her, 'Who's Mrs Fonda?'

'No one you know, Pete,' she says, and they wait. They wait for Ben to give up and return to his car. They listen to the traffic thumping across the bridge downriver on State Highway 2 at the edge of town. Then, without quite being prepared for it, they hear a door slam and the car start up. Over the top of the scrub rises a loud cloud of dust leading back out to the road.

All the way home Pete badgers her about Mrs Fonda. Who is she? Why is it he hasn't heard of her before? The more evasive she is the more he knows he's onto something. Finally she says that Mrs Fonda is an old friend of Ben's. 'Someone he knew before he came to live in South Road. An American,' she adds.

'From where?'

'Texas.'

Here? In their street? It doesn't seem believable. Texas in South Road, Masterton, the Wairarapa.

'That's where she's from, Pete. Where she was born, dum dum.'

Hurt by the insult he doesn't say anything, and Natalie fills the silence with more unlikely information. Mrs Fonda is just visiting. She comes and goes.

They arrive home and outside Natalie's house Pete asks, 'How come Ben was looking for her? Did she do something wrong?'

He can see her trying to avoid his eyes.

'Ben sure sounded pissed off, didn't he?'

'They had a fight,' she says then. 'I think Ben was looking to apologise.'

He laughs. 'Ben apologising. That's a joke!'

She says, 'I don't want to talk about it. I just want to sit here in the shade.' He watches her flop down in the shadow of the elm. She's always so tired these days. Always looking to rest. He feels light as a strip of bark. He hops onto the garden wall to squat and watch the intermittent traffic drive by. Bored with that, he hops down onto the grass and pecks at the leaves. He makes bird noises around the immensity of his friend. When Ben arrives, it's like he has come out of nowhere. A warm wave of air, then the car panting in the drive, the smell of upholstery, then he is on the lawn. Pete gives an involuntary squawk and Ben says, 'What are we today – a kingfisher or a morepork?' Pete stays in his bird character, and raises his 'wings' to squawk defiantly back like a bird protecting its nest. 'Well, I guess that conversation has run its course,' says Ben. He stands there studying Natalie with a thin smile, and jingling change in his pocket. Then he says, 'Well, don't jump up at once. "Hello, Ben" or just a gidday would be nice.' They answer together, 'Hello, Ben,' like kids just starting school. As soon as Pete says that, he's as good as shed his feathers. He's back to regarding Ben with his untrusting eyes. He's thinking about the voice he heard back at the river, its unfamiliar and threatening edges reaching them over the top of the dusty riverbank scrub.

'Why don't you fly back to your nest, eh Pete. Natalie has some things to attend to inside.'

Pete checks with Natalie. He raises his wings, and she smiles and gives him a little wave.

'Thataboy,' says Ben. 'Fly off. Go on. Off you go. Flutter. Flutter. Christ,' he says.

But to show Ben he doesn't take orders from him, he waits for Natalie to go, 'Tweet tweet', and he answers, 'Cheep cheep.'

Ben rolls his eyes and Pete 'flies' off. On the other side of the garden wall he hears Ben say, 'What a fucking disaster that boy is.' Then he slaps his sides and says to Natalie, 'Come on, Mrs Fonda, let's get you inside.'

The last thing he hears is Natalie complain that she's cold and Ben's reply: 'Natalie. That's humanly impossible. It was thirty-one degrees at eleven. It's a summer's day in case you haven't noticed.'

Pete sat at home by the window waiting for Ben's car to leave the drive, and wondering why Ben had called Natalie 'Mrs Fonda'. When his father called for him later in the afternoon to help at the recycling plant, Ben's car was still in the drive.

He didn't see Natalie until the next day. It was as hot as it had been the previous day, the sky a brown exhausted colour, what his father called 'desert sky'. He passed this on to Natalie, and when he complained of her dawdling she said sometimes birds got too hot to fly. After a while he said she was fat. She didn't seem to mind. She said that meant she would float better than him; and at the swimming pool they played a game where she was a ball and Pete was a twig circling in the water.

That's what they were doing when they heard Ben's car for the second time in two days. It could have been anyone's and yet instinctively they knew it was Ben. The car hesitated at the same places that Ben's had the previous day.

This time, though, there was no polite inquiry. Ben seemed to know exactly where they were. They heard him crash through the scrub calling for Natalie.

Pete is more scared than Natalie. Ben is after Natalie. He'll be wild if he catches him there with her. She's the one he is calling out to. All this is communicated in a glance, until Natalie says, 'You can go if you like, Pete. Go on, go.' She seems so calm, like everything that is happening is the way things are supposed to be, and if she's caught then that also is the way things are meant to turn out.

He sets off, weaving through the clumps of broom, and after a while he stops and hears footsteps coming up behind. Natalie must have changed her mind. A scarier thought is answered next by Ben's angry shouting. This part of the riverland is all new. It's like going from one unfamiliar room to another. Suddenly the broom stops and gorse takes over. There's no way other than forward so he presses on, the gorse dragging over his bare skin, until the way ahead is thick with gorse. Nothing has passed through it ever before. Then he notices an opening as round and small as one a rabbit has made to burrow through, and Pete draws in his shoulders and wriggles to the centre of the gorse until the whole world is blocked out by gorse thicket. He can hear Ben now. He's more impatient than before. He's saying what he'll do to her if she doesn't show herself. Pete hears Natalie before he sees her. He hears someone out of breath. Then he sees the Indian cotton shift she wears over her togs and he calls to her – 'Tweet tweet.' Then she calls back – 'Cheep cheep.' He watches her take off the shift and wrap it around her head, then she burrows through to where he is, his knees up by his shoulders, hunched, like a young thrush. It's more painful for Natalie. She takes up more space. The gorse claws at her face. He keeps guiding her with his bird noises until she's almost at his side. She places her face near his – Natalie's is covered with dozens of pin pricks, some with a bright bead of blood.

They hear Ben then, complaining about the gorse. 'This is all so unnecessary. Really, I expected better than this. I thought we were bosom buddies. Natalie! Why aren't you answering me? This is only making things worse. There will be tears at home. Don't think you can come out of this with a clean slate.' He's reached the edge of the thicket. They can see his trouser legs turn this way and that. 'Fuck this,' he says. 'Fuckit! Enough's enough, Mrs Fonda.' Pete can feel the glow of Natalie's face next to his. 'I should have known you were lying through your teeth yesterday saying you were sick and cold and Christknowswhatelse. I'll know better next time, won't I? Okay. Okay. I've got all day. All night if I so choose.' Then the air turns quiet while Ben tries to bluff them out.

They don't move. They don't breathe. They listen to the traffic passing over the bridge downriver. They don't make a sound until they hear the brush snapping off in the direction of the car. They don't move until they hear the gravel spin under Ben's wheels. Then Pete says, 'He's mad. He's a madman, Natalie.' Like she must have known this, what's more she should have told him. Then, in that dry prickly air, he says, 'Why didn't you say you were Mrs Fonda?'

'It's just a game.'

'You said she was from Texas.'

'She is.'

'You're not from Texas.'

'I'm not. Mrs Fonda is. Forget it, Pete. It was a game. That's all.'

'Then if it's a game why can't I play it?'

'Because.'

'Because what?'

'Because it's not that kind of game and because you wouldn't like it,' she says.

They crawl out of the gorse into the larger world. The air is so big and generous after where they have been. As soon as the sun touches their skin all their scratches want to be noticed.

'Man,' says Pete, 'was he pissed off. Was he gutted or what? He was after you all right. What would he have done?'

'Dunno,' she says.

They can see the way Ben went back. There are fleshy bits in the broom where Ben tore branches to the left and right; the snapped brush looks like a temper tore through it.

They have reached the river when Natalie suddenly doubles over. The pain is so sharp she cries out. But it passes quickly and after gingerly straightening up she tells Pete it was something 'like a cramp', only more violent. Near the swimming hole it rips back through her. 'Pete, it hurts. It hurts . . .' He holds out a hand but it is a gesture and too useless to wave away the cramp. Like before, it seemed to enter and pass out, leaving behind sweats and her gasping. 'I don't feel right. There's something wrong with me. Something's the matter.' The Indian cotton wrap lies crumpled at her feet. It is right there but to bend down and pick it up is a task suddenly beyond her, so Pete picks it up. He wraps and ties it around her waist. 'Not too tight,' she tells him.

The next lot of cramps forces her to her knees and she cries out for help, and when it starts to subside, through closed eyes she reports up to him the sensation of two hands trying to drag something out of her. This time Pete bends down to catch her under her arms to help her up. He notices Ben's tyre tracks under where she fell. She is covered in sweat. Her skin is sticky to the touch. He pushes her up the last of the loose metal to the tarseal.

'Oh God, it's too far. It's too far,' she says. He figures she means home. It's never been too far or even far before. Pete is starting to lose patience. She has already lied to him about Mrs Fonda; now this, dragging her feet, complaining of stomach cramps. They are near the aerodrome when the worst of it happens. He said he was looking across the burnt grass to the shimmering tarmac and the limp windsock when he remembered Natalie – he looked behind and saw a wet patch around her feet. 'Bloody hell, Natalie. You've pissed yourself. Look! You've pissed yourself!' He didn't mean to embarrass her. She's looking with him at her glistening legs. She doesn't know what to say. Pete is looking around to make sure that no one else saw; a few cows is all. He says it again, 'You pissed yourself.'

'I know,' she says. 'You said that.'

They walk on until they come to the Beltway and the start of South Road. They pass the iron roofs creaking in the heat; they pass the elderly and splotchy faces toiling under sun hats, holding hoses, and shifting sprinklers. Their spray dries in the air before it lands on the pavement. She says, 'I'm scared, Pete. I'm scared. I've never pissed myself before. Never.'

'We're nearly there. Another hundred metres,' he says.

They are nearly home when the sun glints off the windshield of a car approaching from the top of South Road.

'Ben!' she says, and Pete takes away his hand. She tries to reassure him. The last thing she wants is for Pete to leave her side. She says, 'It's all right, Pete. He won't bite.' He returns his hand but not as before – it's there as a gesture but hardly in the flesh, light in her own hand. Natalie says, 'You don't have to worry about him.'

But he does. They notice the car is in no hurry. Then Natalie catches him looking across to his house and she says, 'Don't leave me, Pete. Please don't. It's just Ben being Ben. Playing tricks. You know what he's like.' She's used to covering for him by now. They watch him slow down for the approach into the drive – then, at the last moment, like a late errand suddenly entered his thoughts, he doesn't enter the drive as expected but drives slowly on, grinning through the side window and wagging his forefinger at them for being the naughty children they've been. This isn't what they expected. Natalie has sat down on the garden wall. So Pete reports back. 'He's still going. He's stopped, Natalie. Now he's turning. He's coming back. Quick! Mrs Austen's.'

They are hurrying as fast as Natalie can go down the drive when they hear Ben tear up the end of the drive at home. Right the length of the drive a hail of small stones flies against the house. 'He's pissed off,' says Pete.

But Natalie is more scared of her body than of what Ben might do. 'The cramps are coming back, Pete. My stomach hurts. It does.'

'Hurry,' he says. They can hear him now – screaming

for Natalie. Pete gets her around to the side of the house where the trapdoor is. It's the only place Ben doesn't know about. It's the only place he can't get them.

'I don't know, Pete. I don't know if I can bend down. I don't know what's the matter with me.'

'If you don't I'll hit you,' he says. The tense threat disappears from his face. He blushes and says he didn't mean it. She can see he's afraid. The cramps have passed so she drops down to enter the trapdoor. As she does they hear Ben in a calm and neighbourly voice call over the fence – 'Is that you? Did I hear you, Natalie?' They hear Ben laugh and they both freeze. He knows. He knows where they are.

Pete grabs her by her hair and drags her under the house; he's dragging her and she's pushing along on her knees. Under the house they hear Ben drop over the fence. 'Was that you, Natalie? Don't you try and hide from me again. I'm warning you.' Pete tucks her feet inside the trapdoor and closes it. Now it is completely dark. She can lie on her back. She doesn't have to hold herself up any more. They lie there and wait; they listen to Ben as he comes around the house. They hear the old basket of clothes pegs kicked over. Then they hear him humming that old Joe Cocker number that he likes. Instead of Marjorie, Ben hums: 'Natalie, where would you be, Natalie . . . Da, da, da, da . . .' Then it becomes silent like he's onto something. His nose has caught a scent. But Ben's patience is not one of his strengths. In a moment he's back to sounding reasonable, and sensible. 'Come on, Natalie, sweetheart. Let's put an end to this nonsense. I feel a hamburger coming on. Ask along Birdbrain too if you think that will add some spark to the conversation.'

That's when the cramps return. She utters a cry and Pete sticks his hand in her mouth.

'Natalie? Was that you?' He's right outside the trapdoor. Natalie's teeth are buried in the flesh of Pete's hand but he leaves his hand there. This time the silence is taking forever to end. This time Ben has turned himself into a rock. Then they hear a stream of water against the house and they realise what he's doing; he's pissing against the weatherboards. Then they hear him rap his knuckles against the side of the house. 'Natalie?' A moment later his footsteps pass up the side of the house out to the street.

Natalie feels so big and useless. It's arm-breaking just to get her over to the hole in the floor. Pete slips through easily. Then he reaches down to collect her under her arms. 'Come on, you big fat cow.'

'Then don't help me,' she says, slapping away his arms. He lets her do it on her own. He stands up, his arms folded, and as she drags herself onto the bare floor she lies there breathing hard.

'Mrs Austen's room,' he says, and this time she allows him to help her. She collapses onto the mattress.

'I don't want to die,' she says to Pete. 'I don't. I don't.'

'You're not dying. You're fat. That's all. You're fat.' Then he thinks to add, 'Anyway, you're too young.'

'What about Mrs Austen?'

'Mrs Austen's a bird,' he says.

'Birds can be fat too. Birds can be anything they want,' she says. 'It's coming back, Pete. It's hurting again.'

'I'll get some Disprin, shall I?'

'No! No, I don't want you to leave me. Please don't leave. Promise.'

That she's so desperate for him to stay scares him.

He says, 'I can get the Disprin and come back. I won't be long.'

'Promise me, Pete?'

'Cross my heart and hope to die if I tell a lie . . .'

He watches her turn her face to the wall.

'I'm thirsty too, Pete.'

'I'll bring over some Coke.'

'No. I just want water. Water.'

He's at the door when she calls him back. 'Help me take this off,' she says. He watches her struggle up and start pulling the straps of her bathing suit down over her shoulders. 'I'm hot and it's too tight.' He watches her raise her hips to roll the suit down the backs of her legs.

'I won't look,' he says.

'I don't care if you look or not,' she says.

She lies back, relieved, and he rolls the togs down her legs and off her feet. Then another attack comes and she clutches the air and cries out this time. Like the other times, the pain, excruciating, passes. She opens her eyes, and seeing the look on Pete's face, she says, 'Get me the blanket. Give it here.'

'I didn't look,' he says.

'I don't care if you did, Pete.'

'I didn't,' he says.

'If it makes you feel better,' she says.

'Well, I didn't,' he says.

'Pete! I don't flippin' care. Get me a cold flannel. I feel like I'm burning up. Bring me a T-shirt as well, and I want a pillow.'

'I'm going,' he says. He doesn't want to be burdened with too many requests. He hears her call out, 'Don't forget what you promised!'

He leaves by the back door this time, and leaves the door ajar. He stops to wonder if he can remember Ben coming back. It's important because if he's home the drive will give him away. So he ducks around the blind side where Ben pissed against the side of the house, pushes through a bunch of camellia bushes and skips out to the road, down his drive and into the back of his house. He can hear the TV on in the front room; his mother is in there watching her programme. He goes to ask her where the Disprin is kept and she sticks up a hand for silence. 'Warren's left Victoria. I don't believe it. I just don't believe what some men do . . .' He walks to his mother's side to see what has her so riveted. On TV is an American living room. The two people, a man and a woman, are immaculately dressed. Neither of them look like they've ever swum in a river or crawled beneath a house. 'Your father called. He wants a hand with loading some bottles. He'll be by in fifteen minutes. So stay put.'

He does a sweep through the house snatching up whatever his eye falls upon. Chippies, towels, a bottle of Coke. Back at Mrs Austen's he opens up the front of his T-shirt and everything rolls out. Natalie picks up a small bottle and reads the label. 'I didn't ask for sleeping pills.'

'I got some throat lozenges as well.' He unwraps one and pops it in her mouth. She looks at him annoyed. 'Water? Did you get what I asked?'

'There's water out in the kitchen.' While he's out there he hears her gasp and cry out; he delays his return until it passes and Natalie's breathing returns to normal. When he comes back into the room, the blanket has slipped down. Natalie hasn't noticed.

'I should get mum,' he says. 'Do you want me to?'

'Maybe,' she says after a bit. 'Maybe.'

His mother will know what to do. She's good at stuff

like this. He's already turned to leave when she calls him back. 'Pete! I need to go to the toilet! Oh shit! Pete!' She's screaming at him so loud that if Ben were home he's sure he'd have heard.

'Natalie. Quieter,' he says.

'No!' she cries. 'Oh God! Something's coming. I can feel it. Oh God oh God. No. Don't leave me. Pete!'

But he's gone. He's out the back door and running for dear life. He runs through the camellia bushes at the side of the house. His father's truck is in the drive. He bursts through the front door – his mother is where he left her, with Victoria saying, 'Please don't' to Warren. His father yells out from the back of the house – 'Pete! That you? I told your mother for you to be ready. I've been waiting here twenty minutes.' They meet in the hall, his father reaching for his hat soon as he sees him. 'Get in the truck. I want the day to end at a reasonable hour.'

For the next two hours Pete helped his father collect the bottles from three cricket clubs. At the recycling yard they sort them into green and brown and clear glass. The last chore is to help his father change the rear tyre on the truck. It was dark before they arrived back in South Road. Then there was dinner to get through. It's nine o'clock before he creeps out of the house and across the road. The lights are on at Natalie's. But at Mrs Austen's the lights are out; the door is ajar just as he left it. He calls out – 'Natalie?' He calls three times. She doesn't answer any of them. There's something about the silence that he doesn't trust. He pushes the door open to Mrs Austen's room. There on the mattress is Natalie. She's fast asleep. There a smell of something, a rich smell with layers of blood and shit and sweat. It doesn't reflect well on Natalie, to stink like that. It's a disagreeable thing. But he thinks he had better wake her. Ben will be out of his mind by now. He crouches beside her, and as he does he sees something tiny and bloody clamped onto her chest. Something. Something that he wouldn't have believed or thought possible.

He wakes her and tells her what she already knows. 'You've had a baby. Natalie, look! It's a baby.' He wants to touch it but doesn't; a bit like touching a dog for the first time. Then he thinks he will. He touches its cheek with his fingertip.

'I'm so tired. I just want to sleep,' she says.

'A baby,' he says. He remembers what Orange Cat did with her litter.

He takes the bloody mess of limbs and something gross that is attached by a cord and plants the lot by her breast. They watch it with its slow pawing fingers and amazingly it starts to suckle.

'It's working,' she says. 'It's working, Pete. I can feel it coming out.'

'Jesus, Natalie. You've got a baby,' he says.

'It's not mine.'

'It came out of you.'

'I didn't ask it to.'

He says, 'If it came out of you then that makes you its mother.'

'Mother,' she says then with a sense of dumbfounded-ness. She supposes she is. She supposes she is just like Vivienne, just like Ben said she was.

'Well,' she says then. 'She's still not mine. She's Mrs Fonda's.'

She watches the pattern of thought on Pete's face. Mystery to begin with, hardening to the surprising discovery.

232

'Ben?' he says. 'He did this?'

'Now you know,' she says.

'Ben. Shit, Natalie. What will your mother say?'

'I knew I shouldn't have told you. I knew it.'

'I haven't said I will tell anyone,' he says.

'I shouldn't have said.'

'I promise,' he says.

'You mustn't tell a soul. Not anyone. Not your mother.'

He's never known anything quite like it; he's never known a secret to weigh as much as this. He can see the lights on in the kitchen over at Natalie's. If he could just pop over there and tell Natalie's mother he would feel free again, like he did when he woke up this morning. He can feel Natalie's eyes looking up at him.

'There's no going back on a promise,' she reminds him. Then she says, 'Can you sneak into your house without anyone seeing you?'

'Of course,' he answers, like it's a matter of pride.

For the second time that evening he steals out of his house with the things Natalie has asked for – a towel, a saucepan and a gas stove (she said she wants some hot water to wash herself), some flannels. By now the baby was asleep. Natalie placed it on the mattress. She went out to the kitchen to clean herself; while she's doing that Pete makes up a bed. He cuts one of his mother's sheets into strips and makes a nest in a carton. When he lowers the baby inside it hardly stirs. Then he goes out to the kitchen to light the gas stove for Natalie. She's standing out there without a stitch on. It's funny, he thinks, that she doesn't seem to care.

Afterwards they shift everything into the front room: a candle, the mattress, the baby's carton, Mrs Austen. Pete has been full of advice, and she has happily gone along with whatever he's come up with.

'You haven't named her, Natalie. You need to give her a name.'

'Choo Woo,' she says. She hardly appeared to give it any thought; or maybe she had been thinking about it while he was across the road. In the front room the name just popped out so naturally that he'd have thought it belonged to someone who had been around much longer.

That night they left Mrs Austen's by the back door. Natalie needed Pete's help. With every step she feels like her bottom is about to fall out, like she's been turned inside out down there. So Pete put his shoulder under her arm and they hobbled from the back door. She stepped on one of the clothes pegs that Ben spilled. How long ago that feels. Time has gathered new edges and divisions. She'd woken up that morning a child; this evening she is a mother – like Vivienne. She looks up the drive and ponders the space between the two houses. The everyday appearance of things; but as they pass the kitchen light from next door she ducks her head like a fugitive. Out in the street, Pete cocks his head for the thin wail of a guitar playing in a pub in town. 'Cheep. Cheep,' he goes. 'Tweet. Tweet,' she replies.

I know the rest. I know about her lingering on the porch, preferring this to that other world where she is responsible for her mother's happiness. Finally, though, she knew she had no choice but to enter it, and the moment she pushes on the door her mother is yelling out, 'Is that who I think it is?' I know the rest from what Viv said; from what she has shamefacedly admitted, to her bailing up Natalie in the hall, demanding explanations.

'I'm sorry, Ma.'

'Sorry for what?'

'Sorry for being late.'

'Sorry for being late where?'

'I don't know, Ma.'

And Viv scornfully reporting back to Ben in the other room with the newspaper spread over his lap. 'She doesn't know where she's been.'

Then Ben coming into the hall holding up his watch, and asking her, 'What time do you call this, young lady?'

Then the two of them pouring it on – first Vivienne, then Ben.

'I was expecting you at the hotel at five. Stewy put a meal aside for you especially.'

'I had to cancel an appointment this evening to go looking for you. But what's an appointment. Why should money be a worry to you?'

'All because of your bloody selfishness.'

'All right, Vivy. All right. Your mother's been out of her mind with worry . . .'

'Ben too. He thought something had happened . . . He wanted me to call the police.'

'Another five minutes,' he says.

Then Vivy dropping her tearful face on Ben's shoulder, 'Does she look sorry? Does she look like she even cares?'

'Leave it to morning, Viv. I think we're all too tired for this.'

But not so tired that Ben can't help himself at the night's end slipping into her room. She's never been this tired and, at the same time, this unable to fall asleep. She thinks about her baby in the carton next door. Choo Woo all alone. Then she remembers that Mrs Austen is there next to her; she remembers now Pete shifted her perch to a place closer to the carton; and she smiles in the dark. She closes her eyes. She thinks she might fall asleep now. Then she hears from the door, 'Goodnight, Mrs Fonda.' She opens her eyes and catches him push off from the door jamb in that lazy way of his; shambling through the dark to smile down at her. 'I wonder where Mrs Fonda got to tonight. Or should I say B'rer Rabbit. I have a rifle. Yes. You didn't know that, did you. I used to like to rabbit-shoot. Don't get much of a chance these days. But I think I'll take my rifle down to the river next time I get a chance. What does Mrs Fonda have to say to that?'

'I'm tired, Ben.'

'Where have I heard that before?'

She closes her eyes. Let him say what he likes, she thinks. Let him waggle his tongue to kingdom come. Then she feels his thumb press her eyes and she cries out at the stab of pain. 'You weren't paying attention, B'rer Rabbit. That's your problem. You seem to have a problem remembering things, agreements, what I said, what you promised, yes! Please don't make things difficult. For me and Vivienne,' he says, in case she missed the point. 'Still, it's not like things can't be put right. I always say it's never too late for that. I remain an optimist in all things.'

It's like listening to old conversations. She recognises old patterns, old needs. He slips his hand inside her duvet. She knows what's next, what is supposed to happen. She knows the inclination of Ben's fingertips and before they run like spiders across her belly she crosses her legs.

'Oh,' he says. 'Oh, what have we here?' She feels his fingers circle back for the place between her legs. 'Choo woo,' he says, but without belief, he's not in character, and it's more habit, more hopeful grasping for old passwords.

Then, seeing that nothing results from the password, he tries this. He says, 'Train tunnel blocked. Train'll crash less the landslide is cleared away. Mrs Fonda, the fate of the passengers is in your hands.'

'They can crash,' she says.

'Oh dear. Oh dearie me. Are you sure, Mrs Fonda? What if I was to tell you that your mother is on that train?'

And slowly she parts her legs.